RUDE BOYS

Also by Gaylord Dold

A Penny for the Old Guy
Disheveled City
Muscle and Blood
Bonepile
Cold Cash
Snake Eyes
Hot Summer, Cold Murder

Gaylord Dold

···

RUDE BOYS

A MITCH ROBERTS MYSTERY

A THOMAS · DUNNE BOOK

ST. MARTIN'S PRESS   NEW YORK

Grateful acknowledgment is given to the publishers for permission to reprint lyrics from the following songs.
"Johnny Too Bad," by T. Wilson, W. Bailey, H. Bexford, and D. Crooks. Copyright © 1980 Ackee Music, Inc. and EMI Music Publishing Ltd. Used by permission. All rights reserved.
"Rivers of Babylon," by D. Dowe, G. Reyam, F. Farian, and J. McNaughton. Copyright © 1978 Ackee Music, Inc., Al Gallico Music Corp. and Far Musikverlag. Used by permission. All rights reserved.

Design by Judith A. Stagnitto and Paul Chevannes

Library of Congress Cataloging-in-Publication Data
Dold, Gaylord.
    Rude boys / Gaylord Dold.
        p. cm.
    "A Thomas Dunne book."
    ISBN 0-312-08286-X
    I. Title.
PS3554.O436R8   1992
813'.54—dc20   92-25838
                                CIP

First Edition: November 1992

10 9 8 7 6 5 4 3 2 1

for Cynthia

and for Harry and Sue Najim,
the captive audience every writer needs

LONDON

By the river of Babylon
Where he sat down . . .
And there he wept,
When he remembered Zion.

—MELODIANS

1

In the third-floor alcove of St. Olave's Hospital Roberts first heard how a young Jamaican had died twice.

Roberts had taken the underground and gotten off in the upper Jamaica Road, finding it entirely deserted at six o'clock on a chilly autumn morning, and then he had walked down through Southwark Park and up the marble stairs of the hospital, and had taken a rickety lift up to the third floor. The lift shuddered so badly that he found himself nervous and inattentive, and so he wandered aimlessly around the empty hospital corridors lost in thought, until he found a young novice with a pale face and huge saucer eyes, eyes that reminded him of a baby kitten's eyes, radish-colored irises that sliced through the gloom, even though her expression looked sad. She was wearing a black habit that surprised Roberts with its austerity, and he must have surprised her as well because he was the only other person standing in the hallway, dim blue light pouring over him like syrup.

As the novice approached, Roberts found that she was quite small and he caught himself looking over her shoulder for the room where he knew James Root, the Jamaican, was

3

lying dead on a hospital bed, dead the second time. The novice smiled and crossed herself, bit her lip and wrinkled her brow, and then tried to explain to Roberts what had happened to the Jamaican in a conspiratorial tone that was like sharing a secret. The sensation of being in the hospital's lonely halls bothered Roberts terribly. Perhaps it was the subtle shades and tones of the corridors, the early-morning gloom bleeding through the polished glass, the tireless tick of heart monitors far away. Roberts had always had an inordinate fear of hospitals, and the gray morning light slipping through the hallways and the sounds of rubber tires creaking over marble only increased his innate existential dread of the place. He was so conscious of time that he thought he could discern each second ticking by, that he could hear glucose dripping through plastic tubes, and he thought he could hear blood running through the veins of the patients. He was that sensitive to his surroundings. Like nickeled mirrors at either end of the corridor, the windows seemed to stare at him, and then Roberts realized he had missed something the novice had said. Cold motes of dust kicked through the air. He felt as though he had been immersed in cold water, part of some elaborate torture.

The novice was wearing a name tag. *Agnes* it read. Agony, Sister Agnes, and Roberts wondered if he should call her "sister." She looked no more than nineteen years old, her face pleasantly framed by Irish-rose cheeks, and those bright saucer eyes that brimmed, tufts of red hair splitting from her white peaked hospital cap. She had been telling Roberts how a duty nurse had found James Root early Saturday morning, just after he had been admitted. The duty nurse had been walking past his room carrying a tray of fresh towels when she noticed that she couldn't hear the heart monitor buzzing. Coming from the room instead was a single dull bleep, unchanging, that meant that the patient was no longer breathing, that, technically speaking, he was dead. At that point the duty nurse suddenly dropped her tray of towels and the aluminum had clanged against the tile floor, echoing down the long corridor, and just as abruptly she had burst into the Jamaican's room and had hammered him once hard right on the point of the chest, a solid blow that snapped his heart into motion just briefly. Then she pounded on his chest again and rang frantically for the cardiac specialist and the intern.

Roberts was listening to the story with *his* heart pounding, while inside he thought: Agnes, Agonistes, *agony*. My God, she is such a child, this novice I've found.

The duty nurse who had found James Root saw that his face had turned an ashen color, with purple circles around the eyelids and dark blue lips the shade of serge cloth, and that he looked like a corpse already. She was frightened by this huge black man lying so unmovingly beneath his sheet, wearing his purple and black tam, his dreadlocks tousled on his chest, and his flat flared nose motionless. He lay there like a ghost, and it scared her. And then the duty nurse touched the man's face, a delicate caress along the cheek, down toward the neck, feeling for a fleeting sign of pulse, some epidermal disturbance that would inform her that his heart was beating again, but there was no disturbance and the heart monitor continued its dull bleep.

The duty nurse could smell rubber and iodine in the room. The metal hospital bed was cold to the touch. Everything was white and laundered, white bedpans, the window glass frosted with early-morning rime, mounds of white sheets, and beneath it all the figure of the huge Rasta, well over six feet tall and seventeen stone, with his coiled black locks on his chest and his empty black obsidian eyes. With her one knee balanced against the metal strut of the bed, she struck the Jamaican a very hard blow on his chest, and heard the heart monitor begin to buzz, knowing now that an ounce of blood had been delivered to the patient's brain, that James Root was momentarily alive, technically speaking.

The duty nurse had broken a sweat. She could taste it on her lip, feel it seeping down her forehead, and when she looked at her patient again, still pressing the emergency button with her left hand, she thought that she saw some color coming back to the Rasta's face, the purple less pronounced around the lips and eyes.

An intern arrived first, took one look at the patient, and filled a hypodermic with digitalis. He injected the drug and began to pound on the patient's chest, and then both the intern and the duty nurse took turns. The heart monitor began to buzz intermittently, and then steadily, and then, fifteen minutes later, James Root began to breathe on his own, though the one thing neither nurse nor intern knew was how long he had been dead the first time. You can be dead only so long before it makes no difference to the brain, the blood will fall on empty cells, the nerves fail to fire. The intern knew that once you were dead you were really dead, truly dead, and that injecting digitalis directly into the ventricle will make no difference, that human hearts will pump and beat, but it means nothing really. Finally, the intern listened to James Root's heart, and pronounced him alive again, really.

And that, the young novice told Roberts, was the first time James Root died, sometime before dawn on Saturday morning on the third floor of St. Olave's Hospital south of the Thames, just across from the docks and the Tower Bridge, there in sooty industrial London. An ambulance had brought him from his flat just off the Jamaica Road where he'd been found collapsed in the hallway of his dirty walk-up. The novice told Roberts what she knew about the Jamaican, how he'd come up from Negril on the west coast of Jamaica, through Montego Bay, and had settled in London on the Jamaica Road, fitting somehow. It was ironic that he had been born in county Cornwall in Jamaica, jungle country named after the ultimate bucolic English place.

The novice said that it took about half-an-hour to really stabilize the Jamaican. Once it happened the patient's face became really black again, and he closed his eyes, and his broad nose quivered with the passage of air. His lips were stretched taut again. The intern had assumed he would survive, and had sat down on a chair and smoked an Oval while the duty nurse cleaned up. Sparrows began to chatter.

Sister Agnes stared at Roberts, a half-stare as if something had stuck to his nose. "You're an American, sir, aren't you?" she asked in her beautiful Irish brogue.

Roberts admitted that he was an American. He told her how he'd lived in London for six or seven months, that he'd come over to be with a woman he was trying to love, an English lady he'd met years before, that they were trying to recapture the past, which was always dangerous. He realized that Sister Agnes was looking at his boots and jeans, the leather bomber jacket, and his unshaved slept-in face that probably made him look slightly dangerous. The young girl was fascinated. Roberts said he'd lived in southern Colorado, that he'd been a rancher and horse trainer, and before that a private detective, and before that even, a combat engineer. He said he'd come to England to explore his future, that flight was what you did when you didn't know what else to do.

"Yes, an American," Roberts said finally, distracted again and hardly able to concentrate as he stood in the ineffable blue glaze of early morning, looking over the shoulder of the novice. An orderly in white was pushing a mop around the tile floor, making a whisking sound like a bat in flight. Sound rustled through the corridors and disappeared as if disembodied from its source. Roberts was looking at a row of rubber-tired wheelchairs with cane backs lined up against one wall, a reminder of the Great War and millions of deaths and maimings. His melancholy was becoming hard to sublimate.

The novice shifted toward him, trying to catch his eye. "Did you know the gentleman?" she asked shyly.

"The gentleman?" Roberts repeated stupidly.

"The Jamaican gentleman," the novice said. "The man we've been talking about!"

"Oh no," Roberts admitted, trying to concentrate now, even though his eyes hurt from lack of sleep. "I do some legal work for his sister, who's a lawyer at Lincoln's Inn." Once in England, Roberts had begun to think about making a living, which was legally impossible on his tourist visa. He had found some work off the books, doing investigations for a Jamaican

woman lawyer at the Inns of Court. Amanda had found him
the work, which was more like charity, accepting money under
the table while he lived in a cellar flat beneath Amanda's house
along the Kensington Park Road. Since moving to England he
had felt like a poor relative, as if something of his personality
had been stolen from him, part of his pride, though he knew
he was responsible for himself. He'd left Colorado behind, and
his ranching and his private detective work, and he'd come to
England expecting to have a new life. Instead, he was still
looking for his life, and now he found that he was constantly
losing more of himself, instead of finding it. Now his rooms
were below ground, under the main house. There was a stuffed
chair, some Hogarth prints on the walls, and a folding metal
bed that Amanda had carried down from her guest room. He
spent a lot of time alone, and when he was there in the late
evenings, he could imagine the thousands of souls in bed-
sitters along the Tottenham Court Road, shop girls frying
bacon and egg, washing their stockings in the tub.

"I'm sorry, you were saying?" Roberts asked the novice. He
was daydreaming.

The novice was telling Roberts about the second time the
Jamaican had died, just an hour ago, right here on this floor.
She'd heard parts of it from the kitchen help, and parts from
the duty nurse. Apparently James Root had gone to sleep
peacefully, and was even awake enough to take some tea, and
he'd filled out a supper form for later in the day. It was
thought that he would perhaps lose part of his stomach but
make a complete recovery. And that was the terrible part
about his second death, that it had come so swiftly, without
any advance warning or meaning, and that he was completely
dead, without any possibility of recovery, and that nobody
could understand why. Nothing of the sort had happened at
St. Olave's before, and nobody could imagine it ever happening again, but it had, and it was both hideous and permanent.
The duty nurse had stopped by the patient's room again, just
a bit later, to take his temperature and had found the Rasta

with a gaping slice across his lower neck, the bed awash in
blood.

There had been a terrible uproar. The duty nurse screamed
and called for the intern, who called for the specialist, who had
summoned the administrator. Later, they had called a priest
and the police. Only just now were they getting ready to take
the Jamaican away.

"He's still in the room?" Roberts asked.

"Oh yes, sir," the novice replied. She motioned down the
hallway, a door open with yellow light pouring out.

"Did he have any visitors between last night when he was
admitted, and this morning?"

"I wouldn't know, sir," Agnes said stiffly, now on her
guard. She backed away, hands on hips. Roberts could hear
sparrows outside, the unmistakable sound of morning, and
some traffic along the Jamaica Road, lorries downshifting
through the tunnels. It was cold and he thought he could see
his breath. The novice moved and Roberts followed her two
steps.

"Do you know the name of the duty nurse?" he asked.

"The same nurse found the poor man both times."

"Her name?"

"Sister Dolores," she answered.

Roberts thanked the novice, who smiled, and swept away
down the hall. She stopped and smiled again, framed in the
blue light, her black habit framed too. Roberts thought about
the Rasta, his room empty now except for the sound of birds.

The novice disappeared at the end of the corridor and Roberts stood in the middle of the hall and then walked down
three rooms until he could look into Root's hospital room,
which was immersed in morning sunlight. There was a row of
high windows and some dusty geraniums on the sill, and
through the windows he could see the warehouses of Wapping, the docks, and the tip of the Tower Bridge. A gold cross
hung above the bed, and there was a movable tray of instruments poised above the iron rung. As he moved inside the
room, Roberts could see the dead man, whose face was

masked by a pearly glaze. His head seemed enormous, dread-locks on his chest, flecks of blood in the black hair, a coil that seemed surreal the more he looked at it, a broth of snakes. The more he stared, the more Roberts knew he was looking at a very remarkable face, a high forehead, arched brows, a flat prominent nose and wide eyes with thick lashes, a single gold earring in one ear. Whatever he had been in life, James Root was impressive in death.

Roberts backed away and rested against the doorjamb. The quiet had returned and he thought it was strange that nobody was guarding the body. It was an English phenomenon, this passive acceptance of the status quo. Inside the hospital room there was a tang of blood in the air, and Roberts looked at the enormous slash on the man's throat, a gape that cut through nearly to the collarbone. Roberts felt ill, and he leaned against the door to steady himself.

Voices circulated up the stairwell, echoes of people talking, hard masculine tones, probably, Roberts thought, somebody from Scotland Yard or the Hospital Administration, people he didn't want to see right now. He cast a last look at the dead Rasta and hurried around the corner and away from the voices that were approaching. He saw the novice again, in front of an open linen cabinet, pulling out piles of fluffy pillows and towels. She had a liquid stare, as if she had been crying.

"Here now," Roberts said, trying to comfort her. They were standing just in front of two huge windows and he could see Southwark Park below, the beeches pulsing with orange and yellow, full of pregnant dying leaves. "You mustn't cry," Roberts said.

"I keep thinking about the poor gentleman," she said.

"Yes, I know."

"We must try to pray for him."

"Yes, we must," Roberts said, a tremor passing through him. *Pray,* he thought. He was a stranger to the secrecy of prayer, to its power. To him, prayer was like knowing how to fly, some occult skill. The novice closed her eyes momentarily, and Roberts felt her stillness. He respected her faith, it moved him, even though he was afraid of it.

"You said Root was admitted when?" Roberts asked when the moment had passed. Roberts was touched by the woman, her gestures, the flush of youth on her cheeks.

"Late last night," she replied. "You'd have to ask Sister Dolores to make sure." She bit her lip, probably aware of her complicity. Roberts was thinking again about the Rasta, the dirty tam on his head, how he would have been rolled in through the grimy dock night on a cart, wheels clanking on tile as nurses and orderlies bustled about the man. Roberts thought about death, how later the duty nurse had dropped her aluminum tray in the corridor outside the man's room. Roberts abandoned the thought when he realized the novice was tapping him on the shoulder.

"Sorry," Roberts said. "I was just wondering what happened to put James Root in the hospital."

Official voices flooded the hallway. Roberts touched the novice, comforting her again, trying to establish a thin bond before he never saw her again.

"I don't know, sir," she said quietly. Roberts said good-bye and started down the wide marble staircase. A sudden wind buffeted the lead-case windows. "Please try to pray for the gentleman, sir," Roberts heard the novice call after him. The gray middle distance held her words.

2

The air outside St. Olave's was thin and cold, as if tiny silver slivers were sifting down from the clouds and were pelting the beeches and elms. The sun had come up over the warehouses and the light was piercing all the leaves. Roberts had come out of the hospital by the back way, through the emergency room, walking along a broad macadam path through the park, across lawns crunchy from frozen dew, flocks of pigeons huddled in the grass. Everything he saw had a sodden autumnal appearance, even the black trunks of the trees, clumps of blue-green moss, the great gray bulk of the buildings along the river with their rows of soot-blackened windows, smoke towering from beyond the docks and shipyards in Bermondsey and Wapping. He walked through a tunnel and emerged by duck ponds surrounded by planted willow trees that seemed overrun with sparrows. He could hear the traffic on Jamaica Road, whispers just out of reach, a presence of cars running through gears, buses laboring down the incline toward Brunel Road. The shadow of the hospital followed him, and he walked through a line of parked ambulances along a high brick wall that was covered by graffiti, coming out on the

Lower Road on a narrow lane choked with delivery lorries. He stood beside a taxi stand for a long time, thinking about James Root, about the two times the man had died. The same few thoughts repeated in his head. They were like sensations against his skin, or bubbles of water rising to the surface of limpid liquid, as if something of himself had peeled away and at any moment something terrible might be revealed, some secret. The sight of James Root had unnerved him and now all of his emotions had needled down to this dim pinpoint of gray morning light that surrounded him like an aura, and he kept thinking about the dead man lying there in the whiteness of his hospital room, above him the blood-red color of a dusty geranium.

He thought about his own life in England, the brief six-month stay in the cellar flat of Amanda's house on Kensington Park Road, and then about his first job with Hillary Root, which had been on the sly, something to make ends meet while he decided his own fate against the backdrop of his discontent. But what really invaded his head and made him think, was the terrible coincidence that now Hillary's brother was dead, found on the third floor of St. Olave's hospital in south London with his throat slashed, the second time he'd died, actually. It was absurd how death seemed to follow Roberts around, and now it was the Jamaican brother of Hillary Root, who was somebody he'd known for barely a month. He hadn't even known she'd had a brother.

Roberts thought about buying the *Daily Mail* so that he could read about the World Series, anything to take his mind off the present reality. He looked around but didn't see a kiosk, not even on the busy Lower Road. There were offices and chandleries, one branch of a Scottish bank, a pub, and a dreary chemist's with faded advertisements in the window. Pigeons circled like vultures and then dropped on the parapets of the union hall across the street. There was a Wimpy Bar on the corner of Gomm Road beside the public baths. The neighborhood reminded him of nothing in particular, perhaps a scene from a Graham Greene novel. A few cabs slid by on damp streets.

And then he saw Amanda approach in a cab. Her face was behind glass, staring out at him like a moon, and the cab stopped and she got out and paid the fare. She was wearing a long blue raincoat and brown boots, and her face was puffy from lack of sleep, and she smiled wearily at Roberts. There was a look of tenderness on her face that made him sad somehow, perhaps because of his love, or perhaps because he was trying to accommodate his own emotions, turn them down a notch and follow them wherever they went. They walked toward one another and touched lightly as mist began to fall.

They went inside the Wimpy and found seats near the window and ordered tea. Everything was too brightly lit, as if the fluorescence was hurrying you along. Eggs and bacon were frying in the back, and you could smell them in the air. Grit had tracked the window glass beside them and they could see mirages of people on the street now that it was fully morning.

"For God's sake," Amanda said, "what's happened? I found your note and hurried right over." For his first two months in England, Roberts had been living without hope. And then Amanda had found him employment with Hillary Root. Now Roberts was trying to pay her back by being on his own. "Is something wrong with Hillary?" Amanda asked.

"It isn't about Hillary," Roberts said, stirring his tea. It was white tea. He'd forgotten that it came that way unless you said something about it. He tasted it. Cheap Ceylon. He laced it with sugar to make it something else. "I'm afraid it's bad news about her brother."

"A chap named James," Amanda said. "I understand he's only just now come over to England from Jamaica."

"Well, he's dead," Roberts said.

The question seemed to dismantle Amanda piece by piece. She discovered her image in the tea and stirred it. "You've been to St. Olave's?" she asked. The Wimpy Bar had grown its own detached stasis. The windows were dripping mist now, obscuring the outside.

Roberts told Amanda that he'd seen James Root before he'd been taken away. He said he'd slipped up to the third floor and had spoken to a novice, and then he'd walked down the hall to the man's room and had seen his blue face. He told Amanda how the man had died twice. "I don't know exactly what put him into the hospital in the first place. I only know that he was admitted sometime last night, and that he'd had an episode of heart failure. He was saved by a duty nurse." Behind him Roberts noticed kitchen sounds. He thought about the sound of an aluminum tray dropping against tile, the dead hum of a heart monitor.

Roberts ordered breakfast, sausage and toast, expecting the worst, some dreadful chunk of fat meat with white freckles. Amanda smoked a cigarette, drank her tea. She looked confused and very tired.

While Roberts ate his sausage, Amanda finished her cigarette and lit another, smoking it thoughtfully. Roberts watched her, thinking how his experience of England was different now, no longer a tourist, but inside the events, part of the flow. He felt as though he had turned back the pages of his personality and a sudden wind had torn them away and they were fluttering down a dusty vacant street. He imagined himself running helplessly behind his own being, just out of reach of his new life. He knew that what was real was the damp cellar, his self-pity, and his sexual frustration.

"How did you learn about this?" Amanda asked.

They had been quiet for ten minutes. Lorries rumbled up and down the Lower Road. Black smoke boiled up, rose through the air, and disappeared.

"Hillary lives in a bed-sitter on Shepherd's Bush. I've been there a few times. The hospital telephoned and the char answered it. I guess Hillary is gone for a vacation and the char had met me once or twice before, and so she rang me up. Didn't know who else to call on a moment's notice."

"I think Hillary is in Wales. I have no idea where."

"When does she get back?"

"Tomorrow night, after the weekend. That's all I know about it. She called me up last week and said she was upset and agitated about a case she has coming up in two or three weeks. She told me she needed a rest before she got down to work. I suspect she didn't even really know where she was going, that she just wanted to drive into the mountains of Wales and find a bed and breakfast. Just somewhere quiet with a dusting of snow."

"She's been working day and night," Roberts said. As a young barrister, and a half-Jamaican to boot, she had been given a cramped corner office at Lincoln's Inn, a shoebox-wedge of wood and damp glass on the darkest side of the law inns, a single nicked desk, a sink and wash basin, one tiny closet, and two smudged windows where pigeons roosted and shit. The windows looked down on a clutch of dark elms and by day there was hardly any light at all. In one corner, she had an electric fire, which she kept glowing all fall. Roberts knew she lived alone on Shepherd's Bush, and that she ate alone at the Lincoln's Inn commissary while ruddy-faced solicitors stared at her as if she had dropped from the sky. She would work late and slip down to Shaftesbury Avenue for curry, perhaps some hot tea after work. As far as Roberts knew she had no close friends. Her first big trial was coming up in three weeks too, a Jamaican Rasta who had been charged with the murder of a bartender during a pub holdup. Roberts wondered how her brother's death would affect her ability to conduct the trial, whether she would be able to continue, or if she would have to ask the judge for a continuance.

Roberts tried to finish his sausage. He thought about how little he really knew about Hillary Root, only that she was employing Roberts to help her with that case—Moseby Demeter, a musician who had killed a man during a robbery. He was grateful for the job, something steady that might give him the confidence to go on gaining an English life for himself. He had known Hillary for only a month, but it took no imagination to see how hard her life was, the cold room in Shepherd's Bush at night, the daily underground ride to Lincoln's Inn, the stares of male lawyers, the permanent foreignness she wore on her brown face. He knew that she was defending mostly Jamaicans and Trinidadians, baleful Pakistanis charged with theft, a few black Africans involved in the drug trade. Roberts thought it was strange you could know so little about another human being, and then be drawn directly into their life, and then perhaps slide out of it entirely, so easily. Roberts looked outside, then drew his finger along the glass so that he could see through a porthole, at the mist and the wind dragging newspapers down the Lower Road.

"You say the char called you?" Amanda asked.

"Yes, sorry," Roberts said. "She was doing Hillary's flat, staying downstairs overnight. Keeps house for the family that owns the building. Apparently there was a long call that no-body answered this morning and finally the char did and it was the hospital informing Hillary about her brother. The char went through Hillary's book until she found my name. She remembered it and called. That was about five o'clock this morning."

"Why didn't you wake me?"

"You were probably beautifully asleep I imagine." They shared a brief intimate smile, something on the way to some-thing else. Roberts and Amanda had these moments together, short sparks of shared feeling that were soon drowned by embarrassment caused by the uncertainty of their relation-ship, a lack of sexual candor. "I decided to leave you a note."

"Yes, of course you did," Amanda said, touching Roberts's hand gently. She stubbed out her cigarette and rubbed her forehead, probably soothing another of her headaches. The waitress had come and was cleaning up. She was a sloppy girl from Southwark with bleached hair and bitten fingernails. She said something pleasant and Roberts smiled at her. Some lorry drivers came through the door making noise, laughing. Rob-erts had nearly forgotten, but it was Saturday morning and people were probably getting ready for the football matches. In his own heart of hearts, all Roberts wanted to do was go to

sleep, then go upstairs to Amanda's house and watch a Stanley
Kubrick film on telly, have some whiskey. While the waitress
cleaned up, Roberts thought about Hillary, wondering about
her trip to Wales, if she was at that moment walking through
the green hill country, showered by wings of fog and mist. He
wondered if there had been an early snow, if the hills were
white and wet, if there was a village in the distance.

Amanda coughed. "I'm sorry," she said. "I'm tired today.
I didn't sleep at all well last night. And now I'm having one of
my headaches." The waitress brought their check and poured
more tea. Amanda said, "Do you know why James Root went
into the hospital last night?"

"I have no idea. Hillary told me nothing about her brother,
and she certainly never mentioned his health. Funny, though,
it didn't sound like an accident exactly." Roberts wanted to
hold Amanda's hand, share some projected grief. He was
thinking how nice it would be to go home to Kensington Park
Road and drink Pimm's all afternoon, get roaring drunk and
sit in a sunny window and listen to England.

"She doesn't know," Amanda said softly, probably thinking out loud. And then, "I knew her father when I was a
teenage girl. My father knew him because he was a diplomat,
but then Mr. Root went off to Jamaica in the foreign service.
The next thing I knew, young Hillary was in England and we'd
have lunch together sometimes in Greek Street. She was studying law then, and that was five years ago."

"The novice at the hospital said James had been murdered."

"For God's sake, what?" Amanda said. "This is terrible."

"I don't know why he was in the hospital," Roberts said,
"but the novice said something about losing part of his stomach."

"Perhaps he was accidentally poisoned."

"You've read too much Agatha Christie."

"Haven't we all!" Amanda said. She seemed to catch herself
then and frowned.

"Listen, Amanda," Roberts said seriously. "What I told

you about James Root is true. He died twice. He was admitted to the hospital sometime last night. Early this morning his heart stopped and he was saved by a duty nurse and an intern who were monitoring his case. Apparently the duty nurse was happening by his room and saw that the heart monitor had stopped. She started heart massage, and then administered digitalis. James Root was stabilized and everything was fine. The duty nurse left him alone for less than an hour. When she came back to check on him she found that his throat had been slashed ear to ear and that he was dead. I saw the man in his room. There was blood everywhere. He had been nearly decapitated."

"Oh God," Amanda said.

Roberts tried to lean across the table and comfort Amanda. "It's terrible, I know." Roberts paid the check and they went outside the Wimpy and up the Gomm Road toward an empty parking garage, just walking. Roberts had to hurry after Amanda, but soon they had gone inside the perimeter of the park where there were trees and hedges. They were under one wing of the huge hospital and you could hear the sound of drayage, the Wapping rail lines humming. "I'm sorry, Amanda," Roberts said, holding her arm. "Sometimes I forget how direct I can be. I didn't mean to bring it out like that." It was true, Roberts had none of the developed social skills of the English.

"Where is Hillary's father?" Amanda asked.

"Isn't he retired somewhere in Bayswater?" Roberts asked. "I think he's in a nice walk-up flat near Paddington."

"Yes, I think that's right. I think he's been retired for some time now on half-pay. As I recall, he married a Jamaican woman and it ruined his career. Reads Maugham, goes to the test matches, and drinks Dewar's. That sort of thing. This is probably going to be terrible for Hillary and him."

Roberts threw a pebble, scattering some pigeons. Ducks were swimming on a dirty pond. "And Hillary's mother?" he asked.

"She lives in Jamaica. Hillary was raised there."

"What is her father's name?"

"Simes Root," Amanda said. "Why all the questions?"

"I'm a curious guy," Roberts said.

"Are you going to get involved?"

"I'm always working," Roberts said.

"Surely the police can handle this."

"Technically that's always true."

"But you're working?"

Roberts shrugged and led Amanda back along the path toward St. Olave's. The sun was fully up now, rising over the warehouses. There were crowds along Jamaica Road. They went across some grass where there were the footprints of children who had been playing near the duck pond. One old man was feeding the ducks, tossing chunks of stale bread.

"I want you to come up to the hospital with me," Roberts told Amanda. The old man was calling the ducks by name, tossing them bread. "I want to see if we can talk to the hospital administrator, see what we can find out. A nun named Sister Dolores found James Root this morning. Perhaps we can talk to her as well." Roberts shrugged again, innocently. "I don't think anybody is going to talk to a disheveled American. But they might talk to you."

The sky had lifted, and patches of blue were showing through thin silky clouds. Roberts could see his breath and his hands were stiff from the cold. Coming off Orange Street he saw children playing. He put his arm around Amanda, who had cinched her raincoat closed.

"Did you ever meet James Root?" he asked her.

"Never," she said. "I thought he was living in Jamaica. I knew he existed, but I didn't know much about him at all. He can't have been here very long."

Amanda stopped them at the corner of Rebecca Street where there was a row of Georgian flats with small gardens, hydrangea bushes and tree roses. "I know you," she said. "You're going to get involved in this, aren't you?"

"If you mean, I'm going to help Hillary, then the answer is probably yes. It doesn't mean anything else."

"Of course not," Amanda said. "I'm not saying you shouldn't help Hillary. But please try to let the police do their work."

The children were laughing and pigeons rose into the towers of the hospital. "It's just that Hillary has given me a job and I feel some obligation to her. When you called her about me I was pretty desperate." Roberts looked at Amanda who looked quite lovely and tired. "James Root was murdered. Maybe I *have* to get involved."

"All right, come on," Amanda said, tugging his sleeve.

Roberts took a deep breath of river air. He could hear Jamaica Road, busy now with lorries and vans, some motor bikes buzzing along. Across Paradise Street there was a moss-bound Anglican church, an antiquity. Suddenly he thought about James Root and found himself in the middle of a silent prayer for the dead Rasta. Here was a human brother, he thought, whose soul was flying up through the falling autumn leaves.

3

Roberts favored solitude. He believed in its healing power and he trusted its purifying properties. Once he had left his home, on the way to England aboard a crowded jumbo jet out of Kennedy Airport, and unable to sleep, he had gazed outside the porthole window. Seeing, after many hours, the arm of Ireland through a dense rain cloud, a slash of green against an endless gray sea, he realized his solitude could have its dangers as well. So far up in the sky and so far away from his home, he was suddenly afraid. Uprooted as he knew he was going to be, and alone despite the noise from an in-flight movie, he had experienced an upsurge of tremendous anxiety and well-being, two gross contradictions inside himself. It was as though his solitude had buried itself inside so deeply that it had gone past all his defenses, and might remain buried there forever, giving him both courage and distress. His solitude was a kind of fretful piety enforced as it had been by long periods alone, until it had almost become a credo, a kind of faith that provided strength, but which was always being tested and was in danger of being lost.

Once in England he took up residence in Amanda's cellar

flat. He had known the woman for years from afar, and now he found himself living a purposeless existence below her three-story attached house along the Kensington Park Road. In the first few weeks his fortitude had been tested, and he felt as if his piety had been broken, as if his character, once a massive oak, had been blown down in a storm. He needed to withstand his solitude, if only to prove his pride to himself. He needed his god-given ritual, and when he thought it might be going away, he missed it.

In the mornings Amanda would fix coffee and they would share an English breakfast in the back garden of the old house. She would bring out china cups of Kenyan blend, and lay the table with some cornflakes, marmalade and muffins, and they would read *The Observer,* rarely speaking more than a few sentences before she would go off to work. She would kiss his forehead and be gone, and he would sit there alone in the cool gray English summer, and then he would shower and catch the bus and wander down Oxford Street, wondering how he would make a life. Finally, after months, he found some work at Lincoln's Inn, and he would often walk all the way from Notting Hill to the Strand, which took him nearly an hour, past Hyde Park, losing himself in the crowd, but happy to have a job he could do.

At times he was almost content in his cellar digs. Amanda had put up her Hogarth prints, and he had bought a Pakistan batik for the walls. She had brought down a desk and a reading lamp, and she had put up a metal bed and had covered it with a German goosedown comforter that Roberts thought was too thick to be comfortable. Still, he tried to adjust to his new life. He bought a collection of Penguin paperbacks, and he had found a black-and-white television, which he watched without buying a license. He tried to follow cricket and football. He began buying a daily provision of cut flowers to brighten the room, some red gladiolas, or perhaps daisies, and he put them in a marmalade jar above the mantel. In the evenings he would listen to the BBC and sit in front of his electric fire.

But more than anything he was trying to love Amanda. It sounded so simple to him, and he thought about it for hours until it became like a political slogan. Going about his daily business he would tell himself over and over that he loved her, sometimes whispering it aloud, and he often said it to himself when he was most alone. Sitting there in his cellar room during the long English summer nights when the sun would still be up at ten o'clock, he would watch its rays tangle in the chestnut trees. Then he would drink some whiskey and close his eyes and say the words. "I love you, Amanda." And sometimes he doubted the words, as if his pact with solitude had been irretrievably broken, that its value as a faith had been destroyed by love.

In reality, what he called his love was actually remembrance. He could recall Amanda as a young woman. He had a wafting nostalgia for her as she was then, when both of them had shared some form of boundless future, only to have that future split suddenly when Roberts went back to America so many years before. In the intervening years he had nurtured Amanda in the only way he could, in memory, a focus that for him remained fuzzy, an outline in the distance. He remembered their bicycle rides through the East Anglian countryside, their visits to Norman ruins, and their nights in music halls and pubs, all their joys. These memories had become a thread, an echo, that with time and distance had become more and more tenuous, until he wondered if it had really ever existed at all. For now he lived on hope and tried to gain strength in solitude. He had broken with the past when he had gotten on the jumbo jet with two bags of clothes, some fishing rods, and his old leather bomber jacket.

When he saw James Root dead in the hospital room, he thought he might borrow some strength by helping another human being, though he knew he might eventually have to pay it back. He thought of himself alone in his cellar flat with Brahms playing on the BBC and the smell of frying cod layered through the flats along the Kensington Park Road, and he realized that he had begun to doubt himself seriously, his presence in England. Alone and without substantial work, he began to pity himself. He knew he had become diffident to a fault, a shade of his former self. He was edgy, and often forlorn. He would fret and pace the floor, turning tight circles on the carpet, and more than once he had left his flat and had wandered through Notting Hill Gate most of the night, trying to control his breathing, which had become shallow and flat. Under the blaze of a midnight sky, he knew that he was becoming one of the Hollow Men, that he was enduring solitude, not learning from it.

They had walked up Culling Road near the edge of Southwark Park now. Amanda had livened, and was rubbing against Roberts as they walked toward the east wing of St. Olave's, in view above the chestnut trees, like a gray cliff against the grainy blue sky. At the top of some marble stairs they found the entrance to the administrative offices of the hospital, partitioned from a hall by frosted glass. Amanda went around the partition and came back five minutes later. They waited on a wooden bench until a matron ushered them into a plush office, a Victorian warren that looked down on the Lower Road where lorries punched through the railway tunnel in a billow of exhaust. The sky outside had turned lavender.

A man rose from behind a huge desk. "I'm Dr. Hughes," he said suspiciously.

The walls were lined with leather-bound books, and there were photographs everywhere. Roberts had gotten hold of himself again, back from his mood, but James Root was still in the back of his mind. "If you'll please sit down," Hughes said. Amanda introduced herself and Roberts to the doctor, who was a burly man dressed in tweed. His muttonchops were bright red and he had tight thin lips. Hughes looked at them with cold gray eyes.

"We came about James Root," Amanda said.

"Yes, well," Hughes stammered. The man regarded them coldly. He allowed the silence in the room to multiply before speaking again. Roberts detected a small tic under the man's right eye. The deep plushness of the room muffled the sound of lorries on the Lower Road. "In what respect," Hughes began, "or rather I should say in what capacity are you asking this question?"

"It isn't official, of course," Amanda said. "It's just that we're both very close to Hillary Root, poor thing. The dead man's sister."

"May I ask you how you learned of Mr. Root's death?" Hughes asked.

"Hillary's char telephoned around straight off. I assure you everyone is terribly upset."

"And this gentleman?" Hughes asked, nodding at Roberts.

"A dear friend of Hillary, from years ago."

"I'm sure," Hughes said flatly.

Roberts had now found his own part, assuming a sense of vague unease, as if he were too devastated to speak for himself. He had decided that keeping his American accent out of the way would be a good thing.

"We simply want to know what happened," Amanda said. Roberts knew that she was acting the part of schoolgirl.

"And where is Mr. Root's sister now?" Hughes said. He had formed his hands into cupolas and was tapping his fingernails on the varnished surface of his desk. He seemed practiced at gestures of political or moral censure. Very old-school.

"On holiday in Wales. We have no idea where. We all thought that she'd been working too hard, and so we sent her away. And she's got a terribly important trial at the Old Bailey in just three weeks. She'll not be back in London until late Sunday night and I'd hoped to learn all I could in order to prepare her." Amanda smiled deprecatingly. "I'm sure you understand." Some pigeons had swooped down to the ledge outside Hughes's window, cooing and gulping. Hughes turned and banged on the glass, scattering the birds.

"Well," he said, "we've tried to inform the father."

"Poor dear Simes," Amanda sighed.

Hughes stood and glanced out the windows and down the Lower Road. Speaking with his back turned, he said, "In all matters such as these, St. Olave's is bound by a duty to the patient and his immediate family to maintain an absolute bond of strictest confidence. In all matters." Roberts sneaked a glance at Amanda during the pontification.

"Oh dear, oh dear," Amanda said, raising an eyebrow to Roberts. "And my own father was with Simes at Harrow. They went up to Cambridge together and we've been ever so close." Amanda had scooted nearer the desk, laying one hand on its polished surface. "I know they'll want to be together during this whole crisis."

"But of course," Hughes said, turning back.

"I did so want to make things so much easier for dear Hillary when she returns."

"But my dear, of course," Hughes said in a comforting tone, placing one hand over Amanda's hand. "The deuce of it is that we don't quite know how it happened. I assure you that St. Olave's is noted for the quality of its care, and the training and experience of its staff."

"I'm sure you are," Amanda said, refreshed. "This is a truly wonderful hospital, I know."

"Yes, well," Hughes said, "nothing like this has ever taken place here before, I assure you. Not on my watch."

"Can you tell me about it?"

Hughes touched his throat. "This chap James Root was brought down to St. Olave's by ambulance late Friday night. I think he lived in a flat on the Curlew Road, not far from here. He was in bad condition. Landlord or char or somebody found him unconscious and convulsed on the landing of the second floor. He'd vomited right there. No telling how long he'd been that way. When he arrived in the emergency room there was barely a pulse and no blood pressure to speak of. I must say, it was a ruddy miracle he survived, but our interns did right by him and pumped his stomach right off. Stabilized the lad, I must say. Flushed his system."

"Do you know what had happened to him?"

"Still running tests when this awful thing happened. Won't get the results back from the laboratory for some time. Just know his temperature was below normal, seemed to be shut down. Had all the classic symptoms of poisoning."

"Beg your pardon," Amanda said, truly astonished.

"Poisoning," Hughes said. "Something he ingested literally stopped his nervous system. His heart was refusing to beat."

"Good Lord," Amanda said.

"Indeed," Hughes said mildly. "I say, my dear, are you quite all right? I know this is a bit of a shock. Would you care for tea?"

"Oh, I don't think so. I'm too upset."

"Naturally," Hughes said. "Quite right."

Roberts felt as though he had disappeared from the scene. He couldn't understand how Amanda had managed it.

"I'm afraid poor James Root had a terrible time of it," Hughes continued. "One awful episode happened early this morning. One of our nurses discovered him without an appreciable heart rate and we nearly lost him. But again, the cardiac specialist team did their miracle and he was revived. And he was stable, I must say." Hughes had leaned over his desk and was speaking directly to Amanda in soft soothing tones. "Bloody miracle, I must say." Roberts smiled to himself, understanding the point Hughes was making continually. The hospital wasn't to blame. "And I'm terribly sorry to say that our Sister Dolores found Mr. Root this morning around five o'clock with his throat slashed." Hughes lowered his eyes, and took another glance behind him at the windows. The pigeons had returned and were dancing on the ledge, five or six fat birds with ruffled throats.

Amanda sat dumbfounded, no act. "Where is James now?" she asked.

"I'm afraid he's been taken away by Scotland Yard," Hughes said. He shook his head sadly. "I must tell you that the father, Simes Root, has been notified by the police. He might even be at police headquarters as well."

"What will happen now?" Amanda asked.

"I'm afraid it is a police matter."

Roberts had been drifting back in time, through his

thoughts too, back to James Root, the dead man and the dusty geraniums and the blood-soaked sheets, the horrible dark blue gash in the man's throat.

"Nothing else?" Amanda said.

"If you mean, do we or the police have any idea who would have done this thing, I'm afraid the answer is no."

"Oh dear," Amanda said.

Hughes sat for a time, embarrassed. "There is one other thing," he added. "I saw the wound myself, and examined the dead lad. Of course I came up straightaway when I was called and examined him. I hope this doesn't upset you, my dear, but the gash in the neck was quite cleanly delivered, without the usual ragged edges from tearing and cutting. The first thing I noticed was how surgical it was." Hughes smiled at Amanda, gently, like someone placating a child. "And then there is the matter of the tongue."

"The tongue? I don't understand."

Roberts sat up, paying attention now. "Yes, my dear," Hughes said. "The tissue controlling the tongue movement had been cut. You're aware of the flap of skin beneath the tongue? Well, that had been snipped in half. Certainly had nothing to do with the cause of death, but odd, mind you."

Amanda stood up suddenly, surprising Roberts. Hughes came around the desk and the two of them shook hands warmly, and Hughes embraced her briefly. He shook Roberts's hand too, stiffly. Roberts followed Amanda outside and down the marble stairways without speaking.

They walked through Southwark Park holding hands, something Roberts hadn't expected. The sun had come up and the sky had cleared and the air was warm. You could see Tower Bridge just over the docks and wharves. They caught a taxi and rode in tired silence. When they arrived at Kensington Park Road, Roberts paid the cabbie and they walked through the house and sat down in the back garden. The air had become tinged with warmth and sunshine was filtering through the last of the mist.

"We're really going to have to talk about Hillary," Amanda

said, taking off her raincoat. "I feel like such a shit acting like some close member of the family."

"I don't know how you did it," Roberts said.

"What on earth do you mean?"

"This fellow Hughes," Roberts said. "When we walked into his office I felt as if he wasn't going to give us the time of day. He was using his duty of confidentiality to hide, and rightly so too. He acted like we had the plague. And then five minutes later he's Mr. Sunny Jim, holding your hand, soothing you like a baby. And spilling his guts I might add."

"Oh, that," Amanda said.

"Yes, that."

"Silly lad," Amanda said, touching Roberts on his cheek. "when we first walked into his office, I noticed his school tie. When he became huffy, I merely made up that story about how my father went from Harrow up to Cambridge."

"So?" Roberts said.

"Hughes went to Cambridge. I could tell it from his tie. We were merely sharing an old-boy experience together. Very lah-de-dah."

"Did your father go to Cambridge?" Roberts asked.

"Good heavens no, he's an Oxford man!"

"I've got a lot to learn," Roberts said.

They shared a sentimental hug. "You'll come up for the Kubrick festival on telly tonight?" Amanda asked.

"Yes, of course," Roberts replied. Until then he would manage his solitude another twelve hours.

4

When Roberts came to England Amanda was forced to feel something for the first time in years. After the death of her youngest child, she had been overcome by a wild and bewildering pain and grief, and a sense of abandonment and injustice that she attempted to subdue by hating God. The simple pleasure that once had been at the core of her life, afternoon on the green at Holland Park with her two children, lunches at Greek Street restaurants with friends, film festivals at Notting Hill cinema, had become odious, weights she could no longer bear. She lapsed into purposeful avoidance, and began to cultivate a disheveled look that surprised her mother and her friends both in its intensity and directionlessness. She awed people with her intense bohemianism, even those with whom she worked at the literary magazine. There were those who feared for her health or her mental probity, who noticed gray in her hair, which had been deeply auburn, the bleaching of her complexion, or the dull, watery look in her eyes. At the center of what had happened to her was a pure existential event, a death so malignant and unheard-of that Amanda had been consciously torn from her own center until a shell had formed around her heart.

She would walk through Kensington Park, across the street from her house, without seeing the big chestnuts, though she walked more and more rarely as time went on. For the most part she stayed inside, sitting in her second-story parlor drinking whiskey as the telly purred in the near background and the cold diurnal shadows of everyday life licked the walls and as the coal fire spit through the vacuous wintry landscape of her life. Night often fell around her without a specific awareness that would prompt her to turn on the lights, and then she would discover herself embalmed in total darkness, as though an invader had come in through the back stoop and had turned out all the lamps. The rain-slick streets would reflect against the windows and mirror her emptiness. She felt no sexual desire, and her other appetites had decreased until she lost weight and began to find that her clothes no longer fit her properly. The fingernails she had prided herself on, long glossy ones, were bitten down to nubs. Her hair went unwashed and lank.

At first, her mother would come down from Ipswich for a visit, or for the theater. They would sit together through long evenings at home, Amanda at the counter of the kitchen watching her mother make chicken salad or a niçoise, and then they would eat silently, Amanda barely touching her food, her mother tired and frustrated and helpless. They would ride cabs to afternoon matinees at Haymarket, or at the Royal Shakespeare on the Strand, and afterward take supper at her mother's favorite pub on Leicester Square. After her son's death, this happened three or four times, when Amanda was abjectly depressed, and then her mother allowed two months to pass without another visit. And then the visits stopped altogether, except for holidays. Even then Amanda would try to visit her mother too, but she had been so distressed that it seemed to serve only to remind her of her children. Amanda dreaded public events, thinking of them as frauds of joy or remembrance. Their trappings made her physically ill. Overcome by the nausea of everydayness, she made anger her talisman of rebellion against God.

Her son Jocko, the eldest, was still a presence, even though he had gone up to university and was home only for term breaks. Jocko would try to engage his mother, aware of her deep depression, and they would talk over supper about his work in philosophy, or his latest girl friend, about poetry too, and even about Amanda and her moods, but then she would begin to cry in the middle of supper at a restaurant, once at a recital in Covent Garden, and they would have to leave. Amanda began to drink heavily, even at lunch, and Jocko would watch her sit on the couch for hours at home, taking glass after glass of Teacher's.

And then Amanda began to receive regular letters from her American friend Roberts. She didn't answer the first few because she couldn't, she didn't know what to say, and was too debilitated to try. Assailed by anger, she couldn't gauge her feelings. She remembered their relationship, so many years before, but she thought that perhaps the memory was tempered or warped by time, that it would no longer fit the truth of things. Perhaps it was nostalgia, she thought, or perhaps they both shared the same unreal fantasy. This lost relationship was something so ephemeral, like wood smoke in a forest. Days and months passed with Roberts threatening to arrive in England, and when the event finally came to pass, she thought that it had occurred almost by default, because she had failed to either stop or encourage it, which was how she made many of her present decisions. She had no resistance, which made her life a series of encounters with fate.

In self-defense, almost out of fear, she cleaned the cellar flat, which hadn't been let for years. She laid some carpet and put up some Hogarth prints, and she brought down the creaky metal bed from her guest room and covered it with a bulky German comforter that she thought would be warm. Her motives were unclear, but she knew she desired a distance from Roberts, that she couldn't have him living upstairs, perhaps because she was still angry and dead inside, or perhaps

because she hated God, but mostly because she no longer
trusted her physical body. Down to her core she wanted no
one to touch her intimate parts. She sensed her troubles had
come from this source, that her womanhood was the spring-
board of her suffering. There was no joy in her viscera. Her
being had vanished. She thought of herself as a vampire who
required night and a box of native earth.

And so they were imprisoned together, Amanda Trench
Smith, the English widow, and Mitchell Roberts, American
cowboy.

She was thinking of these things early Monday morning
while she waited for Roberts to come up from his cellar. The
night before they had watched the Kubrick festival, both of
them apprehensive about the next day. Roberts had spent the
day watching cricket in Holland Park. Amanda was practicing
her speech for Hillary when Roberts finally came upstairs
wearing gray woolen slacks, a wool sweater, and his leather
bomber jacket.

The day was crisp with a light north breeze. There was the
smell of dead leaves in the air. Together they walked uphill to
Notting Hill Gate in a gale of falling leaves. They were waiting
for a bus in front of the wine merchant.

"How do you really know Hillary?" Roberts asked.

"We were at RADA together. I was there two years. I'm
afraid poor Hillary didn't last long."

"What was she like then?"

"She didn't have any dramatic talent at all," Amanda said.
"Just like me. She was very withdrawn and quiet, shy almost
to a fault. She had that same lovely, pure face, those same big
black eyes and long hair and the sweetest, longest eyelashes
I've ever seen." Amanda thought to herself, and said, "It's
true, you know. Our fathers have met. When my father was a
London barrister they would meet in City clubs here and there
when Simes Root was on leave from the foreign service."
Roberts had put his arm around Amanda to keep her warm.
"Anyway, she went away from the Royal Academy at mid-
term the second year. She'd had some bad rehearsals, embar-

rassed silences during scenes, muffed lines, student directors cursing her for missing cues. It's like in the Army actually, only you can't shoot your enemies. She was very young then. We all were, but she was too shy and sensitive to grasp all the emotion and competitiveness in the place, all the ambitious young actresses. There is a lot of politics and jealousy. The environment seemed to be killing her inside."

"How long since you've actually seen her?"

Amanda asked Roberts if they could walk down to Shepherd's Bush instead of taking the bus. They crossed a roundabout and walked downhill, along a stone wall. Roberts was featuring James Root in his mind again and the picture haunted him, the blood and silence in the white hospital room. "I mean, have you kept up with her at all?" he asked to break his mood.

"I'm afraid not, really. I knew she went up to the London School and took her law degree. I must say, I thought that was odd, given her shyness, her withdrawn nature. But she did seem more suited to law than drama, just barely." Roberts had fallen behind, and Amanda tugged him forward. There was a wind blowing off Wormwood Scrubs, and a few buses went past carrying the first of the commuters. The day had turned sullen, and it made Roberts unhappy, and he could barely follow what Amanda was saying next, something about Hillary, a chance meeting not long ago at an Oxford Street music store. "She somehow articled," Amanda said, "and found her place at Lincoln's Inn. I can't imagine it's easy for her with those stuffy solicitors and judges. But then you probably know all of that already."

Roberts had worked only a month or so with Hillary, serving as an investigator for a few small cases, petty thefts, some juvenile vandalism, one stolen car. He had been shocked the first time he saw her because she was so small and uncomplicated, a brown-complected woman in a smart blue suit and man's tie. Later he'd seen her in the courtroom in a white wig and black robe, and the picture was incongruous, but maybe that was because she was a woman and a foreigner. He didn't know where his preconceptions were coming from, and he tried to lay them aside and see the real woman, the lawyer, the Jamaican surrounded by a sea of Salvador Dali eyes, the barristers and defendants and judges all studying her every move, waiting for a mistake or a sign of indecision. Sitting in the courtroom the first time, Roberts wondered how on earth she could make her way in this tremendously hostile atmosphere, how she would be heard in an echo chamber of priggishness. But once he began to work with her in fact, to conduct witness interviews, and once he began to read some of her legal briefs, he realized that she was tremendously intelligent. He'd even gone round with her to do witness interviews in pubs and rooming houses, talking to rough skinhead types who snatched purses and stole cars. Or they would speak with Jamaicans and Pakistanis, or Trinidadians, types who were innately suspicious of Roberts, and whose speech, a patois, he found hard to understand and decipher. While Roberts was regarded with suspicion, Hillary Root handled herself beautifully. Now he thought of them as a pair, the tiny barrister from Jamaica, and the American in jeans who couldn't understand the language.

Hillary lived on Coverdale Road, just off the Goldhawk Road, in a row house on a brick lane of attached houses that had long ago been broken into flats and bed-sitters. They had gone down all the way to Shepherd's Bush in increasing traffic, and then had turned down Coverdale where there was an Anglican church surrounded by a flint wall.

"Anything about Hillary beyond what you've told me?" Roberts asked.

"You'll not get involved too deeply, will you?"

"That doesn't answer my question," Roberts said gently.

"No, nothing," Amanda said, shaking her head. "We have to assume James Root has been in England only a short time. Otherwise, I think we'd have known of him. Hillary hasn't spoken much about her family. She did tell me that her father had been broken by his experiences in Jamaica. But it wasn't any of my business, and she is a very private person."

"Would you tell her about her brother?" Roberts asked. "I think she'd take it better from you."

"Of course," Amanda answered. They had come to a point directly across from Hillary's house. They could see a calico cat watching them from a third-story window. Cars were parked willy-nilly in the street, some on the sidewalk, and there were children playing too, before school. Roberts was trying to string his thoughts into a coherent whole. If he had been in his own country, he would have come down hard on Hughes, asking him to detail duty rosters, security procedures, and employee interviews. He would have grilled the man about staff changes, floor access, and equipment inventories, and he would have been thrown out of the office, of course. There were other questions too, and Hughes might have answered them, but it was too late for that, wheels were turning in other places and Roberts wasn't part of it. When he looked around, Amanda had rung the buzzer after they had gone upstairs.

Hillary's bed-sitter was on the third floor of an old row house, up a flight of carpeted stairs. She opened the door a crack and looked out at them.

She had been crying and her face was swollen. Roberts thought to himself that he had never seen her look so young and vulnerable. She stood there in the door frame staring at them in shock, arms at her side. She was wearing old paint-stained corduroy pants and a man's white shirt. Roberts could see the bed-sitter behind her, exactly as he had pictured it, with its inevitable iron bed, electric fire, and a single drab window that looked out on desolate sycamores and some small garden plots. On a desk there was a heating ring for tea, and a few prints on the walls, relieving the flat yellow finish of the wallpaper. Amanda had embraced Hillary and Roberts stepped back to allow the two women their brief moment together. Then Hillary began to sob and Roberts touched her hand. "I'm so dreadfully sorry," Amanda said in her ear. "We thought you hadn't heard."

"My father rang," Hillary choked. Tears had streaked her

face, but she stopped sobbing. "Thank you," she began, but couldn't continue.

"I'm sorry, Hillary," Roberts managed.

"Come in, come in," Hillary said. "I'm just trying to make some tea. I've got to go to Scotland Yard soon, but I can't just yet."

Roberts explained the telephone call from Hillary's char. Amanda made the woman sit on the bed and made the tea herself. The room was depressing Roberts. He couldn't imagine spending a life in it, though he knew that thousands did, shopgirls, divorced men, clerks, a substantial part of the eleven million people in London. Amanda brought Hillary a cup of tea and she drank it delicately.

"I went to the hospital early Saturday morning," Roberts said. He was standing in one corner of the room feeling useless. "When the char rang around I went straightaway. I've seen your brother and we've talked to a Dr. Hughes."

"My father said he was murdered," Hillary said. She had gained enough composure to look white-faced and in shock.

"Yes darling, I'm afraid so," Amanda said gently.

"I'm afraid his throat was cut," Roberts said.

Hillary put her face down on the bed, spilling her tea. Amanda bent over her, rubbing her shoulders, eyeing Roberts in disapproval. Hillary sat up abruptly and said, "All right, I'm all right now."

"Feel like talking?" Roberts asked. He knew shock when he saw it. He crossed the room and sat down on the windowsill. He looked at the soot-caked facades outside, dog pens, rubbish heaps, wash fluttering on lines.

"Why not?" Hillary said dully. "I haven't talked about James in my whole life. Why not now?"

Roberts took the woman's tea cup and refilled it and gave it back to her. "First of all," he said, "promise me you'll put off this Moseby Demeter trial you have in three weeks. The way things are now, I don't want you extending yourself. This is quite enough to deal with all at once."

Hillary wiped her eyes with a handkerchief. "The trial," she said. A crazed smile lit her face. "The trial is in three weeks and we haven't done much work on it. We haven't interviewed the major witnesses. My client has been in jail for a long time. Do you actually think I could postpone it now? He's counting on me."

"I'm not trying to start an argument," Roberts said. "I just don't think you should be thinking about Demeter right now. Believe me, I know what I'm talking about. I've worked on dozens of tough cases, and you have your work cut out for you. Unless you're under control emotionally and physically, a criminal trial can be a true test. I know you can handle this, but just postpone it a few months."

Hillary went to her tiny basin and rinsed her face. Roberts was impressed at her ability to conjure strength.

"Moseby Demeter goes on trial in front of the King's Bench at the Old Bailey in three weeks. He's accused of robbery of the Zion pub off Jamaica Road, and of killing a bartender named Calliope. He says he's innocent. He says he wasn't there that night. He says he has an alibi, that he was drinking and smoking ganga with another Jamaican somewhere around Curlew Street. We have to interview the witnesses, and devise a defense strategy to get this defendant an acquittal, if that's humanly possible. He's been in jail the better part of a year. He can't raise a bond, and if he could, the judge would just raise it higher. Do you think my personal troubles are any greater than his? Have you been to Wormwood Scrubs? Every day in prison is a sentence that he has to serve without being found guilty." Hillary took one gulp of air and turned ash-gray. Amanda helped her sit down on the bed.

"I don't know," Roberts said, accepting another harsh glare from Amanda. "Somehow we have to find out who killed your brother. Both things are important."

"We have to make time for both," Hillary said, her breathing shallow. She got up and put on a winter coat and a pair of mittens, then got her notebook and put it in a pocket of the coat. Roberts was heartbroken for her. She looked frail, her smoothly oval face framed by pale sunlight.

"Let us come with you to Scotland Yard," Roberts said.

Hillary closed her eyes. "I'd like that," she said.

"On the way, you tell us about your brother," Roberts suggested. "Tell us about his life in Jamaica. Tell us how he came to England, where he lived and what he was doing. Then we'll talk to the coppers."

Hillary's calico cat followed them to the door downstairs. They walked six blocks to the tube stop and caught the Central Line. Right now Roberts could see ahead about a week. The rest was a tunnel without end.

5

Roberts didn't know what he had expected, but he hadn't expected ten floors of glass and steel with television cameras surveying every scene, and listening devices—a twentieth-century Scotland Yard crammed with late-twentieth-century technology, blue-white technical noise and metal detectors. They were in the outer alcove of a stuffy office while a man named Drummond shuffled papers in his frosted glass cage. Amanda was sitting next to Roberts in the fluorescent glare, which Roberts thought should have been Victorian gloom with high ceiling panels and walnut desks, guys walking around with magnifying glasses. Instead it was all drop-ceilings and insulated pasteboard and slick blue tile that reverberated with the hush of computer language. They had come all the way across central London on the Central Line, then had walked half a mile through a warren of alleys and cul-de-sacs, then found the girdered steel building without any character, as airless and dry as computer printout paper. Drummond had met them in a hallway and had made them sit outside his office while he shuffled paper and looked out at them occasionally with his official squint, fixing on them a

41

beady stare that emanated from his hard glassine eyes. He was wearing a neat blue serge suit and a freshly laundered white shirt. He looked a young fifty years old, as if he did sit-ups every day and watched his diet and didn't eat too much chocolate, one whiskey before dinner and off to bed at ten. He probably enjoyed his stamps and flowers and he probably had a son at Eton he saw twice a year. Hillary was pacing the floor nervously, still without much color. Roberts thought she was holding up damn well under the circumstances, better than could be expected. He was proud of her.

Drummond ushered them inside his office and then sat down behind his desk. "Miss Root," he said, "I hope you can answer some questions for me. I understand your friends are here just for support. I know how hard this is for you." Drummond smiled officially, but not without feeling.

"I'll try," Hillary said.

Amanda had taken Robert's hand. It was a gentle thing to do and he was grateful. He thought that maybe this terrible event would bring them closer, break the wall of embarrassment between them. Already he had decided to help Hillary in any way he could.

"Your father has already identified the boy," Drummond said. "So that won't be necessary. Your brother is downstairs now. I'm afraid there will have to be an autopsy. I hope you understand."

"Yes of course," Hillary said bravely. Roberts was glad she wouldn't have to see the body right now.

"By the way," Drummond said, "your father was completely exhausted. I've had one of our men take him home. You can see your brother when we're finished. Before the . . ."

"Yes, thank you," Hillary said.

"Well, then. Suppose you just tell me about your brother. Perhaps that would be easier."

"I don't know," Hillary said. "I don't know where to start actually."

"Suppose you tell me about his enemies. Who would want to kill him?"

"I wouldn't think he had any," Hillary said. "Enemies, I mean."

Drummond shrugged. "He had one enemy, didn't he? In a situation like this there is an obvious element of premeditation. We have to assume there is an element of revenge or passion of some sort. Somebody came into his hospital room and willfully murdered him, after all." Drummond paused, waiting for the conversation to jump-start itself. "I wonder if your brother was involved with a woman?"

Hillary stared at the floor. "I'd like to tell you something," she said slowly.

"Please do," Drummond said.

"My brother holds a British passport. He came here from Jamaica not long ago. In the short time he was here I'm sure he couldn't have made many friends, or even met many people. He was not a violent person. He was quite sweet and gentle. I don't know if he was seeing a woman. The most important thing about him was his love of music. He was very talented. And he was very quiet." Hillary looked at Roberts for support, and he nodded. Drummond was staring at them through the blue-white fluorescence.

"Go on," Drummond said.

"He was twenty-two years old," Hillary said. "He was born in Jamaica. There was no work for him there. I'm sure you know there isn't any work for men in Jamaica. They stand around on street corners and they drink rum. They cut sugar cane when they can or they wash cars or they find jobs cutting the grass at tourist hotels. James had little education and he decided to come to England to make something of his life. He knew I was here and he thought he could make a new start. He wanted a future."

"How long had he lived on Curlew Street?"

"He found those rooms shortly after his arrival."

"Who bought his air ticket?"

"Is this necessary?" Hillary said.

"Please, miss," Drummond said. "I don't know what's necessary and what isn't."

"My father bought his ticket," Hillary said.

"Your father is a retired civil servant?"

"Of course, you must know that."

"What did your brother do? Did he have a job?"

"He was looking for work," Hillary said. She thought for a moment longer. "But it's very difficult."

"You provided him with funds?"

"My father and I were helping James, yes."

"That's very good of you," Drummond said. Roberts was trying to read the man, but it was hard. He maintained an official tone, and his expression never altered. "I understand that James Root was your half-brother."

"Yes," Hillary said. "As long as you've discussed this with my father, I may as well tell you what you already know. My father is not James's father."

"And tell me, miss, did James have trouble with the police in Jamaica?"

Hillary stared at Drummond for a long time, her face coloring. "Aren't you forgetting something?" she asked.

"What would that be, miss?"

"My brother has been murdered. He isn't charged with any crime. He isn't guilty of any offense. He's only just been found dead in his hospital bed."

Hillary had begun to cry again and Amanda stood to put her arm around the woman. The air in the room was dry and Roberts could hear the click of computers.

"Very well, miss," Drummond said. "I'll tell you what the Yard is doing right now. We're in the process of interviewing every member of the hospital staff who was on duty at the time your brother was killed. Our men are scouring the neighborhood where your brother lived and attempting to talk to every shopkeeper and pub owner in the area. We're searching the hospital and its immediate area for the murder weapon. Our medical people are taking care of their analysis right now. Tomorrow morning we'll sit down with the results of all this and see where we are. We'll try to reconstruct every move your brother made since he's been in England if we have to, talk to his friends, any employers. I assure you we have no intention of sweeping this under the rug. If it's humanly possible, Scotland Yard will find out what happened to your brother and why."

Hillary sat down on a bench beside Roberts. She had stopped crying and was dabbing at her eyes with a handkerchief. "Yes of course," she said, exhausted. Roberts knew that some of the air had gone out of her, that she had a stunned look.

"I must tell you," Drummond said, "that we've searched your brother's room already." He looked away, then back at Hillary. "We discovered several packages of marijuana wrapped in brown paper, then put in pink plastic sacks and wrapped with rubber bands. I'm sorry, miss."

"Oh dear," Hillary said.

"Yes, I'm afraid this puts a different light on things. Did you know of his involvement with drugs, miss?"

Hillary bit her lip. "Of course, of course," she said, as if to herself. "You don't understand." Fighting back tears, Hillary had closed her eyes. "Ganga isn't uncommon in Jamaica. You have to understand that sometimes it's seen as a sacrament almost. Many young men smoke ganga and it's readily available on the streets. You see it everywhere. It isn't some sort of evil that isn't spoken about."

"But this is England, isn't it?" Drummond asked, for the first time some animation in his voice. Roberts grew away from the scene, thinking about James Root again, something he couldn't get out of his mind. He wondered about the man's life, living by Curlew Street on the docks of the Thames, the dark alleys that smelled of garbage and river water. While Roberts thought, Drummond read through his files, but Roberts was hardly aware of the policeman. Hillary was crying softly, without resistance to the present. "And at the same time," Drummond said, "that you were supplying James with money, he had quite a large amount of marijuana. Ganga, as you say."

"It doesn't matter," Hillary said. "To him it was sacramental. He would never turn it into a commodity. To sell." Roberts had returned to the scene with an urge to speak, prolong things, take the bite out of Hillary's pain. But he didn't. He didn't want to take twenty minutes explaining himself for nothing.

"Your father told us much the same," Drummond said. "I'm afraid he didn't know of any acquaintances either."

"Yes, that's true. My father was just being kind, buying the ticket I mean." Hillary sat up straight. "My brother was fully Jamaican. He had no blood tie to my father. James was at odds with himself, but he wasn't a drug seller."

"You were in different spheres?" Drummond said. "Would that be a fair statement?"

"No," Hillary snapped. "Both of us are in different spheres from you."

"Aha," Drummond said. "Was your brother a rude boy, miss?"

"I've told you no," Hillary said. Roberts could sense her resistance breaking. "If you mean to say that he was a *ska* man or a Rasta, then the answer is probably yes. He'd lived in Kingston and he'd played music in the slums and he'd lived with Rasta all his life. But if you're asking me was he a gangster, then the answer is no. Some people can't tell the difference."

"But the marijuana," Drummond said.

Hillary was sitting down, looking entirely exhausted. "You have to know Jamaica," she said. Hillary looked at Amanda as if to ask for help. "What should I say?" she asked rhetorically.

"Go home, Miss Root," Drummond said suddenly. "We'll do our interviews and tests and we'll let you know what's happening next."

Roberts stood. "Check the tongue," he said.

"I beg your pardon," Drummond said.

"Check the tongue," Roberts said again.

"Ah yes," Drummond said. "Doctor Hughes told us about that. Rather odd at that."

Amanda was busy with Hillary, helping her on with her coat. Roberts followed them outside, past the frosted glass divider and into the hall.

They rode the underground in silence, surrounded by the flash and roar of stations going past, a white glare of toothpaste posters. Amanda left them at Notting Hill Gate while Roberts rode one more stop down the line with Hillary. She was pale and tired and she had only a few words to say. While they rode, he studied her, finding her quite lovely in a faraway, lucid sort of way, with a strange intensity in her eyes. They got off at Shepherd's Bush and walked down Goldhawk Road until they arrived at Coverdale, which was empty and forlorn with its gray rows of flats and parked cars and empty Anglican church. The sky had lowered itself into a gray mat that seemed to press down on the dreariness. Roberts followed Hillary upstairs to her flat and he helped her off with her coat. She sat still on the bed, looking out the window. Roberts put a shilling in the electric fire.

"Will you be all right?" he asked.

The windows faced west and there was no light in the room.

"Yes, of course."

"I'm sure you'd be welcome to come around and stay for a while with Amanda. It might not be a bad idea."

"I'd rather be alone."

"Please think again about postponing the Moseby Demeter trial. You know we haven't interviewed the witnesses. I haven't even talked with Demeter himself. There's a lot of work to do and you're going to need some time. Just give it some thought."

"Actually, I'd rather do the case. It will give me something to think about other than James."

"Perhaps you're right," Roberts said.

Hillary sighed. "You know, I never really knew James at all. And now he's gone."

"I'm sorry," Roberts said. Roberts walked to the door and surveyed the room. Five steps across, barely a room at all. "Perhaps I can help with James, too." He continued to calculate, two steps from bed to desk, three steps from desk to door, two steps from door to bed. "Would you mind if I asked you about rude boys?" he asked.

Hillary paused. "Jamaican men who've taken a certain attitude. It comes from reggae. They're angry and can't find work and they roam the countryside and then one day they go to Kingston and become rude boys. They steal what they can. They exist on the edge of something none of us can readily understand."

"Gangs, you mean?"

"Gangs," Hillary said dreamily. "In a way, I suppose. What was the Mafia? In one generation it was a fruitseller forcing protection on small store owners. In the next generation they organize huge rings of prostitution and gambling businesses. In the next they run labor unions and buy politicians. And in the next trucking businesses. And finally they become corporation presidents."

"I'm just trying to understand," Roberts said.

"Then you have to understand Jamaica. In my country there is tremendous poverty and injustice. Any gang is just a response to the social conditions that are ever-present. In Jamaica there is a heritage of colonial exploitation and the rude boys are responding to it. Poverty is an injustice, and wherever there is great injustice there is great crime."

"I think I do understand."

"It's more than that," Hillary said. "You'd have to understand about Ras Tafaria too. You'd have to understand the religious significance in the music and the drugs."

"It's existential then."

"If you wish. There is a religious significance to the ganga. Zion has a special place too. Slavery and sugarcane and *mento* music and piracy and *ska* beats and English colonization all have their place in the iconography of Jamaica. You'd have to understand displacement and pain and servitude and ignorance. You'd have to understand the whole of the Caribbean experience. But it isn't a simple matter of selling drugs and being a rude boy." Hillary stood and walked to the window and looked out at the English row houses. "My brother was a Rastafarian," she said. "It was his religion. He probably had the ganga for that reason too, not to sell it. He wasn't a rude boy. He was lost and looking for Zion and he had no work and no friends and he was in a strange land. But he was not a gangster." Hillary sighed again. "I'm going over to be with my father for today. Can we get to work first thing in the morning?"

"Of course," Roberts said.

He jumped—she had screamed, one shrill piercing scream. Hands to her face, she collapsed on the bed. Roberts hurried to the window and looked down into the garden below. The calico cat had been strangled and was hanging by a wire from the wash line.

"Why would anyone?" Hillary cried.

....

6

His morning went by in a dream, as if some piece of himself
had uncoiled in a tuft of cloud and was drifting away across
the checkerboard rye fields of England. He shaved and dressed
and smelled the aroma of bacon and egg, but he had the
feeling that he'd forgotten a name, that it was on the tip of his
tongue and some force was making it impossible to speak. He
rode the Central Line amid a welter of foreign faces and
cigarette smoke, squeezing his eyes closed, trying to recall
what it was his mind couldn't focus on. Later, walking
through the rain-sodden edge of Lincoln's Inn, it finally came
to him, and he remembered hurrying down from Hillary's flat
to the alley below, between rows of identical facades. He had
gone round to the back garden from where he could see Hillary's face looking down at him from her window with a
wide-eyed broken expression of pure dread and grief, while he
found the cat with its neck broken, distended from a wire. He
wanted to hide his movements but he couldn't. Hillary was
directly above him, her face pressed to the glass. He had cut
down the cat and had searched for a spade, and had buried the
poor thing behind an ash heap, as far back in the garden as he

could, beneath a barren mulberry. Those minutes had seemed endless, one repetitious tick after another until time seemed as drawn out as a bad cough. He could hear the traffic on Goldhawk Road. He could hear the wind clicking in the trees.

While he climbed the stairs to Hillary's office he thought about the dead cat, its thickly wet fur and empty gauzy eyes. He felt as if he were swimming through murky water, his lungs bursting, and he wondered if he had a fever. He found Hillary in the office, sitting over a cup of tea.

"Are you all right?" he asked stupidly.

She poured another cup of tea and shuffled some papers. For a while they sat in silence while Hillary pretended to work. Roberts read a police report on the Demeter case.

"What do you think of the report?" Hillary asked.

"I think I've got the general picture. Robbery and murder. Demeter walks into the Zion pub and pulls a gun. Calliope comes around the bar and somehow Demeter shoots him."

"Is alleged to have shot him."

"Alleged, yes," Roberts said.

"As you know we've been through the preliminary hearing and Demeter has been bound over for trial. There are three witnesses who will testify that Demeter came into the pub and pulled a gun. A man named Howard gave him some money from the till. The robber then took a watch from a man named Treacle and four quid. When Calliope came around the bar he was shot in the stomach and died on the spot. Demeter is said to have run from the pub with the owner behind him. He disappeared and the police were called."

"Look here, Hillary," Roberts said, trying to make her stop the manic work. He knew she was operating in a frenzy of denial and avoidance.

"Please, let's get to work," she said.

"All right." Roberts smiled gently. "The police report indicates that the robber was wearing some kind of mask. A carnival getup."

"A devil's mask with horns."

"Then how could three people identify Demeter positively?"

"They all say they could recognize his voice and his mannerisms. They knew him, you see."

"Is that good enough?"

"It's circumstantial, of course. The police found the mask in a trash bin outside Demeter's flat. Apparently Moseby Demeter was a regular at the Zion pub. He came in the place all the time and cadged drinks and ran up a bill but never paid. He was a pest and probably a rude boy himself. I'm afraid their claims are going to be hard to break on the stand."

"Still, it isn't enough to convict, is it?"

"I don't know. He's certainly a fool to go into a place and rob it when he's known there. Or hungry or desperate. Why don't we decide for ourselves when we visit him?"

"You want me to interview the three witnesses?"

"Yes, do give it a go today."

"Maybe I can make some progress with them. Plant a seed of doubt, you know?"

"Please give me a written report in detail about their testimony and the results of your interview." Hillary smiled now, trying to lighten the load. "But please be careful. Even if these men aren't Rasta, they're Jamaican and they're going to be suspicious of you. But you're the only investigator I've got, and lucky to have you."

"Surely a voice identification isn't enough," Roberts mused. "It's a murder case."

"You've read the report," Hillary said. "Demeter lives in a bed-sitter off Old Jamaica Road, not ten minutes from the Zion pub. The police searched the area and found a weapon in another trash bin. They think he ran down toward his house and dropped the mask in one bin, the gun in another. I do suppose it could have happened that way."

"No fingerprints on the gun?"

"Yes, but too smudgy to identify properly. And Demeter says he was wearing mittens on the night of the murder."

"What's this about the four quid found in the toe of a sock?"

"Yes, that's right. Four quid rumpled in the toe of a sock. Exactly the amount taken from the till and found in Demeter's flat thirty minutes after the robbery. Demeter admits he put the money in the sock, but he says that's all he'd managed to borrow or cadge over weeks and weeks. That's a bit of a stand-off because there is no way to positively identify the money as having come from the Zion till. But it is one more circumstance working against the defendant."

"I see why you waived the jury now," Roberts said.

"Juries don't like technical defenses."

"The report says Demeter was wearing a watch."

"He says it was one he'd had for years. One of the patrons, this Treacle, says it's his, but Demeter says it isn't, that he got it years before in Kingston. There are probably thousands of those old watches around. But juries are impressed by connections like this."

"Maybe he did it."

"He's innocent right now."

They were quiet, Roberts noticing how tired Hillary looked. "You need some rest," he said.

"I didn't sleep last night."

"Take some time away from here. I still don't think you should do this Demeter trial, you know."

"Never mind," she replied.

Roberts took his tea to the tiny wood-frame window and looked out at the autumn gloom. Hillary put on her coat and they went downstairs and caught a cab at High Holborn and went across the West End toward Bayswater and Wormwood Scrubs to keep their appointment at the prison with Moseby Demeter. There were crowds in the streets, old women with shopping bags, young women with prams.

Roberts leaned his head against the window glass. "How is your father?" he asked. They were near Paddington and you could see the crowds at the station.

"Inspector Drummond was right. When I went to see my

father yesterday, he was very tired. I think my brother's arrival in England had unnerved him somewhat, and now that he's dead, I think my father is very confused. About his role in my mother's life, and his reactions to my brother's death. As you know, he wasn't the father of James. But he loves my mother very much, and whatever causes her pain, also causes my father pain. Perhaps more so." Hillary looked away at the crowded city streets. It was one of those dull, featureless days. "We sat together in his flat and drank tea and he finally took a nap."

"Perhaps you two could go away together after this is all over. Majorca or Sicily."

"Perhaps," Hillary sighed. Roberts wanted to talk more about James, but he saw that Hillary had slumped against the seat and had closed her eyes.

"I'm sorry about your cat," he said.

"Why would anyone harm my little Jeremiah?" she asked.

"Children are cruel."

"But to hurt him like that."

Roberts realized he had no further answers, and wished he hadn't brought up the subject. He could remember the feel of the dead cat in his hands, its almost emphatic weight, like holding a wad of starlight. Roberts began to think about the odds against this remarkable woman. She had suffered the death of her brother, the loss of her only pet, and in three weeks she would face the King's Bench in her first murder trial at the Old Bailey. He remembered burying the cat, looking up at the window on the third floor, seeing Hillary as he shoveled away at the dark English dirt. When he went back to the Kensington Park Road cellar, he had stood alone in the dark for fifteen minutes trying to make sense of existence.

"Let's see what Demeter has to say, shall we?" he asked, changing the conversation's focus.

The prison sat on the edge of a dale, surrounded by thick brick walls. The walls were topped by barbed wire, and at every corner there were glass conning towers and spotlights. Some of the bricks had turned green with moss, and Roberts could see guards moving along the top of the wall with machine guns and field glasses. They were let in through a front gate after being searched and presenting their identification, and then were led down a series of locked hallways, until they were made to stand in the glare of bright lights in a waiting room. At one end of the room a door opened, and Demeter was led to a small barren desk by a guard who made him sit down, and then chained him by a ring to the desk. The table was made of cheap plywood and there were two metal chairs on the side opposite Demeter. The room stank of tobacco smoke and urine. They were alone in the room, except for the guard and some television cameras following their every move.

Hillary sat down and smiled at Demeter, then patted his hand warmly. The man was very skinny and tall, with a tangle of greasy dreadlocks that had a tint of red. His nose was flat and flared and he had the look of a man in prison, tired, unself-directed, without will. Prison had obviously worn him down with its bad food, lack of privacy, noise, and regimentation. Roberts thought of the long hours alone in a tiny cell, and he could tell the etiology of Demeter's red eyes and shaky hands.

"Are you being treated well?" Hillary asked the man.

"I not my own man here, I," he said. "You from Jamaica," he continued. "You my saviors, jah!" Roberts recognized the sarcastic tone for what it was. While he spoke, Demeter remained in perpetual motion, his head bobbing, hands relentless against invisible boredom. "Hard on me, jah," he said.

Roberts was impressed with how Hillary went about her business. She had worn a gray suit and blue blouse, and a pair of wire-rim glasses, and Roberts thought she looked quite professional. She was in control of her documents and her questions, and he was delighted to see her controlling the Rasta. They were having their own inner confluence and they seemed to understand one another perfectly, even though Roberts had a difficult time with the patois and the repetitious slang. A dirty institutional glimmer settled over the room, and occasionally Demeter would look at the bulbs and cover his eyes, and then hum softly to himself, listening to another voice. Hillary would follow him in these digressions, not letting him get away from her. Every so often the guard would stroll by, check Demeter's chain, and then move away.

"Now listen to me," Hillary said. "The witnesses against you are the three men at the Zion, Howard, Lemon, and Treacle. Of course, a police officer will testify about the money and the watch. There will be laboratory reports offered about the gun. Do you understand?"

"You know I didn't do nothing at all," Demeter said.

"I know, Moseby," Hillary said. "But we have to make a defense. You will have to take the stand and explain the watch and where you were that evening if you can. When the prosecution is making a case based upon circumstantial evidence, the one way to certainly create reasonable doubt is to present a logical explanation for every circumstance. And of course the three witnesses will claim to identify you by your voice and build and manner. I must find a way to counter their identifications if I can." Hillary glanced at Roberts, who was making some notes. "Do you understand me, Moseby?" she asked. "You have to say something to the judge."

"I get that old watch in Kingston. Some ruddy trash," he concluded.

"Do you remember exactly when and where you got the watch?"

"Down in Kingston town I told you, I," Demeter said. He had closed his eyes again.

"But do you remember who you got it from?"

"I had it years now."

"Can somebody testify to that?"

"Oh, lady, no," Demeter said. Demeter's eyes lidded, and then opened, levers to his thought. "Time don't mean nothing to Demeter for years. You think I need a watch in England. I have to get to my good job, hah."

"You play in a band?"

"Jah, mon," Demeter said.

"Those boys with you in the band ever see you wear a watch? Could they testify to that?"

"Don't them know. Why they know about my watch?"

"What about the four quid?"

"They going to hang Demeter for four English quid? That the thing? You know the truth, Miss Hillary, if I had a hundred quid in my jeans they would hang me for having that. They would hang me if I had a silly penny in my pants. They going to hang a right Englishman if he have four quid in his sock?"

"So the members of the band hadn't seen you wear the watch?"

" 'Cause I don't wear the watch, that's why."

"Do they know anything that would help you?"

"No, miss, they don't. Why should they? It wasn't them I was with that night they say I robbed the Zion."

"You've said you have an alibi."

"Now there you go," Demeter said. His patois was very thick and Roberts could barely understand him. Demeter flashed a poignant smile. "That night some boy robbed the Zion I was smoking ganga with a Jamaica fella. You find him and he gonna tell you that. He tell you old Demeter didn't rob no fool Zion. He tell you Demeter didn't shoot Calliope, hah."

"Let me get this absolutely clear," Hillary said. "You were with a Jamaican the night of the robbery?"

"Jah, I told you that."

"You smoked ganga with the man."

"Sure, no problem," Demeter said.

"No problem," Hillary said. "Just tell me who this man is and we have no problem."

"Don't know him from before. Just a boy I met in an alley and we share some rum and then some ganga where he lived."

"You went to his flat?"

"For sure I was a little drunk, miss, jah," Demeter said, smiling slyly. "Just stay up at his place and watched the water roll by."

Roberts was writing furiously now. "Do you know where this Jamaican lived? His address?"

Demeter rolled his eyes and laughed. "I told you the truth that I was spinning around that night. Like some crazy Rasta fuckah that night, jah."

"You'd been drinking?"

"Sorry thing," Demeter said.

"You don't know where the man lived?"

"Jah, no."

"What was his name?"

Demeter didn't seem to hear the question.

"Moseby," Hillary said loudly. "Can you describe the man you say you were with the night of the robbery?"

"Big boy, not a Creole. Black like me."

"Dreadlocks?"

"Jah, mon," Demeter said.

"Skinny?"

"No, mon. Big boy, strong. You know."

"Did he have a mustache or beard?"

"He didn't have no beard or mustache."

"Scars or tattoos?"

"I don't know, miss. We was drinking rum."

"Did he have the ganga?"

"Blue mountain the same," Demeter said. "He had the best ganga I see for a long time."

"The man you met had the ganga," Hillary said, Demeter nodding his head in agreement.

"Do you remember his room?"

"Sure, some."

"Was it near your place?"

"Right near. I remember it only take me a few minutes to walk home from there. But I never been there before or since."

"Was his room upstairs?"

"I think we go upstairs, jah."

"On the right or left side as you went up?"

"Jah, the right I think. This going to help?"

"I think it might. If we can find this Jamaican boy."

"So, you going to be my savior."

"Just some more questions, Moseby," Hillary said. "Please try to tell me if you remember anything about the room you were in. If we can find this Jamaican boy, we can make him testify." Hillary continued to press the man. "Just try to remember the room itself right now. Were there any pictures on the walls? Was there a window you could look out? What could you see if you looked out? Things like that."

"Sure, there was a picture. Big Ras Tafaria on the wall. The Lion of Zion!"

"Now, can you remember the boy's name?"

"He told me he was Jimmy," Demeter said, looking and sounding bored. Roberts had a brief premonition, then made some notes. The guard moved in and looked at them curiously.

"All right, Moseby," Hillary said, snapping shut her notebook. "We'll see what we can do. We'll interview the witnesses at the Zion pub, and we'll see if we can't find this man you say you were with the night of the robbery. Maybe we can."

Demeter had opened his eyes and was staring at Roberts. "You the white man Hillary here told me about?" he asked.

"I must be," Roberts said.

Demeter raised a hand and looked away. "Jah, you go down to the Zion then," he said. Hillary slid a package of English cigarettes across the table and Demeter opened it and smelled the tobacco. Hillary had taken off her glasses and was watching Demeter, who was quiet, staring into space. The guard was waiting for them to finish. "We been talking now," Demeter said, "and you ain't telling me you can handle this case. You sure nothing on your mind? You all right?"

"I'm fine," Hillary said.

Demeter was very cold now. "You look a little sick to me, girl." Demeter smiled without emotion. "You going to get old Moseby off this thing? If you're not too sick?"

"Don't worry, Moseby," Hillary said, annoyed.

They left Moseby Demeter in the gray light of the prison interview room. Roberts followed Hillary down the anonymous corridors until they reached the front gate and were searched. Once outside, Roberts realized he was a little shaken from the experience of claustrophobia, the rigors of circumspection, all the imposed terror. They walked away from Wormwood Scrubs and found a cab going into the City.

"How do you like my client?" Hillary asked, once they got going back to Lincoln's Inn.

"I don't care for him," Roberts said. "The question is how will the judge like him?"

"A Rastaman?" Hillary said. They were on Bayswater in heavy traffic. "No English judge is going to like Moseby Demeter. That's why we have to try to find this Jamaican he says he was drinking with the night of the robbery."

"I'll ask around."

"You'll interview the pub witnesses?"

"Don't expect much from them. If they were the dead man's chums, then they'll have an ax to grind."

"I don't expect much from anybody," Hillary said. "But see what they have to say, will you?"

"They'll talk to me," Roberts said.

The cab was caught in Paddington traffic, moving slowly in the clutch of commerce. Hillary was distracted again. Roberts thought of suggesting a lunch of pink gins, but he let the moment pass. "I'd like to help you with your brother," he said instead. "In any way that I can."

"All right, maybe," Hillary said. "But Demeter comes first."

"Don't you worry about that."

Roberts watched Hillary collapse against the leather seat, her eyes brimming. He looked out at the rail station and the gray brick buildings. Pretty soon they got going again, but by then there was nothing left to say.

7

Roberts had given himself six months to find work and settle into an English life, to become something other than an alien presence in an environment of eleven million. He counted on Amanda and he needed some strength and hope from her, but now for the first time he felt that he was achieving some independence, that his work with Hillary, and his sudden interest in the death of her brother, as horrible as that was, had given him a reservoir, some room where he could succeed or fail on his own. He wanted to help Hillary, and in helping her, help himself to a new personality, or at least a new hold on the fragile thread of being, which now ran through a cold cellar flat, a nervously embarrassed love affair, long walks alone in Kew Gardens.

He said good-bye to Hillary at Notting Hill Gate, and watched her taxi speed away in the noonday traffic toward Hyde Park. He walked downhill to his flat, thinking about how they had barely spoken during the last twenty minutes of their ride while a slow gray summer drizzle began to fall. It depressed Roberts, and he was angry that he couldn't resolve the woman's pain, but he knew that it was too great for that.

And then she had begun to cry, just as the drizzle began, as if the weather was a signal for her sorrow. Roberts tried to comfort her by touching her gently on the shoulder, pouring as much feeling as he could into the gesture, but it had remained empty, and he noticed that the taxi driver was staring at them in the rear-view mirror. He let Hillary continue to cry. He thought that perhaps Demeter's behavior had prompted some of her tears and in the back of his mind he wondered about the "James" who would serve as an alibi, and he pondered Demeter's last few cutting remarks about Hillary's competence and emotional stability. While he watched the taxi disappear into the mass of traffic, the gray English rain, he wondered how she could possibly find the strength and courage to pass through the next three weeks.

Roberts ate lunch alone in the back of the Kensington Park Road house. He poured himself a single glass of red wine and he ate a cheese sandwich and some almonds, and he watched the drizzle slip down on the bricks of the garden path where there were some dying mums in patches of damp earth. Again his mind turned to the mental image he had formed of James Root dead in his hospital bed with his neck slashed, cleanly cut through to the nerves and arteries. Mental images came to him in waves, the blue light of the corridors at St. Olave's, the sound of sparrows, frosty windows, and all of a sudden he decided that he would call around to Simes Root and see if he could get the key to James Root's flat on Curlew Street, the one the police had searched, and see what he could tell about the Jamaican man who'd just come to live in London. He knew the police would never allow him to search the room, but it was something he thought he needed to do if he was going to help Hillary.

Just before they had gotten to Notting Hill Gate, after those horrific twenty minutes of silence and tears, Hillary had tried to recover. "Howard is the name of the Zion pub owner," she said, getting back to business. She handed Roberts a scrap of legal paper with the address of the pub scrawled in red ink. "I've written down their names," she said, referring to the witnesses. "Howard Boston, James Treacle, and Arthur Lemon. Remember Treacle is the one with the watch." And then she had said something Roberts would never forget: "Please be careful," touching his hand. It sounded to him like an epiphany. He could hear the drizzle on the hood of the taxi, swirls of it sliding down the window glass. People on the sidewalks were unfurling their umbrellas and the pubs were filling with lunch drinkers. For a moment Roberts wanted to ask her something more, but then the taxi stopped and he hopped out and walked down to have lunch at the house.

After lunch Roberts caught a bus across the Thames to near south London. On the forty-minute ride he tried to get his bearings again, thinking about Hughes, what the man had said about James Root's tongue. "Frightfully odd," he put it. And then he thought about the marijuana the police had found in Root's Curlew Street flat, brown packages of the stuff, placed into plastic sacks. He tried to square all of this with the picture he had formed of Hillary and her life, and it didn't square.

Roberts got off the bus in upper Tooley Street. The drizzle had become a light mist, and he could see the Tower Bridge. He decided he would walk down Jamaica Road to get a feel for the place, even if he got wet, because he thought it might give him a perspective on life near the docks, maybe provide him with some insight on how life worked in this part of London. Ducking in and out of doorways, under awnings, he made his way down the busy road. There were flower stalls and chandleries, cheap licensed workingman pubs, greengrocers and betting parlors. Most of the people were East Indians or Pakistanis, Jamaicans, some Africans. He could smell roti, curry, and rotting garbage.

When he saw the Zion he thought it wasn't much, just a gray storefront pub where Abbey Street jutted back at crazy angles from Old Jamaica Road, a wide three-cornered boulevard with a traffic island in the middle. The glass window in front was covered by a painted mural depicting an island scene, a huge black face with a ganga cigarette in its mouth, and childlike flowered designs of starfish, African lions, and guns. The door stood open to the mist and he could smell the aroma of ale seeping out into the street. Through the opening he could see a fat man with wiry gray hair sitting at one of the tables that were scattered randomly around the room. It had once been a classic English pub with rows of glasses above the bar and a mirror in back, and a bandstand in one corner. Two swinging doors went back into the kitchen area. Roberts went inside and looked at the fat man.

"Jah, mon," the fat man said in greeting, before Roberts could speak. He was wearing dirty yellow trousers and suspenders. Some of his teeth were missing and there were boils on his face. "Raining like snakes," he said.

"That's right," Roberts replied. He went to the bar and sat down on a stool, Gary Cooper–style.

"Welcome to the Zion," the man said.

This must be Howard, Roberts thought. "I was looking for your best pint."

"Now don't you talk funny," Howard laughed. He rose and stuck a thumb under one suspender. He was a clumsy man whose belly folded over his pants. A large gold medallion hung down his chest, a lion's head. "You must be from foreign lands."

"America," Roberts said, not knowing what else to say. Howard walked around the bar and drew a pint into a ribbed glass.

"Now you say," Howard said. He pushed the pint over the bar to Roberts, who waited for the froth to subside. Gusts of rain blew through the door. Roberts was waiting for something clever to come to him, a way to begin all of this, but instead he took a drink of the warm beer. "Since you've come so far to have this pint, the first one is going to be free." Howard smiled widely. "Don't you say Jamaica don't be good to you."

Roberts thanked the man.

"No problem, mon," Howard said.

Roberts savored the beer, warmly bitter. "I hear you had

some trouble in here with Moseby Demeter. That must have been something."

"That's for sure," Howard said. "Seem like trouble follow Howard around."

"It must have been pretty bad," Roberts said in an airy tone. He was trying to maintain his composure. Howard had leaned back against the bar mirror, hands on hips.

"You know," Howard said, "I come down to Trench Town in Kingston from a little *ville* in the country, and then I come to London. But you know, as bad as Trench Town be, I never seen nothing like this London town." Howard had narrowed his eyes, and was studying Roberts with an air of suspicion. Roberts felt a chill from the rain. "Yeah, mon, that little *ville* was better than Trench Town, and Trench Town was better than here. Seems like the farther you go away from home, the worse your loss going to be."

"This is a tough town all right," Roberts agreed. Roberts was looking behind the bar at dozens of photographs and postcards tacked to the wall, so many they covered it entirely. On the marred surface of the bar itself there were tiny statues and dolls, ceramic figures of all sizes and shapes. The configuration of the images gave the bar the feel of an altar or shrine. At the far end of the bar was a poster of a lion-maned man in military uniform, stern-gazed with a wispy mustache. It was Ras Tafaria under a peaked cap too large for the tiny face. "What happened that night of the robbery anyway?" Roberts asked.

"Mon, you take a mighty interest in this bad thing," Howard said angrily. His face was blotched the color of a pumpkin. "This terrible thing, why you want to know about it?" Howard walked away from the mirror and was leaning over the bar with his face directly over the pint of ale. Roberts could smell his breath, strong and sour. "Say, what is this thing you got for Moseby, that man?"

"I work for Demeter's lawyer," Roberts said. "There is going to be a trial in three weeks. I'd like to find out what you saw that night."

"Well, I tell you, mon," Howard growled. "This skinny rude boy come in here that night and he stole the money in my till. He waved his gun around like a fool and like some big man he ain't ever going to be, and then when poor Calliope come around the bar here, doing nothing, mind you, that Moseby he shot Calliope dead. That's what Moseby Demeter did to Calliope. Now that what you want to know?"

"Demeter was alone?"

"Like a baby in a cradle," Howard said, glaring at Roberts.

"That was pretty risky."

"The boy is a fool. He was born a fool. The band had gone home and all the girls were gone and there was just me and some of the boys in here. That fool rude boy think he going to rob us and he just kill Calliope for nothing."

"Moseby got four quid?"

"Jah, four quid. That's what that rude boy shot Calliope in the stomach all about, hah." Howard flared a nostril. "How you like that, Mr. American?"

"Calliope have a gun?"

"You crazy, he didn't have no gun."

"Then why did Moseby do it?"

"He crazy mon, he."

"And the watch," Roberts said.

Howard squinted at Roberts for a long time, catching him like a small fish in his gaze. He walked to the end of the bar and back, then came around and stood behind Roberts, crowding close to his shoulder. "He took that damn watch off Mr. Treacle, who was drunk too."

"Demeter say anything while he was in here?"

"Just about give me the money, that's all."

"He was wearing a mask?"

Howard rubbed his chin. "Say, mon, what's your name?"

Roberts told the man his name, then turned and took a sip of ale. Howard took the beer glass in his hand, and for a moment both men held it, poised together in midair, until Roberts released his grip and Howard set the glass down and pushed it away. Outside the door, Roberts could see that there was nobody on the street because of the rain. It had gotten colder too, and he could hear church bells. "Hey Lemon mon," Howard shouted. "Lemon mon! Hey Lemon mon."

Roberts's mouth went dry instantly. He licked at his upper lip and studied the floor for some reason, the rain feathering down on the gray grimy surface. Through the back door came a tall muscular Rasta who was wearing a black vest and white T-shirt underneath, bell-bottom pants with a gray stripe down the legs. His hair was linty and thick, and he seemed to have just come from a deep sleep.

"Jah, mon, what it be?" he asked Howard.

"Fancy mon here want to know all about the stickup and that fool rude boy Demeter. He is a curious man who works for some lawyer going to get Demeter off, some fancy mon."

"All right," Roberts said. "I just want to know your version of what happened that night. There isn't any harm in that."

"That fool killed Calliope, that's the harm," Howard said, while Lemon watched.

"Every man deserves a defense," Roberts said. He was fully tensed now, every nerve alive, watching the Rasta named Lemon come awake, standing just behind him.

"And what defense Demeter give poor Calliope?" Howard said. Howard had broken a shiny sweat, even in the cold pub air.

"I'm sorry about Calliope," Roberts said, turning slightly on his stool so he could see both men clearly. "But Moseby Demeter still deserves a defense."

"Moseby he shot the man," Howard said. His face had contorted into a half-pucker. It was like a rubber face, only more terrible because it was attached to a deep bass voice.

"Moseby says he didn't. He says it wasn't him. He says he wasn't here that night, that he was drinking rum with a Jamaican down the street."

"What you think he going to say, that mon?"

"The robber was wearing a mask?"

"That thing?" Howard asked, sarcastically. Lemon shared a smile with Howard. "Skinny rude boy Demeter he come in the Zion all the time. You think we don't know how he talk? You think you can't tell rude boy like Demeter even though he wears a silly mask, like some fool?''

Lemon laughed loudly. Roberts was about to speak again when the Rasta named Lemon put his hand on Roberts's neck. It was a slick move just as Roberts was about to get off the stool, the hand finding Roberts's neck, guiding him back to the stool where he sat stiffly in front of the dolls and ceramic figures, the altar. Roberts thought about whirling and taking a punch at Lemon, trying to run out the door, but the thought passed, and then it was too late. He tried to concentrate on the moment, to let it take hold of him. He didn't want to get ahead of himself.

"Calliope come up from Trench Town like me," Howard said. "He got a wife and some little children, but they got no Calliope now. How you like that?"

"I'm sorry for that," Roberts said. He was angry, but his anger had no place to go. It was humiliating, this pose of abject surrender, but he endured it.

"And what Moseby Demeter got?" Howard said.

"What's he got?" Roberts answered.

"He got him four quid and an old watch. Four damn quid. Just a fool rude boy come up from Kingston who wants to rob and loot, you know? I hope they hang that rude boy for what he done to Calliope. Somebody try to help that rude boy, they ought to hang too. That right, Lemon?"

"That right, mon," Lemon said tonelessly.

"Moseby has an alibi," Roberts said.

"You said that before," Howard snarled.

"White fool," Lemon said. It was the first time that Roberts heard the man clearly. He spoke in an incongruous child's voice, a face like a boxer, wide eyes and bulging muscles. Just in a second, Roberts thought, he would spin and take a punch, maybe land one solidly on Lemon and make a run for the door. It felt like the moment had come, and then it was gone, just as Lemon forced Roberts's face to the bar surface. "It was Moseby done the thing, fool," Lemon said.

"Jah," Howard announced finally. "And to think that Moseby come in here and drink and play music. Him drunk and making his noise and when he ain't got no money too, mon. Who you think give him rum when he run dry and start to cry? He drink for free in here when he need to. And then he do this thing. All that nonsense he do. And you come in here and tell me he didn't do this thing, when we know he do it. What kind of man are you? Say?" By now Lemon had pushed Roberts's chest to the bar as well, and he was pressed flat. Lemon and Howard were breathing hard. Roberts realized his whole approach had been wrong, a big mistake. He remembered that Hillary had told him to be careful. He wondered what he could have done differently. "And when he come in here with that mask, we know him right away, jah! Everybody in here know right away it was Moseby. That fool. Jah, it was him."

"Jah, mon, it was him," Lemon said.

Howard poured what was left of the ale over Roberts's head. Roberts felt something cold tick his right ear, and over his shoulder he could see the point of a machete, the short sharp blade, double-edged. Lemon was standing back like someone about to behead a chicken, both hands on the taped grip of the knife. His forearms were rippled. Roberts closed his eyes.

"Lick the mon," Howard said.

Roberts raised his head slightly, and then felt steel slide down his neck, opening the leather bomber jacket neatly like a tomato skin, without sound. The jacket scarred open, once or twice, until the leather was in tatters. Roberts felt blood trickle down his neck, just behind the right ear where Lemon had sliced it. Roberts put his head back down on the bar. He could see his own face in the mirror. "All right, you've had your fun," Roberts said.

Howard hitched up his suspenders and moved back two steps. Lemon tapped the machete blade on Roberts's right shoulder. "Sure, mon, sure," Howard said. "One more thing. You tell that lawyer you work for that she don't know nothing about Moseby. That Demeter he killed Calliope for four quid, jah. You tell her she better stop what she's doing."

Lemon picked the machete off Roberts's shoulder. "Stay off the Jamaica Road," he said.

Roberts left the pub and walked the curve of Jamaica Road down to where Druid Street came in. Rain was pouring down and everything was wicked in the weather. He was getting wet through his tattered jacket, even though he tried to stay under awnings. Over the docks Roberts could see the masts of ships, and he could hear tugs working the Thames. He wanted to take off his jacket, but it was cold, and so he kept it on even though it made him ashamed to be seen in it. He was so angry, he didn't know if he was looking for a bus, or if he was just going to walk on alone. It was a long time before he made up his mind which it was going to be, and by then he was soaked to the skin.

8

Roberts was so cold he couldn't pour Teacher's into a cut glass. Amanda had taken off his boots and his wet socks, and he was sitting naked beneath a heavy blanket, trying to warm himself enough so that he could put on dry clothes. Outside the rain had stopped, and he could see a vivid draft of sunshine dropping through the chestnut trees across the street in Kensington Park, and beyond that a ragged row of black clouds clubbing along toward the West Country. There had been a brief rainbow, then a shadow of evening purple, and then a brilliant sunset, which was rare for London. He had walked all the way across Central London in his tattered jacket, feeling thoroughly depressed and aimlessly angry, like a child who'd lost his candy money. There was a swatch of dried blood on his neck from where the Rasta had nicked his ear with the machete. When he got home he let himself into the upstairs flat, and when Amanda returned and found him she made a coal fire in the corner of the sitting room, stripping off his clothes later. She took away the bottle of Scotch, and poured him a glass neat. Roberts sat in a wing chair, too demoralized to speak.

There had been a moment, somewhere near Marble Arch, when he thought he might go directly to his cellar digs and become wildly and extravagantly drunk on Algerian wine. He thought he might flatten out his mood with alcohol, but before he finally made up his mind what to do he reached the Serpentine and the evening traffic had started to thicken and the fog dropped down through the gray trees, and he decided that he wouldn't do that after all. Something snapped inside him. He would be brazen, or brave; he flagged a taxi and went back across London in a fit of pique.

He dropped off at Jacob Street, about two blocks from the docks in a warren of abandoned tenements, warehouses, and flats. Streams of water were running in the gutters, and there were wrecked cars and refuse scattered in parking lots, and some children were playing football in the streets. After asking around, a Pakistani woman told him that James Treacle lived in a row of flats across from Jacob Street. Roberts read her the address, and she pointed a finger south, and walked Roberts part of the way across Jacob Street in the rain. The flat he was looking for was on the third story, and Roberts walked up the stairs and pounded on Treacle's door, behind which Roberts could hear music.

It was obvious that the man had been drinking rum. Staring out from red eyes and a gray face, the man looked vague and disheveled, and he seemed to stagger when he pulled open the door, then recover, just enough to fall back inside the room. He was an old Jamaican, shriveled and in his cups, but with a look of pleasure on his features.

"Mr. Treacle," Roberts said politely. The man was wearing a black and green tam over his short gray hair. Roberts edged inside the room, into the filth. He could see a stove and fridge, an iron bed in one corner. The window was sooty and dark. "Are you Mr. Treacle?" Roberts asked.

"Yah, mon, that's me," Treacle said.

"I'd like to ask you about Moseby Demeter," Roberts said. The room was cold, hardly warmer than outside, and Roberts could see his breath. The faucet dripped.

"He stole my watch," Treacle said drunkenly.

"That's what I want to talk to you about."

"Irie, jah!" Treacle said. Roberts thought he recognized some form of chant, an intonation like song. "You got my watch, mon," Treacle exclaimed happily. Treacle seemed to drift away, as if his legs had turned to jelly, until he fell back all the way into a chair just under a wooden table in the center of the room. He wiped a hand across his dirty paisley shirt. He was very thin, with a hollow chest and stick arms. Treacle poured two shots of rum into glasses.

"You a copper?" Treacle asked.

"Something like that," Roberts said.

"Jah," Treacle said, raising his glass, spilling some of the rum. His teeth were stained dark brown and his skin was wrinkled. "That Moseby Demeter he one rude boy, jah he is. Why he want to steal my watch?"

"Why do you think?"

"Bad rude boy," Treacle muttered, drinking some rum.

"Can you tell me what happened during the robbery?"

Treacle pushed one glass toward Roberts and nodded politely. "They asked me that before," he said.

"One more time. Just for the record." Roberts drank a shot of the rum, which tasted like molten brown sugar.

Treacle cackled loudly, having a good time. He picked up a spliff and lit it with a wooden match. The spliff sparked alive under the condensed flame of the match, and then Treacle inhaled the ganga deeply. A brown glaze hung in the room and Roberts could smell the sick-sweet aroma of the drug. The ceilings were water-stained with lathe flapping down. Treacle kept at his spliff until it went out. He tried to light it again, but he didn't have the coordination. His lips were wet with rum. "Jah, mon, that Demeter he some kind of fool, say I."

"Why is he a fool?" Roberts asked.

"Oh, him and that devil mask. You think we don't know rude boy Moseby under that mask? Hah, that's why he such a fool."

"You knew him right away?"

"Jah, mon, no problem."

"What time was it when he came in?"

"Getting off work time. My woman she come home. I went on down to the Zion."

"You saw Demeter come in the Zion?"

"Him and that mask."

"You saw the man in the mask shoot Calliope?"

"Sure, mon, I saw that. Calliope he come round the bar and that's when Moseby he shot him. And that fool he took my watch before that."

"The devil mask covered his whole face?"

"Jah, mon, I told you." Treacle poured himself some more rum, and nearly lost his balance in the chair.

"How long had you been in the Zion before Demeter came in?"

"I don't know. Maybe an hour."

"Drink rum that day?"

"Sure, mon, why not?"

"Who else was in the Zion?"

"Howard, he was there. And Lemon and me. And then there was Calliope." Treacle paused and closed his eyes and drank his rum in one gulp. Roberts thought he might lose the man to oblivion, but a moment later Treacle opened his eyes and smiled. "Hey, mon, I tell you something," he said, leaning over the table. "That old watch, I don't care so much about that old watch. It don't run for ten years. I just be wanting to wear it around, you know? But why he want to take that old watch?" Roberts could smell the rum and ganga on the man, and he was very weak-looking, but he had to admire the man's sense of humor, and his generosity. This old guy belonged somewhere else, in some other scene, maybe beside the sea, not in a cold flat south of the Thames. Roberts admired the man's openness, his lack of pretension, talking freely to a stranger without fear. "That old Demeter, he be surprised he find that watch don't run, jah!"

"Did the coppers show you the watch?"

"Jah, they did, jah." Nodding happily.

"You think it was yours?"

"Why not?" Treacle said. He tried to light the spliff again, offering it to Roberts, who turned it down. Treacle took two huge puffs, holding the smoke inside his lungs, letting it out in a slow euphoric moan. "They show me the watch," he said.

"But you think it was yours?"

"Say now," Treacle said, "what you think happen to that rude boy Moseby Demeter?"

Roberts gave up trying to get an answer. "There's going to be a trial. The judge will tell us all what's going to happen to Moseby Demeter. Who knows?"

"Now isn't that the way it got to be?" Treacle laughed. "You don't know what going to happen until it happen."

Roberts thought he saw a little opening. If the watch the police found in Demeter's room was in working order, then it would prove he hadn't stolen it. "Where did you get the watch?" Roberts asked, following his train of thought.

"Jah!" Treacle shouted. "I got that old time piece back in Kingston."

"You know Demeter a long time? You know him from before you say he came into the Zion?"

"Long time, mon," Treacle said. Treacle waved an arm, tracing his memory back. "That boy from Trench Town. That boy you see him in the street. He come into the Zion all the time wanting rum. Sometime he play music too."

"Does he live near here?"

"Jah, he does," Treacle replied. Treacle made an undifferentiated gesture. Roberts watched the man fondle his empty glass and gaze at the empty bottle. "That Demeter he one rude boy who love to *fete.*"

"How did he get money to *fete?*"

"He beg and steal, jah. Sometimes he play music."

"He sell ganga?"

"I say he rude boy, I," Treacle laughed. Treacle was massaging his empty glass, moving it in circles on the table. "How anybody make money in London town?"

"Do you know a man named James Root?" Treacle seemed puzzled. "A Jamaican, just moved into the neighborhood?"

Treacle shook his head.

"Did you hear of the Rasta poisoned last Friday night? Down around here some place?" Treacle was vacant now, and Roberts didn't know if it was the question or the rum. If something registered, Treacle didn't show it, moving his glass in circles. There was something Roberts liked about him, the musicality of his speech, the strong sense of play. It wasn't just the rum. "The Rasta who got poisoned is big with long dread-locks and black eyes. He was new around here. You ever seen him?"

"I don't think so, mon," Treacle said finally. His voice was weary now, out of rum.

"Do you know any of Moseby Demeter's friends?" Roberts asked.

"No, mon, I don't know them boys at all."

"Do you know exactly where Demeter lives?" Roberts tapped Treacle on the shoulder, trying to get his attention.

"No problem," Treacle said dully.

"Suppose we get a bottle of rum across the street," Roberts said. "Maybe you could take me to where Demeter lived."

Roberts had Demeter's address in his notes, but the area was a true wilderness, most of the flats without numbers, street signs vandalized. He watched Treacle stagger to his feet and break a wide grin. "No problem now," he announced. "Trea-cle, he take you, jah!"

They went downstairs and across the street to the market where the Pakistani woman sold them a bottle of rum. Treacle led Roberts down Jacob Street until they reached a backwater jetty full of floating cotton packing, slicked by oil. Now Trea-cle was clearly confused. He had opened the rum and was taking deep swigs from it while he walked. A constant drizzle was pelting them, and rain ran down Treacle's face. He looked both happy and confused, and Roberts was too cold inside his tattered bomber jacket to make much of a fuss about how long it was taking. They went up and down the jetty without any real purpose, and then out into Curlew Street, which was utterly deserted in the late afternoon. Roberts thought they were lost once or twice, and was about to give it up, but then they went up Gainsford Street about fifty yards and Treacle began to do a jig, drinking from his rum, until he had danced to the front of a dismal cleaning shop, across the street from an equally dismal row of four-story flats. Many of the windows in the flats were broken, and there were only one or two lights showing through.

"Back up there, mon," Treacle said, waving the rum bottle at a second-floor window.

"Second floor," Roberts said.

"Sure, mon, no problem."

Treacle tucked the Myers's rum in his pants and gave Roberts a warm hug. "Thank you, mon," he whispered. The bottle was half-empty, and Treacle backed away from Roberts and took another drink from it before he waddled back down Gainsford Street, stopping twice to wave good-bye. For a moment Roberts thought he should walk back with Treacle and make certain he arrived at his flat and didn't get knocked down in the street by a lorry or a cab, but he didn't because he didn't think it would do either of them any good. Roberts knew there had been, and would be, dozens, if not hundreds, of afternoons like this for Treacle. He went back to his study of the upstairs flats, the rows of dirty windows and peeling facades, the moonish gray dusk emanating from inside. A Jamaican was watching him from behind the windows of the cleaning establishment, so Roberts hurried across the street and up the stairs of the row flat. He was stiff from the cold and the nick in his ear was throbbing. He went up stairs that were lighted by a single bulb.

The first door at the second-floor landing was locked. He knew it was Demeter's flat, and so he listened intently, leaning on the wooden doorjamb, his senses focused on the silence. Rain was pelting down outside now, and he could hear it dripping from the eaves of the building in a steady, lugubrious patter. He thought he could hear radio music filtering through the halls and for a moment he thought he might walk back to his cellar and get drunk, then go upstairs later and watch telly with Amanda, maybe even have a pub supper on Portobello Road where he knew a place that served roast beef and home-made horseradish sauce. Instead, he stood against the wood frame of the door turning up his courage a notch, steadily increasing the pressure against the door, which was rotten from water damage. The latch snapped and he pushed very hard until the door gave and he was suddenly inside the flat. Every nerve was screaming at him and his heart beat fiercely until he thought blood would run out of his eyes, but it didn't, and he stood quite still in the dark listening to the rain. Something in the room smelled candy sweet. On the wall over his right shoulder was a huge color portrait of Bob Marley.

There was a single divan in the room, and one broken-down reclining chair, pillows scattered in disarray. In one corner an old gas stove stood covered with rust and grime, and there were guttered candles stuck to the bare floor. He stood in the center of the room, with the door open a crack, and smelled the accumulation of ganga, beans, and pickapeppa sauce, until he was seized by dread and wanted to run away. Instead he sifted through the room, opened the single closet and observed some women's clothes hanging from a dowel rod. In the same closet he found a guitar, and in a box some women's undergarments and some white orthopedic shoes, cosmetics, and handbags. He even found some spliffs rolled tight in a jewel box, and a few photographs of Demeter and his reggae band in full regalia.

He got on his knees and unwrapped a brown paper sack and found about five or six pounds of ganga, bricks stored in pink plastic and held by rubber bands. He was transfixed for a moment, looking at the ganga, remembering what Drummond had told Hillary about her brother's flat, the ganga the police had found wrapped in brown paper, pink plastic sacks. He closed the closet door and stood at the flat windows, looking down on Gainsford Street where he could see the Jamaican face staring at him from inside the cleaning establishment. Roberts thought about the Zion bar, the dolls and obsidian figures in a line, the guttered candles too.

Roberts went out and closed the door behind him and walked down the stairs to Gainsford Street where he stood in the rain looking up and down the deserted road, expecting to see the police. By his reckoning, Curlew Street intersected a few blocks toward the docks, and he thought about James Root, who lived maybe five or six hundred yards away. Lives were intersecting now, Root and Demeter, Treacle with his slave name and frail face etched with troubles, Demeter in Wormwood Scrubs prison. Roberts wondered who was living in Demeter's flat now, and he thought it was probably a woman.

That was when he thought he'd walk all the way across Central London and get uproariously drunk by himself. He did walk all the way, but he didn't get drunk. . . .

In the upstairs flat Amanda fluffed his blanket. "Good Lord," she said, taking the Teacher's bottle from his hand. "What on earth happened to your lovely jacket?"

Roberts shivered in his wing chair. Amanda began rubbing his feet, which were numb from the cold. Roberts explained about his experience at the Zion pub and sipped his whiskey. He felt as inert as radon gas.

"There's another Stanley Kubrick on telly tonight," she said shyly. She was still wearing her work clothes, a woolen skirt, high boots, and a long purple scarf.

"I'd like that," Roberts said. The windows looking out on Kensington Park Road had turned a shimmering blue and Roberts felt inexplicably happy.

9

Roberts woke up with a fever. He had watched the Kubrick film, sharing whiskey and small talk with Amanda, and then he had slept a sleep full of dreams, the night passing in a cacophony of futile tossing and turning until he had awakened suddenly with a dull headache. He drank some coffee and ate a breakfast of toast and marmalade, and then he took the underground across to the Strand, hoping to meet Hillary at Lincoln's Inn, even though he was getting a late start. For an hour he sat in her office, writing out a complete report of his interviews with Howard and Treacle while Hillary was busy in court. He was in reverse shock, with his mind racing through a million changes of gear, a tiny whine inside his head that was perfectly lubricated. At first, he had been numbed by the violence at the Zion, and then angry, and only later, after a hot bath and some television, had he come alive to something that was happening just beyond his reach. But it was there and it was making an indelible scratch on his brain, something that wouldn't go away, something that was giving him pain, discomfort. He would touch his ear where Lemon had ticked him with the sharp machete point, which had left a red stripe all the way down the right side of his neck. The vision of the ganga in Demeter's room kept recurring, part of his dream-state, and the shredded leather jacket was a symbol of his anger, his hope for retribution.

Finally Hillary came back from court and Roberts gave her his report. She looked pale and drawn, even smaller than usual, and he realized that she probably hadn't slept for two or three days. A desultory weariness was written plainly on her face, and especially in her eyes, which were dull and watery, like a sick animal's.

She took Roberts's report, but didn't read it. "How was your trip to Zion?" she asked, trying to smile.

"You told me to be careful," Roberts said. "I tried, but it didn't do much good. It's all in the report."

"What happened?" she asked. "Something bad?" Hillary poured hot water into two cups, then dunked a bag of Earl Grey in both.

"It's all in the report. I had a lovely chat with Howard and Lemon. It was all cosy and warm at the point of a machete. They weren't very hospitable."

"You had some trouble," Hillary said.

Roberts explained how Lemon had gotten behind him, pinning his head to the bar. He explained the glass of beer on his head, the surprise of the machete ripping open his jacket. "On top of that their testimony is not going to budge. They claim they knew Demeter from the Zion, that he'd come in many times. All of them will say they recognized him immediately, despite the mask. They want revenge on your client, I'm afraid. It's become a personal thing now. They claim they can identify Demeter by his voice and his manner, just as you said they would. He's played music in the Zion, and cadged drinks, and borrowed money from Howard more than once. He was evidently a fixture on Old Jamaica Road and I think you'll have trouble breaking this guy Howard down on the witness stand. He's no fool."

"I thought as much," Hillary said.

"There's something else," Roberts said. "They're not surprised that something like this happened. He was known in the pub as a rude boy. Apparently he's known to have been a thief. He probably sells ganga on the street. Their story is pretty tight and I think they'll stick to it. They've even got a grudge against you for being his attorney."

"Of course," Hillary said. "And I'm a woman too. Their real grudge on that account is cultural."

"They tore up my bomber jacket. I've got my own grudge."

"I told you they were difficult. I'm sorry about your jacket. I know you've had it for a long time."

"I'm not complaining. It's part of the job."

"What about the four quid?"

"Howard told the police he handed it over. Just about then Calliope came around from behind the bar and Demeter shot him."

"The perpetrator shot him."

"Yes, that's right. Sorry," Roberts said, smiling. "The whole story makes a lot of sense. Demeter lives within walking distance of the pub."

"I never thought this case would be easy." Hillary put on her wire-rim glasses and read Roberts's report. "You interviewed Mr. Treacle?" she asked.

"One and the same."

"Did you get much out of him? I think he likes his dark rum."

"Treacle is with the rest. He doesn't seem to bear a personal grudge against Demeter, but I think he was drunk that evening in the pub. It might be something you could use in the case to discredit his testimony. I like the old man, but he was drunk when I interviewed him and he was probably drunk off his top when the robbery took place. On the other hand, I don't think he'd lie. Even he told me he thought it was Demeter who came into the pub with a gun. He sounded as if he thought it was some kind of joke at first, and was a little surprised when things got serious."

"You think he's a dead end?"

"As far as it goes. You can attack him on the stand for

being drunk. I think you'd make some points if you can get him to admit he was drinking the whole afternoon and evening. I don't think he'd deny it. He's genuine as hell."

"So I have to attack the only genuine witness."

"Why not? But there's another thing. He told me the robber took the watch right off his arm. But he also told me the watch hadn't run in years. If the watch the police found actually runs, then you've got something. You could prove that it wasn't the watch taken in the robbery, and you'd break the chain of circumstantial evidence."

"How wonderful!" Hillary exclaimed, truly excited.

Roberts was thinking hard now, trying to condense himself through the effects of his fever, the cold, close dampness of the room. There was ancient dust in the air. It lay on the furniture like a shroud. Roberts watched Hillary finish the report. He liked the way she handled herself, her white blouse and gray skirt, the schoolgirl hair done up with a velvet ribbon in back.

"How is your father?" Roberts asked, just to break the flow. "Is he going to be all right?"

"I saw him last night again. I'm afraid he fell asleep in his chair, he was so all in. Right in the middle of a Stanley Kubrick film."

"You're tired too," Roberts said.

"Don't start this," Hillary said good-naturedly. "You can't make me postpone the Demeter trial. You know this is my first big trial. If I back out now, it will get around Lincoln's Inn that I'm not only a bloody Jamaican nigger and a woman, but a quitter to boot."

Roberts was surprised. "No problem, mon," he said.

Hillary smiled and placed her face in her hands, resting. Roberts couldn't imagine how she was going to manage a murder trial and her brother's funeral, all the questions from the judge and the pretrial briefs and motions, along with the inexplicable undercurrents that went along with all of it. He had almost forgotten the calico cat that had been strangled and hung up like wash in the back garden. He wondered if he should mention the ganga he had found in Demeter's place, the ganga that looked like what the police had found in James Root's room.

"I'll be all right," Hillary said. "Really, I appreciate your concern. I'm not being stubborn. You just don't quite understand my place here. I'm not only suspect as a woman, but as a Jamaican as well. When I go into court I can almost hear the whispers following me."

"Don't you worry," Roberts said.

"That's all right. Thanks awfully."

"There's another thing," Roberts admitted. "When I was in the neighborhood I broke into Demeter's flat and looked around." Roberts sensed Hillary's surprise, and shrugged mischievously.

"You what? You can't do that."

"I did it. I wanted a look."

"I'm sure our friends at Scotland Yard would appreciate the irony."

"That's why I didn't ask their permission."

"You shouldn't have."

"It was an impulse. I had a hunch and I was angry. I thought it would give us a chance to get acquainted with Demeter without the police being around. Get a jump on the opposition." There was a moment of silence while Hillary looked out the window. She sipped her tea and frowned.

"Well, don't keep me in bloody suspense," she said with a vague smile.

Roberts told her about the flat, its dreary shrine of guttered candles and dolls, the women's clothes in the closet, and the five or six pounds of ganga wrapped in brown paper inside pink plastic sacks. Hillary listened with a perfect reserve of silence and attention. Pigeons were circling the chestnut trees outside and a cold bright crimson sunshine was falling through the limbs. Roberts was surprised by the beautiful bronze day, a blue sky pulverized through some wispy clouds.

"And what did we learn from this felony of yours?" Hillary asked.

"I learned about rude boys, ganga, and burning candles.

There was a picture of Bob Marley on the wall. I'm just wondering who lives there now. I think it's a woman."

"Perhaps we should ask Demeter. Do you think it makes any difference at all?"

"Maybe she knows something."

"Demeter would have said."

"And another thing," Roberts said. "The ganga in his flat had to get there after the Zion robbery. Otherwise the police would have confiscated it after they arrested Demeter."

"Well, that's right," Hillary said, noticeably interested. "But still, the main thing we're looking for is the identity of the man Demeter says he was with the night of the robbery. With an alibi witness, we could win the case. It would mean everything if we could find this man."

"I've got a line on him."

"You think it might have been my brother, don't you?" Hillary asked, just then breaking over her rationality and beginning to cry softly. Roberts got up and put his arm around the woman but she flinched away. "I understand what you're trying to say. You think my brother was selling ganga and Demeter was one of his customers. That would explain why the ganga was found in the same brown paper bags and pink plastic sacks. That's what you're trying to say. Well, if that's it, it wouldn't do Demeter any good. My brother isn't going to testify, is he?"

"I'm sorry, Hillary, perhaps I shouldn't have brought this up now. But it does seem a possibility." Roberts wanted to make the woman see reason, ask her to take a week off and spend it quietly in Cornwall watching the sea break on rocks.

"Damn it, damn it," Hillary said. "Demeter keeps after me about the trial. He's done nothing but hammer away at me like a child, wondering out loud whether I can go on with the case, if I'm competent, if I don't need a rest. Of course I've got to go on with the trial. Don't you understand? Lincoln's Inn is a fiefdom of gentlemen and good old boys, prigs from public schools with flats in Mayfair and summer homes in Devon, prissy wives with blue-rinsed hair and noses in the air. You can't imagine how they treat me, looking at me from across the serving line at the commissary, how the judges look down at me from their mahogany benches. I could scream." She looked at Roberts with a disconcerting glare. "Don't you see I can't break down now like a simpering idiot? I can't go and get some rest. My client is in Wormwood Scrubs and the judge has set down the trial for three weeks. Everybody is so concerned with my competence, even my client. I suspect they want me to have a nervous breakdown during testimony and then run away and hide, to writhe like a ninny on the floor until some man in a white coat takes me away to Bedlam where I'd eat porridge and milk toast before an afternoon of crossword puzzles. They'd expect just that from the Jamaican creole half-breed, wouldn't they?" Hillary was staring at Roberts and he thought he was included in the indictment. He knew she was right, but he didn't know how to properly apologize.

"Well, then," Roberts said.

"You think I'm being selfish?"

"Not at all. I'm trying to understand."

"Sorry," she said.

"Suppose we go over and have a chat with Drummond. I want him to take us to your brother's flat on Curlew Street. We can set our minds at ease that way."

"Of course you're right," Hillary said. "I'm sorry if I've spoken a bit frankly. I'm not a crybaby. It's just that I've had it up to here with those overgrown country squires and their priggy stares and their law degrees and their school ties and their musty offices and their pink gin lunches and pub suppers at the Owl and Thrush. I'm afraid the little Jamaican creole isn't their cup of tea. And besides, Demeter really has been in Wormwood Scrubs too long to postpone the trial. The evidence won't be any different in two months from what it is today."

"That's right. To hell with the prigs."

"Yes, indeed," Hillary said.

They took a fifteen-minute bus ride to Scotland Yard and

then sat around the reception room for half an hour waiting for Drummond, who was busy in meetings. Finally the man ushered them into his office, which had a good view of West-minister, part of Green Park. There was no sun on that side of the buildings, and it was cold.

"The autopsy report is complete," Drummond told them before either could speak. "I do imagine you'd like to hear the results." Hillary nodded, but said nothing. Roberts could sense something complex moving inside her, the telepathy of emotional tremblings. Whatever it was, it had some connection to Jamaica, an experience he could not relate to. "By the way," Drummond said, "we can release your brother's body anytime you wish. Perhaps later we can make arrangements if you'd like."

"I'll make the arrangements," Hillary said. "But I'd like to hear the autopsy results now, if you don't mind."

"Of course," Drummond said, sliding open a manila envelope. "Your brother was poisoned by arsenic, probably dissolved in a cup of tea, but we can't be sure. That was the cause of his original admission to St. Olave's."

"Arsenic," Hillary murmured. "Could this have been accidental?"

"I don't see how. We made a search of the room he lived in on Curlew Street. We didn't find any arsenic in generic forms like rat poison, for example. This stuff is very common on the docks where you'll find a lot of rats in these old flats and tenement buildings. We're trying to check all the places that you can buy arsenic-based poison in the neighborhood, but there are dozens and dozens of small shops and groceries, not to mention the Marks and Spencer and Woolworth's too. I've got a man making inquiries. He's going to ask after the clerks and shopkeepers, but I don't mind telling you that it's a very long shot that any one of them will remember much of anything. I don't suppose you've had time to think over some of my questions of yesterday. But I'd still be interested to know if your brother had made any enemies, or if there was a woman in his life. Sometimes the smallest detail can provide a lever we can use to pry open a case. I'm sure you're aware of that as a lawyer."

"I'm afraid not."

"As for the autopsy, the immediate cause of death was loss of blood from his neck wound. The wound itself was two inches deep, which is quite serious, of course. He would have been in shock immediately, and probably unable to ring for the nurse. Only instant care could have saved him in our doctor's opinion, so I don't think much blame can be laid on the hospital for that. Are you sure you don't know of anyone with a motive to kill your brother?"

"I don't know of anyone. He was new to London and I didn't know much about his life."

Drummond tapped his desk with a pencil. "There was tremendous force applied with the weapon to make such a deep incision." Roberts studied the man's gray eyes and hawk nose. "And then again," Drummond continued, "there's the matter of the wound itself, which was hardly serrated at all." Hillary moved to the edge of her chair expectantly. "Which means that we're dealing with an instrument of almost professional sharpness. It is very unusual to encounter a wound of its kind."

"I don't quite understand," Hillary said.

"Our doctor thinks that perhaps a scalpel was used."

"From the hospital?"

"It's a good theory. It's unusual to find an instrument that sharp out in the everyday world. And for another thing we think the murderer was left-handed."

"Is that what you think?"

"It seems likely the murderer leaned over the hospital bed and delivered the slice in a single motion. That would mean that the left hand was used, particularly when you think of the strength involved to make such a deep wound. It would require the person's strongest side. The left in this case, in order to account for the angle and direction of the slice."

"What about a machete?" Roberts announced to the surprise of Drummond. Hillary was staring at Roberts dumbly.

"Yes, I suppose so," Drummond said. "But for right now I'd like to work on the assumption that the murderer used a hospital instrument. My men are making an inventory right now of anything that might have been stolen from any of the surgical kits or doctor's offices on the premises of St. Olave's. Perhaps if we can make a match with a stolen instrument we can find out who had access to the room from which it was stolen. Maybe narrow down the field a bit."

"Someone on the hospital staff?"

"I'm sorry, but we can't make that assumption quite yet. In point of fact, I'm sorry to say, but we have to assume that your brother was involved with marijuana and its sale. I know you've told me that isn't true, but we've got to account somehow for the ganga found in his room. Do you know if he had any trouble at all with the police in Jamaica?"

"No, I don't think so. I told you he was my half-brother. All the news of him I had was through my mother who still lives in Jamaica. She didn't say anything about trouble with the police."

"I see," Drummond said. "And then there is the strange matter of the slice under your brother's tongue." Hillary sat back in her chair. Roberts admired her courage and tact, the way she handled herself. "I wonder if this means anything to you?"

"Nothing right now," she said.

"Please, Miss Root," Drummond said. "We have no idea why anyone would poison your brother and we have no idea why anyone would take the risk of going into your brother's hospital room and killing him and slicing his tongue. I think you know how difficult it is for the police to gather information down on Old Jamaica Road. I'd like to know about his friends and acquaintances in London, anything that would help us reconstruct some of his activities. This kind of information would be very helpful to our investigation. I have no wish to pry into your own affairs at a time like this, but your father hasn't been any help to us so far. He doesn't know anything."

"He couldn't know anything about James. But I'll try to do some thinking. I've already told you I didn't know much about him either."

"Just jot down what you can remember on a piece of paper and send it around. For now we'll continue our inquiries at St. Olave's and around the neighborhood."

Hillary stood. "I'd like to see my brother's flat in Curlew Street if you don't mind."

"Ah, of course."

"If you don't mind."

"I don't see why not," Drummond said. "I'll have the sergeant outside drop you over in one of our cars. He'll let you in and he'll let you out." Drummond continued to tap his pencil on the desk. "Please don't take anything out of his flat quite yet, miss."

Drummond exchanged a glance with Roberts. Hillary was already out in the hall talking to the sergeant.

10

They ate lunch in a bistro on Greek Street, hoping that Amanda would join them. They suffered through a terrible bout of silence, despite the fact that the restaurant was very gay and crowded with Soho types, broadcast journalists, fashion freaks, and trendy middle-aged women in leather skirts. You couldn't hear above the shouts for shandy and wine, and the smoke was very thick. Never in his life had Roberts been in a room so filled with smoke, worse than the underground smoking cars that were so densely dark that you thought you might suffocate. He sat and looked out the window at the crowds coming around the corner of Leicester Square and tried to eat some of his sole, and then he would gag on the air and try to make some conversation with Hillary, who was quiet, sunk into a mood of despair.

She had ordered some bread and cheese and a glass of mineral water, but when the waiter delivered her lunch she didn't touch a bit, sitting like a statue over her Brie while brilliant sunshine poured through the windows and made patterns on the checkered tablecloth. The noise was deafening, and Roberts thought that perhaps he could have made a better choice, but he and Amanda had eaten in the bistro a number of times, always finding it enjoyable. Roberts had some spaghetti with his sole, and a glass of Orvieto, which tasted sharp and rocky. The wine was lightly chilled, and he had to admit to himself that he enjoyed the fish and pasta, the sips of wine while the sun warmed him. He tried to think of something positive or constructive to talk to Hillary about, but all he could think of was the bloody weather, or the Kubrick film he'd seen on telly the night before. He kept a watch out for Amanda, who he thought might come up Greek Street through the narrow passageways of bookstalls and flower vendors, but she didn't come, and then when more time passed, he knew she wasn't going to make it at all. More and more his thoughts turned to the sacks of ganga in Demeter's flat, the same ganga that James Root must have stored in his apartment too. . . .

The sergeant had driven through the traffic to Curlew Street in a Cortina. He talked to them nonstop as they drove over the Bermondsey docks. Roberts was hunched in the backseat with barely room enough for his legs, his knees knotted under his chin. His back ached and he suffered from a slight fever. He tried to think despite his illness, entertaining some hope that his news about Treacle's watch would prove useful to Hillary during the trial. Back at Scotland Yard, Hillary had gone downstairs for thirty minutes to make arrangements about her brother's body. Roberts had wanted to go with her, but she insisted on going alone. He watched her disappear down the fluorescent-flooded corridors that turned things inside out. When she returned she was ashen and shaky, and the sergeant had escorted them to the little Cortina parked in the police garage.

Down on Curlew Street they parked on the sidewalk. They were in front of a townhouse that had been chopped into flats, and then the flats into bed-sitters. The buildings had an institutional feel about them with their identical facades, graffiti-marred doors, and broken windows. He could smell garbage, and there were mounds of furniture piled in sodden heaps out front. They went after the sergeant up a flight of stairs to the second floor. "I'll be just outside," the man said, leaning against the jamb. Roberts followed Hillary inside, not knowing if she'd ever been in the room before or not.

The room itself was about ten feet square, and Roberts felt claustrophobic standing just inside the door. He could sense the fear in Hillary, and her desperation, and he could hear her sigh as she walked inside and began flicking through drawers, opening the single closet door. Roberts began to flip his mind through angles and distances, thinking now about how far it was to Guilford Street where Demeter lived, and another few blocks to Treacle's flat. He thought about all these Jamaicans living anonymously in the city of eleven million, how the calculus of their lost social life was right there in front of his nose, if he could only understand it. These people, he thought, shared a single life, aspects of it reflecting in everything they did. There were a few books on a shelf, and Roberts fingered through them, tracts on mentalism, a volume of Edgar Cayce, an astrology handbook, and some guitar chord charts. He found a few personal items like a flowered shirt from the islands, glass beads, and an old swimming suit, too. Hillary was looking at the strikingly beautiful photograph of a woman with her hair blowing in the wind, behind her a tropical sea with the sun glinting off it in shards. Hillary touched the photograph gently, then put it back down on a table, tears in her eyes.

Roberts could smell ganga too. It had sunk into the wallpaper and into the drapes. He walked to the window and stood there looking down at Curlew Street, the Thames and docks in the near distance, farther a slice of Jacob Street where Demeter lived. Hillary was crying now.

"There's really nothing to take away, is there?" she said. "All this bloody pain, but nothing you can touch. I should have done something."

"It isn't your fault. There wasn't time."

"Rubbish," she said. She dried her tears, and began to pace around the room aimlessly. Roberts noticed a poster on one wall, a frisky-stern portrait of Haile Selassie, the Emperor with a wispy beard and a breast full of military ribbons. What Roberts was thinking gave him chills, but he thought he should mention it to Hillary.

"I have to say something," he told her.

"Yes, I'm sorry," Hillary said.

"I'm just now remembering everything Demeter told us about the man he claims he was with the night of the robbery. It was somebody named James. It was somebody who lived in a second-floor flat on the right. There was a picture of the Lion of Zion on the wall nearest the door. You could see Guilford Street from the window facing Curlew."

"Dear God," Hillary said. The sergeant was pacing up and down outside the flat. Roberts expected him to duck inside soon.

"And you have to remember the description that Demeter gave us of this James person. A large Rasta with dreadlocks and dark eyes. He said he didn't know him because he was new in the neighborhood. I spoke to Treacle, and he didn't even know of the poisoning. Your brother matches the description and he was new to the neighborhood. By my reckoning, this is quite likely the flat they were in that night, if Demeter is telling the truth. Of course, it could be just a lie. It could have happened, of course. But it could have happened on an entirely different night. Perhaps he's made it all up just on the hope that we'll work harder for him. I've been involved with all kinds of criminals and sociopaths in my time, and they often don't know when lying is in their interest, and when it isn't. They just lie because their consciences don't compute things like that."

"Or it could be quite true," Hillary said.

"Anyway, it's all here. The portrait of Selassie on the wall."

Hillary had slumped down onto a dirty divan. Roberts sat down beside her. "I told you," he said quietly, "that when I went into Demeter's flat I found brick-size ganga packets wrapped in brown paper covered by pink plastic sacks. You heard Drummond describe the ganga they found here. I'm sorry, but you know I think it could be the same ganga. It might explain why Demeter and your brother could be together." Hillary had covered her face, and was crying softly. "But look," Roberts continued, "this is all just guesswork. It doesn't establish an alibi for your client Demeter, and it doesn't explain why your brother was killed. I just don't know if we should tell Drummond."

"Even if it *is* true," Hillary said, "my brother isn't going to testify, is he?"

"Look, Hillary," Roberts said gently. "I don't know if there was a connection between Demeter and your brother. We don't really know if James was with Demeter on the night of the robbery. I don't even know where we go from here. All I know is we have a handful of problems and you've got a difficult trial ahead of you."

"This is terrible," Hillary said. The sergeant walked inside the room and he gave them a ride up to Greek Street.

By the time Roberts finished his sole, the restaurant had calmed down. Hillary picked at her Brie. "I want to tell you some things," she told Roberts, who was glad that the silence had been broken.

"Go ahead, get them off your chest. It might do you some good to really talk to me."

"It's about my father," she said. "He's English. And I mean he's very old-school English, complete with a public school education. He played cricket for a county side and his family had a house in Gloucestershire. He started his career in the foreign service and his very first posting was to Jamaica. He met my mother there. She's a creole from Negril and they fell in love and got married. It was all very romantic, but it wasn't a popular thing to do. He was in the diplomatic corps, but it wasn't diplomatic to fall in love with a Jamaican woman and marry her. I was born in Montego Bay where my father was attached to the consulate. After they were married, my father's colleagues made things very difficult for him personally and professionally, and things were made very difficult for them socially." Hillary took a deep breath. The restaurant was half-empty now, and there was a semblance of disheveled silence. "My mother still lives in Montego," Hillary sighed. "I haven't seen her in nearly five years, but we write very often. When I was young, she always wanted me to come to England and get an education and be a success in my father's world. Their marriage came apart pretty soon after I was born because of all the talk that swirled around them in the English community. You know how it is with small talk and gossip, it covers a person like dust." The waiter came and Roberts paid the bill. "At any rate, a few years later my father was forced out of his position in the foreign service. You wouldn't say he was sacked, but he was passed over for promotion, and given progressively worse positions, and then finally he gave it up and returned to England. That was over twenty years ago. When he came back he found work in a bank. In Jamaica, he found that people wouldn't speak to him, or they'd talk behind his back. Now he's retired on half-pay and he has his flat in Bayswater and his plants and a few friends in London. He goes up to Scotland and shoots grouse. We have dinner twice a week." Hillary drank some of her mineral water. "I'm afraid he thinks his life has been a failure." Hillary wiped away some incipient tears. "I think he still loves my mother."

Roberts waited for a long time. "And your mother," he said, "what does she do?"

"She's an artist," Hillary said proudly. "It isn't really very sophisticated work. She paints island sunsets, goblets full of tulipans, and tropical fish. She caters to tourists and she has a small shop in Montego." Hillary smiled wanly. They were the last two customers in the bistro, and the waiters were busing tables. "She's a very striking woman, my mother. I think she still loves my father."

"Perhaps she does," Roberts said.

"And of course, there's James," Hillary said. She was dabbing her eyes, through the worst. "As I told you, James was my half-brother. His father is a Jamaican. He and my mother never married. I don't even know if they really loved one another, but it was just one of those things. All I know about the man is that he lives somewhere in Kingston and he and my mother never see one another. I don't even know what he does for a living." Hillary smiled again. "That's the way life is in Jamaica. It also explains why I know so little about James. He was younger than me, and I was away at school so much of the time. And when I came to England I had much less contact with him than before. It was silly of me, but I had dreams of going to drama school and becoming a famous actress. I had no talent for that of course, and so I went to the university and took my law degree. When James came over here, I hadn't seen him in years and I was very involved with my new career. That's why I didn't tell much to Drummond about James. I'm not very proud of myself for ignoring him all this time." She thanked Roberts for the meal.

Roberts left a tip and they walked out into Leicester Square. They bought some warm chestnuts from a vendor and walked on down the square under a clear blue sky. A few clouds had bunched on the horizon, but the air was crisp and clear. They walked west toward Bayswater, thinking that sooner or later they would have to hail a cab, or just walk for an hour. It was pleasant, and they scattered the pigeons as they walked.

Hillary took Robert's arm. "There's something I'd like to ask you."

"Be my guest," Roberts said.

"We're friends, aren't we?"

"Certainly," Roberts answered.

"I don't have any real friends, you see. Amanda has been lovely, of course. But I don't have any real friends of my own. I see my father and I work, but there isn't anyone that I can rely on outside of my father."

"Friends, then," Roberts said.

"I've made arrangements to have James sent home, back to Jamaica. I wonder if you'd go with him? I can't go now with the trial and everything."

"I don't know, Hillary."

"I'd be so happy if you would. I can't stand the thought of

James being bundled up like so much cabbage and I don't want my mother there alone when he comes home. I'd just like you to go along with him, take him home to my mother."

"But we've got the Demeter trial."

"In three weeks. There isn't much more to do for you. And another thing, I'm very upset about this ganga business. Drummond keeps asking me about James, his life in Jamaica. I just thought you could ask after his life while you're there. I'm afraid Drummond is going to sweep poor James under the rug, forget about him. I don't want this to be the end of his life. I thought perhaps you could make some inquiries while you're there to try and find out if something in Jamaica caused his death here."

"I don't know, Hillary," Roberts repeated.

"I'll pay you, of course."

"Nonsense," Roberts said. "It isn't a question of pay. We're friends, right? It's just that I don't know Jamaica at all. I've never been there, and there's a lot to do here with your case. I'm afraid it's out of my range."

"Please," Hillary said. "You've heard Drummond wonder out loud about my brother's past activities. I've thought that there might be something to that, that I don't know for sure. And you're the only one I know who could help me do this. I don't know anybody like that in Jamaica. But I do know there is a man named Eli Churchill in Montego who was my brother's best friend. He knew James better than anyone. He could help you. And then there's my mother. She would help you too. I'm sure you'd like her ever so much. I'm not talking about a major investigation, just a few questions. I just want you to ask after James, to find out what he was doing there. I have to know if he was killed for something he was doing there. Then you can come back and tell Drummond what you've found. Be perfectly honest with him. I'm willing to hear the truth about him." They had stopped walking, and were alone in an alcove. "I just don't want James to be utterly forgotten. Then you come back and we conduct the Demeter trial."

"All right," Roberts said. It was against his better judgment, but he couldn't say no. "When do I leave?" he asked, laughing.

"How about tomorrow afternoon?" Hillary said. "There's a British Airways direct flight to Sangster. You fly at night and arrive in the morning with the sun coming up over the bay."

"You knew I'd say yes."

Hillary pulled Roberts back out onto the sidewalk. "I *hoped* you'd say yes," she said.

"I suppose you have a ticket already."

"No, but I have a reservation for you," she laughed. They hailed a cab. "Tourist class, of course!"

The taxi delivered them to Queen's Gardens where Simes Root lived in a Georgian attached house. There were tree roses in the garden across the road, and you could see the crowns of elms in Hyde Park above the skyline. It was a quiet neighborhood and all the houses were porticoed, and there were small patches in front of each, filled with hydrangeas. When they went inside the house, Roberts thought it was odd that the front door was slightly ajar. Inside, the room smelled of dust and furniture polish. He found Simes Root on his back, with his throat cut. The flowered carpet had soaked up a lot of blood, and a Siamese cat mewed on the windowsill. A radio was playing classical music, and a walnut table was laid for lunch. It was a long time before Hillary stopped screaming, and Roberts could telephone for the police.

JAMAICA

Walking down the road
With the pistol in your waist,
Johnny you're too bad.
Walking down the road
With the machete in your waist,
Johnny you're too bad.
Just a-robbing and a-stabbing
And a-looting and a-shooting,
You know you're too bad.

One of these days
You may hear a voice say, come.
Where you gonna run to?
You're gonna run to the law for rest
Where there will be no more run.

—Slickers

11

Roberts ordered a Red Stripe from the veranda barman and carried his beer to a canvas chair, as far away as he could get from anybody at the hotel on Harbor Street. The beer was very cold going down and when he finished the first he immediately ordered another, just sitting at his corner table in a wedge of sunshine, sweating slightly in a flannel shirt, studying the people on the promenade. He was away from the main bar and the lobby, up about five feet from a hedge of tulipan and hibiscus, a green traffic divider in the street and then the boardwalk along the beach of yellow sand and the bay. The ocean shimmered in the harbor and Roberts squinted at it. The sun was shockingly bright, and he could barely see a jetty, where the sun was glinting on gray rock, some seagulls whipping down for bait fish. His head felt light as a feather, as if the sun and heat had soaked in, dried him out, becoming part of his skin. He breathed in the sharp salty air, watching all the people go by, kids dressed in white pressed duck pants and a policeman in stiff English blue wool with a pukka hat, tourists and hawkers and beggars. It was as if he was under a wall of heat that separated him from the hot pavement, the burning

103

sand, all the green water. There were lots of people swimming in the flat breakerless water, heads bobbing like corks, kids on jet skis.

There was a gentle calypso beat coming from the hotel lobby, somebody's radio, and a breeze was clicking in the palm trees along Harbor Street and in the dim distance. The sun was so bright he could see the customs house where they were unloading James Root right now. Way out he could also see a huge yacht, the *Mary Lou,* anchored. Roberts savored the beer, it was as thick as honey and seemed to disappear against his tongue as soon as he tasted it. He was so tired his experiences were abstract, everything going down in dream-like slow motion, the sandy ring around the bay burning yellow, the fishing boats chopping out toward the open sea, and all the blue-green water swelling out toward the line of infinity that was the horizon.

He resisted the temptation to drift into a reverie. He took off the flannel shirt, it was really hot now, and wished he had some white cotton pants and a flowered shirt and a cane woven hat and some sunglasses, maybe some flip-flops too. His legs were stiff, he'd been flying all night, and though he'd tried to sleep on the plane, all he'd had was a fitful hour after a movie, coming away from himself into vaguely remembered nightmares. The whole flight had been a floundering of consciousness, his arrival at Gatwick in heavy fog, the wait in international passenger areas, being herded into the jumbo, and only one moment of clarity as the clouds had parted at thirty thousand feet and Roberts was stunned by the brilliance of the view, the emergent sun behind the plane, an island down below in a green sea, some beach houses, and then they had landed. He went through customs and gave an official five dollars to take care of James Root, and then he had walked all the way down Harbor Street from the airport, maybe five miles, and had come up to the first good-looking bar he'd seen, a bar where he could be alone on a veranda and stretch his legs and drink two or three cold beers. He couldn't remember how long it had been since he'd had a decent night's rest, maybe ten days, maybe more, though it might have been the night he watched the Kubrick festival with Amanda, maybe that night he'd slept six hours altogether. Now, though, he was completely relaxed, into an insouciance that had a slightly hermetic tone, something magical in it, as if his mind was resonating. Maybe the beer was doing it, too.

When he tried to think, he could only remember Hillary screaming. One long dreadful agonizing horrible scream, and then a series of broken guttural screams, and then another long keening wail as she screamed and screamed until she collapsed. When he had come up the steps of the Queen's Gardens Road house, inside the foyer, he had definitely seen the door to the flat slightly ajar. It worried him at the time, and he had hurried on ahead of Hillary, pushing open the door with his foot, slightly apprehensive, wondering if he was even being too silly, but he pushed it open anyway. The silence in the flat bothered Roberts too—a little classical music and the rush of traffic along Hyde Park, but nothing else. Hillary said something to him as she stood behind, and then he saw her smiling face beside him, and then Roberts saw the body in the same instant he heard Hillary scream and he rushed around her and tried to hide her from the sight. Root was on the floor, spread-eagled on his back, in a circle of dried blood.

And there was the walnut table set for lunch, a crystal glass, a bowl for soup, a wedge of melon, and some cut daisies in a goblet. A bright autumn sunshine was filtering in through the bay windows and the air was swept by motes of dust and the windows were wet with steam. The room had a sense of serenity about it, and Hillary's screams pierced it like a knife through cloth, and then Roberts had grabbed her wrists and tried to usher her outside. She was staring at her father, who was neatly dressed in tweed lounging trousers and a white cardigan turtleneck. His hair was a gentle and distinguished gray. A trail of blood led from the door to where he'd fallen over, as if someone had rung the bell and had slashed his throat when he opened the door, and the man had staggered back across the room to where he'd fallen.

Roberts held Hillary until she fainted. She went limp in his arms, losing her consciousness in one great gust, though she was still standing, leaning against him, his hands over her wrists, until he felt how rigid she'd become and how a strange, senseless vacancy was coming into her eyes. For a moment Roberts felt absolutely lucid. Someone honked a car horn down the road. Leaves skittered on the street and the Siamese mewed and rubbed the wet window glass. Slowly, he placed Hillary in a Queen Anne wing chair and telephoned for Drummond. He saw that he'd gotten blood on the toe of his boot when he'd come inside, and that he'd tracked it around. There were flecks of blood on the door frame, where Simes Root had been standing when he opened it. Hillary's complexion was gray as stone, and Roberts went to get a wet washrag.

As he sat wiping her forehead, a density caved in on top of him. Hillary began to mumble: "Who is doing this?" she said. *"Who is doing this?"*, chanting the words to herself again and again in some kind of trance, a hypnotic phase until the words lost significance and became mere sounds. She looked around the room, which had filled with a vague yellow light as the sun creased through the chestnut trees. Roberts saw her shudder, her skin grew cold, and her eyes rolled back again and she nearly fell out of the chair to the floor, but Roberts caught her and saw that she was unconscious again. He put his arm around her. In about five minutes he heard the police siren wail through traffic, and a few minutes later Drummond came through the door with a couple of bobbies.

They took Hillary to the hospital and Roberts stayed behind with Drummond while the man worked over the body, the room. Drummond let Roberts wait outside. He'd had enough of the room, and sitting on a stool he watched the bobbies come and go, and the lab men and the photographers, everybody eyeing Roberts as they passed, Roberts wondering how Hillary was doing. They'd taken her to St. Mary's on Bishop's Bridge Road.

Drummond followed the stretcher out and stopped to talk to Roberts as the morgue crew worked their way outside. They watched the men pile the body into an ambulance and drive away down the Queen's Gardens Road. Finally Roberts agreed to get some tea with Drummond and they went downhill to Craven Hill and found a restaurant with velvet settees and windows full of red geraniums, potted petunias, and African violets. They were served by an elderly woman in a blue apron.

"This is a bloody right mess," Drummond said. "I wish you'd tell me what you know about this. What is your part in this woman's life?"

Roberts told Drummond the exact truth about the Demeter case. He saw no reason to be cute with the guy, to hold out on him now, things had gone too far for that. He wasn't going to lie about his lack of papers. His own life was inconsequential.

"I could have you deported," Drummond said.

"Sure you could," Roberts replied.

"But I appreciate your candor."

"My only interest right now is Hillary."

"All right then, old man," Drummond said. "Then I'll come right to the point. I don't bloody well care if you work the rest of your bloody life in London, don't pay income tax, or live in a rent-free squatter's hovel over in Brixton. What I want to know is what's the connection between the deaths of James Root and Simes Root?"

"Yes, that's the question. I don't even have the slightest idea why either of them died."

"Then we're starting from the same bloody dead end." Drummond sat back on his velvet cushion and surveyed the quiet streets around Craven Hill. In the late afternoon, the sun had gone behind a row of flats and the streets were draped in shadow and everything had a quiet hollowness. A jet roared over for Gatwick.

"I think both men died of the same kind of wound. I bet you'll find deep incisions from an incredibly sharp blade, no serrations on the wounds, an almost scientific precision."

"I've already concluded that, old man," Drummond said. "This was done by someone with a scalpel."

"Or a machete."

"Yes, there's that too. Now suppose you tell me what you know about James Root." Roberts did, telling him everything Hillary had told him at lunch.

"This is hard to make sense of," Drummond concluded. "If I say James Root was killed on account of some drug scheme gone bad, or a soured deal, then it wouldn't make sense to involve Simes Root as well. From what you say that man wasn't even his father. There has to be some other connection. It has to be something else entirely, something we can't see." Drummond had leaned across the table, fixed on Roberts now, almost tense. "Are you sure Miss Root is telling you everything about her brother? About her father? I haven't looked into this, you know. I'd hate to find she was leaving something out. Something she should have told me. Perhaps she's ashamed of something. That sort of thing."

This is *insane*. Roberts was staring at Drummond, this official in a french cuff shirt, pointy collar, and silver hair, and what was going through his mind was, *This is insane*. Nobody could connect a retired civil servant, this gent who lived in Queen's Gardens amid lace curtains and hydrangeas, with a kid just over from Jamaica who smoked ganga and played guitar. For a moment, Roberts entertained the thought of telling Drummond his own truth, that he'd broken into Demeter's flat, but then he realized he couldn't do it, not yet, before the Demeter trial when he still owed Demeter a duty of some kind. Besides, what good would it do to tell Drummond about the connection between James Root and Moseby Demeter? Here he was with Drummond in a tea shop on Craven Hill, cultivating the guy, trying to achieve a level playing field with him, and he was thinking about throwing it over, for what? That was what Roberts was thinking, For what? . . .

He realized he had finished his second Red Stripe. The lager was still cold, tasting like a dream, sparkling in his glass, then gone. Now that he had thought it all through, he realized he needed to get back to London as soon as possible, even though he enjoyed the heat, the unbelievable green sea, and all the glare, he had to make certain that Hillary would survive her ordeal. He had left Amanda in charge, together there in the Kensington Park house with Hillary bunked in the main room upstairs, sleeping on the couch after two days in the hospital, exhausted and in despair. There was a murmur in Roberts's head, the traffic on Harbor Street. For the first time Roberts noticed the bay arcing around to a row of green hills and some pink and blue houses in the jungle, halfway up to the top of a mountain, palms whipping in the wind.

Roberts paid the tab and walked down to Harbor Street and followed the curve of the bay north until he crossed the road. He walked down to the beach and skirted the surf, it was low tide, until he got just below Gloucester Road where there were bathers everywhere, and higglers with carts of soft drinks, beer, and goat meat sandwiches, woven beach hats on racks. The sand was white there, and soft, he could feel it inside his boots as he walked. He made his way to a collection of administrative buildings that were slightly seedy, painted green with pink tile roofs and a smell of urine inside. The official paperwork on James Root had been completed and Roberts stood outside in the heat waiting for a cab to come by.

Certain voices came back to him. A breeze was kicking up sand from the beach and there were two customs officials standing outside in the shade of the bulwark along the beach, one a skinny fellow in a gray-green disheveled uniform that had stains on the breast, and another, nondescript and sleepy-eyed, who was smoking a huge cigar and blowing puffs of blue smoke out toward the sea. He could hear Drummond telling him that there was no connection between the two deaths, none that he could see, no connection between the men either, James Root and Simes Root, just two names. Roberts started walking back down the beach the way he had come. The chief of customs would be holding James and so Roberts wanted to get away. Roberts thought through his whole conversation with Drummond, the two of them together for nearly an hour sharing confidences, and then Roberts had gone over to the hospital and visited Hillary while she tried to eat some clear broth and failed. Amanda had come then, and together they watched over her for most of the late afternoon and into the evening.

Roberts found a cab back at the hotel. His head was buzzing from the beer and he had begun to break a good sweat. It was so bright that he couldn't see outside the windows of the cab as they got going, just a furze of blue sky and some brilliant color over the water and the green palms clicking in the wind. They went straight up into the hills, past Sam Sharpe Square and all the tourists dressed in bermuda shorts and straw hats and sunglasses, and then right on through the square up Albion Road where there were wild lemon trees along the road, and farther up, orange trees that were in full blossom. Mounded up around stone fences were huge piles of untended hibiscus and bougainvillea, some logwood trees up in the hills, and later oleander growing wild too. It was cooler up in the hills and the breeze felt good. He saw banana trees and down below in the bay there were sailboats. The colors out in the ocean had become more varied, a mottled turquoise and a welling onyx gash of surf and then the incredible horizon that made a crystalline white line in the far distance. Roberts paid the cabbie and got out. All the way up there had been loud calypso on the radio, which was tied by a thong to the rearview mirror. Roberts watched the cab go back down the hill.

He was standing in deep shadow. A wooden walk led steeply up and the tip of a tin-roofed house painted blue showed amid the trees. When he walked up the stairs he could see it clearly in a little opening, with a sagging porch, akee trees hanging over it, some gingerbread gables, and sloping roof. The clearing was noisy with birds. Roberts was being watched by a woman wearing a cotton skirt. Her hair was black and piled on her head and her skirt was whipping in the wind. He was below her about fifteen feet, sweating heavily.

"Mr. Roberts," the woman called down to him. She had a great solid face like one of Picasso's monumental browns. "You'd be sent by Hillary from England."

Roberts called up to her, a greeting. He was sure a hummingbird had streaked across the path, a blur of green color. He climbed up the porch, feeling lightheaded, sleepy. Wind chimes purred steadily and everywhere the jungle rose up, the air smelling thick and damp.

"I'm Arcadia," the woman said.

From Montego Bay came the sound of calypso. It drifted gently out to sea.

12

He was eating callaloo soup from a white porcelain bowl, spooning up portions while he sat at a wrought-iron table under a big tamarind that had grown over the house like an umbrella. Way up the hill beyond there was a grove of untended lemon trees and all their blossoms were drifting down toward him in the Doctor's Breeze, white flowers shedding on the ground like a carpet. Both of them had maintained an embarrassed silence, Arcadia directly across from Roberts, dressed in a flowered muumuu, hair wrapped in a brilliant, hand-painted scarf. When he sat down after his sleep he had felt strangely vibrant, maybe it was the coolness and shade of the veranda, or the sweep of the wind, which had its own brilliance and tone, but right now he didn't feel the great tug of grief. Arcadia had made him come inside the shop, which was also her home, and she had found him some clothes, a loose pair of cloth trousers, a cotton shirt with big flower prints on the pockets and even epaulets, and a pair of canvas sandals. He had dozed for a while as the woman gathered the clothes and tended the soup, which Roberts could smell, and then later they'd gone outside to a table where she'd made a

112

spread with cold beer, a platter of mangos and papaya, some cheese, and the delicious homemade callaloo.

They were on one side of the hill with the house tipped above them, while below there was the wooden walkway and an expanse of dense forest, and beyond, where a few boats were bobbing up and down, the arc of bay and the town center. The sun was behind them now and the hills were bathed in a bright red glow. Roberts sensed that the wind had begun to change direction and was coming up from the gulleys that cut into the hillsides from the beach, rustling in the forest caps. He felt himself coming to life. After the long flight and the lack of sleep, it was like shedding a skin.

"How do you like my callaloo?" Arcadia asked. Her voice was musical and she had an accent Roberts couldn't place, he'd never heard anything like it. It was hard to understand at first, but he knew, instinctively, what she was saying. The words were transparent, they floated wingless before him on the wind. "It is the special dish of Jamaica." Yeah, Roberts was certain now, there were hummingbirds everywhere, on the sides of the hills, in the air, and the trees were full of swallows too, he could hear their wings thrashing through the lemon trees. "Sometimes the people they don't like this soup too much, at first, yes?" The woman was giving Roberts a nice smile.

"It's wonderful," he said.

"I want to thank you for my Hillary. And for me too. Hillary has written to me about you. And then she sent a telegram about James."

"You know about James," Roberts said flatly.

"Oh yes, I know," Arcadia said.

Roberts wanted to be accurate now. He didn't know the rules and he didn't know this woman. He thought he was probably in a place and situation where all he needed to do was be natural, allow his feelings to surface, and then he'd be as transparent as he wanted to be to things and people. It was a trick he thought he might master if he had long enough in the sun, some more Red Stripe, about ten hours of sleep. No doubt about it, there was a whirlwind of hummingbirds, it was amazing.

"They have James at the customs house," Roberts said. He was drinking his beer. He hated the talk part of this, what he was going to have to say to Arcadia when it got right down to it. It seemed especially cruel in this beautiful spot. "We can go down and get him when you're ready."

"Yes, that's good," Arcadia said. "We get him by and by, no problem." Roberts was in awe of the woman's face, the way she held herself. "I done my cry for two days now, don't you worry," she said. "But I want to know, how is my Hillary? It has been such a long time I've not seen her. What is happening to her now that there is all this violence and my husband is dead too?"

"Hillary broke down, I'm afraid. She's recovering. We took her to the hospital, and now she's staying with Amanda Trench Smith. When I left, she was resting, trying to see to her father."

"Will she be all right?"

"She has a trial starting in two weeks. I've tried to get her to take some time off, but she won't. I want her to get away from London and take a rest. She's very headstrong and very proud, and I think she's trying to prove something to herself and the English lawyers at Lincoln's Inn."

"I'm glad but I don't understand this about Simes," Arcadia said, looking away.

"I know. I don't either. I'm sorry."

"My poor child," Arcadia murmured. The wind was blowing strong up the hill now, straining off the sea. "Her health, you've not said exactly."

"She's pretty grim. She'll be all right."

"And what about the hospital?"

"She spent two days. The police took her over there and I thought that was a good idea. Amanda and I were with her most of the time and now she's at Amanda's. She has a pallet made up in the upstairs room and she can see Kensington Park across the road, watch telly, get some rest. We made her promise not to go back to work until her father's funeral arrangements are made. I don't know if she'll obey."

"She's a very sensitive child," Arcadia said. "Not at all like her mother—" The sun went down fully behind the house and they were in dense shade, though it was still quite warm. As the wind rose, Roberts thought it was going to rain lemon blossoms. He had never seen such color and he couldn't explain the rose and violet hues on the water either. "She inherited her sensitivity from her father." Arcadia had been thinking, eating a slice of mango. "I'd like to tell you it was intelligence from me. But that wouldn't be true. I suppose what she got from me is invisible."

"She looks like you," Roberts said.

"No, can that be true?"

"Yes, she does."

"Poor child," Arcadia said, smiling. Now the game seemed natural to Roberts. There were tears bunched in the woman's eyes, and she was playing too. "No, I think maybe Hillary has from me an intuition about people, you know? We can unsew them and sew them back up good as new." A tear rolled down. "You know about that?"

Roberts said he didn't know, but he had an idea. Roberts told the woman his power was with things and words, not with people. It was that way sometimes. Roberts tried some of the mango, which was very sweet.

"Tell me," Arcadia said, "do you think my child is happy there in London? There in Lincoln's Inn where it is cold all the time and there are all these lawyers?"

"Happy," Roberts repeated dumbly. "I don't know her well enough."

"Please," Arcadia said, "you are a man."

To Roberts this was an expression of something deeper than the surface. "She's out of place," he said finally.

"Ah yes, but I already knew that."

Roberts tasted the papaya, this yellow ethereal fruit. He said, "But I don't know if she's happy or not. Really."

"Then tell me about her brother. Did they meet? Did they know one another?"

"I'm sure they met. She told me about him, about his life in Jamaica, what she knew. But I'm afraid they didn't know one another very well. There were a lot of reasons."

"I'm sure. They were very different. It was no secret that they were only half-brother and sister. I just wondered if they had a chance to talk."

"I'm sure they did," Roberts said.

"Hillary is confused."

"Yes, she's confused," Roberts agreed. "But she's at a place and time where happiness isn't terribly important in her life. She isn't at a carnival having an upset tummy or enjoying the rides. I'm afraid she's involved with the world in other ways. And it's a world that isn't easy on outsiders, especially young Jamaican women. They've given her a corner office on the north side of a building. It used to be a char's chambers. It's cramped and drafty and damp. She eats alone in the cafeteria and she lives in a bed-sitter in Shepherd's Bush and rides the underground to work six days a week. She fries egg and bacon on a little ring in her room and sleeps with a hot water bottle. But whether she's happy or not I couldn't say. There are other things in life."

"Yes," Arcadia said. "You see a lot."

"It doesn't take much."

"But it does," Arcadia insisted. "You answer my question right now. Here in Jamaica, where she was born, oh, you know, the notion of happiness is taken very seriously, you see. *Irie* is the word. You'll hear it now that you've come, and we use it to explain how you should exist. I don't even know how to tell you what it means. It means you see the red of the poinciana, the cloud up there going over the hills. You take happiness in the sight."

Roberts said, "Then Hillary isn't happy."

"That's what I know," Arcadia said. "I wish she would come home. I don't know what she would be doing here, maybe like her mother she would sell trinkets to the tourists. But maybe she could be happy."

Roberts had finished the callaloo. He ate some more fruit, but he didn't have much appetite anymore. He was drowsy and afraid of having too much talk. His skin was hot and he could see pink on the backs of his hands, already a sunburn, just from wandering around on the beach this morning.

"You are tired," Arcadia said.

"I'm tired, yes. But we have to talk about James and your husband too."

"But you look so tired."

"Please," Roberts said. "Tell me about James."

"I know what happened to him," Arcadia began. "I know how his throat was slashed. Hillary, she telegraphed me all about it. Like I told you, I had my cry. You know, James he went away to Kingston five years ago and he didn't come back to Montego Bay at all. He was a very restless boy." Arcadia had looked away again, down the hillside, as if transfixed by the frame of bay and mountain. Roberts saw that the clouds had banked up on a spit of land that went out into the sea, just at the western edge of town where land ended in the Caribbean. "It is hard to understand what the Rasta belief has for a Jamaican boy. And why he holds so tightly to it. My James, he wanted to be away from Montego Bay where the only thing a man can do is higgle trinkets on the beach or sell hats and wash cars for the big hotels. This hurts a man's pride, you know? It hurt my James, who wanted to be somebody, who wanted to become something real. There are so many boys like him, you see them all over the island. They have nothing to do, no education, no hope. They have no work, and when they marry they have no way to support their families. When you strip a man down that way, he can become angry or desperate, you know?" Arcadia had turned back, looking at Roberts now as if she were willing the words at him. Before, she had been talking, looking at the bay bathed in sunset hues. The wind had a cool bite now, which made his skin more hot. "Kingston is a bad town, Mr. Roberts," Arcadia said. "And James was not a boy to write his mother. I can only imagine what he was doing down there."

"When did he go to London?"

"He was unhappy. He went a few months ago."

"Do you think he could have been running away from somebody or something? That somebody wanted to harm him?"

"He could have been. I don't know. You'd have to ask his friend Eli."

"I'm sorry to say this," Roberts said hesitantly.

"Go ahead," Arcadia said.

"The police in London found ganga in his flat."

"Oh, of course now."

"The police thought maybe his murder had something to do with the drugs."

"What do you think?"

"I don't know what to think. Now that Simes is dead too, the police aren't sure what to think. A man named Drummond is handling both cases and he doesn't see any connection at all."

"There was no reason for Simes to be killed."

"I'm sure."

"No," Arcadia said. "There was no reason." Roberts was surprised at the sudden intensity of her gaze. He was searching for another right word, the truth.

"I'll tell you, Arcadia," he said. "Hillary is defending a man named Moseby Demeter on a murder charge. It's possible that Demeter was with James on the night of a robbery that the police say Demeter committed. Now that James is dead, Demeter's alibi isn't good. Several days after James was murdered, Simes is murdered as well. And I found ganga in Demeter's flat too. When you start thinking about all these events, you tend to get confused. There are a lot of things going on, and nobody has a clue what it means. I'm one of those people."

"About the ganga," Arcadia said. "All the Rastas have that stuff."

"I know, but the ganga wrapped up in James's room was

from the same batch, same brown grocery bag and plastic wrapper." Roberts leaned back. The clouds were thick in the mountains now. All the lemon blossoms were blowing wildly down the hill. The hummingbirds had disappeared but he could hear the swallows still, thick in the trees. "Do you know if James was a drug dealer?" Roberts said. It was terrible, but he had to ask.

Arcadia sighed, put her hands over her face. "I don't know what he was doing down in Kingston." Tears flowed around her fingers, you could see them clearly. At the same time, Roberts smelled the rain in the hills. "I told you he went off. He was just a teenager. I asked him to keep going to school, but he wouldn't do it."

"Can you tell me about where he lived, who his friends were?"

"His friend Eli can tell you."

"That's fine then," Roberts said. Rain was beating through the forest far away. The trees had begun to tremble, it was like the sound of silk, rain marching across the tops of the huge akees and tamarinds, clouds purple and mauve, and all the water out on the bay roughed up and bruised.

"Did my husband suffer so much?" Arcadia asked.

"No, I don't think he did." Roberts touched the back of the woman's hand.

There was a hammock on the porch. Roberts slept in it while the rain slammed down. He thought he could hear Arcadia moving around in her shop, just before he went to sleep, singing in a deep, lyrical voice, but he wasn't sure. By then his eyes had closed, and he was engulfed in lemon blossoms.

13

From his hammock on the porch Roberts could see blue light pouring over the mountains like dust. It sifted over everything, the huge akees, swept in by the breeze as the trees growled. He woke with a start, not knowing fully where he was, first recognizing the sweep of bougainvillea and the stone fence at the bottom of the property, which was bounded by wild banana trees under which a goat prowled against its tether. There was a dirty irrigation ditch, probably filled with garbage, a clutch of huts across the road, and more buildings hidden in the forest. Once or twice during the night he had awakened and had seen the darkness filled by shapes of cloud, the sea toward Montego Bay, and a few lights out on the water, which he knew were boats, and a few houses that clung to the hillsides along the beach, but then he had slipped back into dreamless sleep only to wake again when Arcadia had come out onto the wooden porch and covered him with a blanket, leaving him to fall asleep again as before. He felt wonderful recognizing the blue light as dawn, smoke from wood fires rippling through the forest, just as the last frogs stopped croaking. Just then the clouds ignited as the sun slipped from behind the hills.

A line of black men walked downhill, he could see them sliding single file back into the jungle, across the stone fence, five or six of them in white cotton pants, their T-shirts ghostly in the moonless light, woven sacks over their shoulders. They were humming together, some lost tune or other, he couldn't tell if it was a song or a chant, or just the Doctor's Breeze. Arcadia had been talking to the men, and then she came back onto the porch with her hair bunched up behind her head and a string of conch shells around her neck.

"Hey, you sleeping man," she said cheerfully.

Roberts tried to move, but he was buried in the folds of the hammock. He was trapped in a cocoon, and he smiled as Arcadia carried a tray to the table on the porch and unloaded an English tea service, porcelain cups, wedges of fruit and cheese on plates.

"I can't believe I slept this long," Roberts said.

"All night too," she said. The coffee smelled wild and strong when she poured it. He took a cup from her and tasted it. There were wedges of chocolate on the saucer. "Break the chocolate into the coffee, put it in. That's how you do it in Jamaica."

"There were some men," Roberts said. He gestured down the hillside where there was nothing but the goat now. The sun had come up behind the house again, some of the heat from it on the porch already. He threw off his blanket and sipped the coffee, broke the chocolate and stirred it in. He ate a slice of orange.

"Those are my higglers," Arcadia said. "They take my crafts down to the beach and sell them to the tourists. Come back the next day and do it again, all over. All year, every year."

"The coffee is terrific," Roberts said. He hadn't slept so well in days. He was astonished that in the middle of all this terror he could sleep so long, nearly the entire afternoon and night. Now that he was awake he could hear the birds singing in the jungle. It was wood smoke that created the lambent blue color in the hills.

"We have to talk now," Arcadia said, "before Eli comes up from town."

"Eli is coming?"

"He's coming. He's the closest thing in the world my James had to a friend. You'll see. If you want to know anything about James, Eli Churchill will tell you. He drives a cab in Montego Bay now, but he went to Kingston with James. They want to be reggae stars, these boys, but they end up driving cabs or higgling on the beach. You know, they go off to Kingston town and hang around the record stores and dream about driving big cars. Eli came back here when James went off to London. Now he drives a cab."

"Good, I'd like to talk to him."

"But we have to talk first."

"All right, Arcadia," Roberts said. He ate some more orange slices, and some fresh mango, and drained the coffee. He decided it was Jamaican Blue, from the mountains. Everything here was blue, the mountains in the morning, the water, all the smoke slipping through the trees. Now that the wind was high in the forest, it was as if everything was in motion, the house and the hammock included.

"I want to know how my husband, he died," Arcadia said. She put her coffee down, stared at Roberts. He studied her in the light and shadow, her huge dark eyes and her flat face, the flared nose, her skin colored caramel. She had handsome features, almost masculine.

"He was in his flat in Queen's Gardens. Someone came to his door and probably knocked or rang the bell. He opened the door and his throat was slashed. He stumbled back across the floor and collapsed by a walnut table he had set for lunch. It was set for one, so he didn't expect anyone. He was too badly hurt to call for help."

"Did you see the room?"

"Yes, I was there."

"What do the police do about this?"

"I talked to Drummond. He searched the room looking for anything that would link James and Simes. He didn't find anything unusual at all. The man is as confused as we all are about these things. As I am."

"Simes did nothing."

"I'm sure of it," Roberts said, aware that something was on Arcadia's mind.

"No, no," Arcadia whispered. She had placed her hands in her lap, gazing at Roberts in a distracted fashion. He felt as if she were miles away, in another time, too. "No, Simes did nothing wrong, I'm sure. Nothing, nothing at all. That's why you are so important to me, why you must be so important to Hillary. She is alone in London now. Her father was her only link to her past, to her own real life. You know how it must be, you've known her."

"I think I understand," Roberts said. "But there are serious problems. There has to be a connection between the deaths of James and Simes. I don't know what it might be, but it has to be. I've only got scraps and tag ends of things on my mind. Moseby Demeter is one. James may have been his alibi in a crime there. Then James is killed. I found ganga in Demeter's room that is the same as that in James's room. Then Simes is murdered in the same way as James. These things come together, Arcadia, but I don't know how."

Tears had welled again in Arcadia's eyes. Roberts got to his feet and poured himself more coffee and waited. A scrawny dog crawled onto the porch and sat under the woman's feet, licking her ankles. She hardly noticed, still immersed in memory.

"You have to know one thing," Arcadia said. "Simes was a good man and he wouldn't do anything bad. He would not lie or cheat or steal. That's what I say."

"I believe you," Roberts said simply.

"We met when I was very young." Arcadia paused, gathering herself, trying to get back and hold on. "I was just a girl really, and my husband was older than me. I was in school, think of me, with my school uniform going back and forth to St. Lucie on the hill in Negril. Simes had a temporary job there then and we would see each other in the early morning when

I was out walking and he was on his way to the office, and we would stop and talk. Then we would see each other again at night when I was going home. He was so wonderful to talk to, me so young, he was so handsome too. You know when we got married we loved one another like a man and a woman love one another. I didn't know it then, but there was no way such a love could work. I know it now, but not then. And it didn't matter then. We would walk along the beach and he would tell me about England and his books and his work. We got married pretty soon after I finished school and moved up to Montego Bay.

"Maybe Hillary has told you, but they finished him in the civil service, made him do small jobs, hurt his pride, made him feel bad for me. We had five years together, and then everything was over for both of us. He missed England and he missed his friends, and he missed being part of something real. By that time he had no real work. Those silly fools would laugh at us behind our backs, stare and wag their tongues. It was sad, but he had to go home. There was nothing left for him here and he couldn't live so far away from home with no work to do, nothing useful to keep him going. You know how that might be?" Roberts knew exactly how it might be. He was feeling some of it himself, so far from home. "So Hillary she stay with me and go to school and visit in England twice, and then when she was old enough to go, she went to England for a real education." Arcadia stopped crying, probably with the effort of remembrance. Roberts thought she had spoken beautifully, with the accent of a Jamaican educated at Catholic school.

Down in the harbor people were taking to the beach and the quays as the surf came in. "Don't talk anymore," he said.

"I want to say two things," Arcadia said.

"All right. Just two."

"I want you to find out who murdered my husband and my son if you can."

"Of course, I'll try," Roberts answered. He was feeling nervous again, just as he'd felt when he left Gatwick, when he'd talked to Hillary lying pale and tired on her sofa in Kensington Park. He was making hopeless promises, it was his good nature, but he was frightened too. "There isn't much to go on," he said. The sun had fallen on Arcadia's hair from behind. Hummingbirds and butterflies were streaking on the hillsides. "But look," Roberts added quickly, "there *are* some things we have to go on."

"I know," Arcadia said. "You do your best, that's all. I know you will."

Roberts heard loud music coming from below the stone fence. Arcadia went to the edge of the porch and called down to someone in the banana trees. A small, spidery man hopped over the fence and up the wooden steps. He had on dirty plaid trousers and a clingy, fluorescent long-sleeved shirt and a flat green-and-black tam.

"Eli! Eli!" Arcadia called, obviously happy to see the man.

He shouted up. *"Irie* gal, how *irie* woman!"* Arcadia had gone down the porch steps and Roberts watched the two of them talking in an embrace, and then the man took off his cap and they stood together for a long time in silence, the man with his arms around Arcadia, though he was much smaller, holding his cap in one hand while the woman cried. They were in the shade of an old akee and the tree was full of swallows, one ragged parrot in a lower branch. Roberts had time for more coffee because the two were together for a long time, swaying there in the shade of the tree as the wind whipped around them. Their voices had become hushed, the man was almost swallowed by the woman's huge form and her flowing dress. She was nearly a head taller. Finally, they came up the porch steps together, slowly, with the man holding his cap in both hands in a manner of supplication, quiet embarrassment. Roberts could see that he was missing some teeth and that his skin was bright-slick black, the face wrinkled. He was so skinny you could see his ribs against the long-sleeved shirt, his wrists were hugely knuckled.

"Hello, mister," the man said. He was wall-eyed.

"This is Eli," Arcadia said, sitting down at the table again

while Eli stood uneasily at the top of the stairs. Roberts stood
and introduced himself, shaking hands with the man whose
grip was light as bone. He had a wisp of chin whiskers and
deep lines around his eyes. He reminded Roberts of a lemur.
"Eli was my son's best friend. They've been through a lot
together. They lived in Kingston town."

"That true," Eli said quietly, turning his cap around and
around in his hands.

"Arcadia told me," Roberts said. "I'm pleased to meet you,
Eli." Eli Churchill, Roberts thought to himself, a slave name,
like stamps on a pouch of tobacco, tags on a cow's ear. "I'm
glad you've come to help me. I know Arcadia appreciates it."

"Jah, I've come up here all right," Eli said.

"I'm sorry about James," Roberts responded. Eli was
standing stock straight, looking across the hillsides now, obviously uneasy. "James is down at the customs house."

"I'll go see to him," Eli said to Arcadia.

"This afternoon, Eli," she said quickly.

"I'm told you can help me," Roberts cut in.

"I knew James," Eli said.

"I've got to go now," Arcadia interjected, crossing the
porch now. "I want to go down to Montego and see my son.
You two carry on without me." She went inside the house and
Roberts could hear her in there, cups tinkling in the wash
basin, her dog scuffing after her.

"We go away from here now," Eli said. He had started
down the stairs without Roberts, who scrambled to catch up.
They went part of the way down the hill and Eli slowed. Sun
was splashing through the trees and the flies and gnats were
thick. Eli bounded down the wooden stairs and gained the dirt
path and was already hopping into a Chevelle when Roberts
broke through the wall of foliage. The car was rusted-out
under the wheel wells and the gray vinyl roof was worn
smooth, ripped in spots. From inside the car, Roberts could
hear the jagged metal sound of *ska* coming from a radio
thonged to the rearview mirror, metal drum and a guitar line.

Roberts got in the passenger seat and they roared away

down a narrow road that led through wild acacias toward the beach. The wind was blowing hard down the mountainsides from behind them and he could hear the ocean breaking against the cliffs as they went downhill. There were gulls whirling above the cliffs too, and puffy clouds floating just offshore. Eli stared straight ahead, as if transfixed by the music, his head moving up and down as the drums banged away. The whole cab smelled of sweat and burning motor oil. They passed other cars going uphill, jalopies, other Chevelles, and older-model Impalas. Everything was suffused with music, steel drums, a laughing riot of sound in the stifling heat.

Eli made a hard right up another, steeper hill bounded by tended lemon groves, and they weaved up a lane guarded by logwood railings, a steep cliff of red rock down one side to the pounding surf. The banana trees were clicking in the wind and farther up Roberts saw a cane field banked against the emerald-green hills. Eli kept glancing at Roberts, perhaps trying to gauge his feelings, this black face slashed by a wide grin, brown teeth, and then he would show Roberts a blank stare. They were turning into a summit framed by brilliant sunshine and the green succulence of a bermuda lawn fronting a huge wooden house with a veranda. The roof was made of wood shingles painted green.

"Richmond Hill," Eli said, pulling to a stop outside the hotel restaurant. They were on a spit of land over the ocean and way out in the bay Roberts could see a cruise liner chugging through purple haze, its wake-white fading behind the ship for miles. Eli put on mirrored sunglasses and sat listening to a *ska* tune, old-time reggae with a backbeat, calypso with venom. "This a fine place for the view, mon," Eli said.

"You didn't bring me up here for the view, Eli," Roberts replied. The car was superhot, he was glad for his cotton pants and sandals. There was a glaze over the water that gave it a white sheen.

"You gonna find who cut James?" Eli asked. The man turned a look on Roberts that was luminous. Roberts could see himself dancing on the dual surfaces of the sunglasses. It was a pure *ska* image, hot lessons in Jamaica's heart. "You gonna find out who done that," Eli said again. "No problem, huh, mon?"

14

"Hey, doan you get drunk now, man," Eli called, Roberts sitting on the hood of the Chevelle, feeling really good, one leg over the grille, and a sandal on the bumper, drinking from a bottle of Bacardi dark. "You hear now, man. Doan you get drunk!," a big smile on Eli's face. Roberts's white cotton trousers were damp, but he could feel the breeze in his clothes, the Doctor's Breeze that roared down from the mountains all day. It was stiff now in the afternoon, scudding the clouds and making a white surf line just beyond the arc of the bay where the ocean ran in a ragged blue-green swell. All around him, the oleanders were churning, you could smell the dusky aroma of the leaves. There were swimmers on Fletcher's Beach, and beyond them small boats bobbing in the waves and some people driving power boats farther out toward open water, one guy naked on the bow with a parasol. Everything had a burnt orange haze to it, maybe it was the rum, Roberts couldn't quite tell, but he didn't want to think too much either, he was satisfied to swig rum, watch the logwoods dance, and enjoy the sun straining down through the forest over his right shoulder. The metal of the car was hot and he could feel his skin right against his body like an ointment. Maybe that's what he needed, to feel his skin, be outdoors, get drunk. "Doan get drunk now, man," Eli said, going away.

Eli walked up to the restaurant bar of the hotel and came back with a loaf of French bread, some crab salad, and another bottle of rum. He told Roberts he wasn't allowed to eat at the bar, so he'd gone to the kitchen where he knew a boy who washed dishes and bused tables for the white tourists. Their first bottle had come from the trunk of the Chevelle. Eli had brought it out just as the sun came up over the mountains, and Roberts had watched Eli take a long drink, the black man staring out at the ocean with his wall-eyed gaze, enjoying the rum and the sun both, very comfortable in his dirty polyester plaid pants and his broken-down sneakers and his scruffy wisp of chin whiskers. Maybe it was the morning, or the way the blue dust seemed to burn away from the edges of the hills and ridges, or maybe just the way the two of them had sat on the hood of the Chevelle while the breeze riffled down the valleys, but Roberts sensed some deeper spiritual emotion inside this tiny Jamaican cab driver, something romantic and practical at the same time, something just beyond his ability to understand it right now. But they had enjoyed some rum, and Eli kept telling Roberts not to get drunk, taking his own deep swigs in rhythm with the ocean and the wind. Roberts had taken the bottle and had a long pull and smiled at the cab driver, wondering if there was anything to share with him right then. He didn't want to get drunk, but he wondered what difference it would make. After all, Eli was drinking right along with him. In between drinks, they sat the bottle on the hood between them.

"I won't get drunk," Roberts said to Eli when he came back with the bread and crab salad. Already slurring his words just a little. The rum settled in his stomach but he felt wide awake, like a sleepwalker. Down on Fletcher's Beach there was a volleyball game going on, American tourists with their oiled bodies already reddened by the sun. "How long did you know James?" Roberts asked.

Eli hopped off the hood and squatted in the grass, arms folded, hands between his knees. He reached up to the hood and took the bottle and had a long drink, staring out at the ocean, the long spit of land that jutted into the sea. "Jah, I know the man all my life. We were kids up here in these hills, you know?" He had looked at Roberts, then away, trying to establish a rapport, maybe wanting to see how authentic things were going to get. Roberts had a scruffy beard and a flowered shirt, a pasty London face going red, and Roberts thought that Eli was using the rum to test something between them, see how far their sharing could go before it snapped into something else. Roberts ate some bread, tearing off a hunk and spreading some of the crab on it with his fingers. The heat had begun to roar in his head and he could sense activity behind him at the hotel, waiters scurrying among the veranda tables, people talking and dance band music. "You know, man," Eli said, pulling up some bermuda grass, "I can't believe the boy is dead. It seem so soon he just go to England now. I seen him go down the road to the train station with his suitcase in his hands now. He had some record albums and a guitar and then he went to England, way over there." Eli turned his head slightly, glancing at Roberts, who looked at his sweaty face with its wrinkles, older than it should be. "Hey, we live in the same flat down in Kingston for two years. We shuffle around that town and you get to be close, you know."

"Arcadia told you how he died," Roberts said.

"She tell me. You think you know who did this?" From Eli it came out: *Yuh tink yuh know who deed tis?*

"Not yet."

"You going to find out, man?"

"I'm going to try. That's part of why I'm here."

"Why you doing this, man?"

Eli had turned his back to Roberts. They were locked in phase with the breeze. Roberts decided to take a drink, sink himself in the rum, which would maybe give him an experience that he could share with the Jamaican man. Perhaps it was a mistake, thinking he could share something like this with the guy, but he thought it was worth a try. You can't make music unless you pick up an instrument.

"I want to help Hillary Root. I like her. Her father is dead too. Did Arcadia tell you that?"

"Jah, man, she told me," Eli answered.

"Did you know Simes?"

"I was a little kid, man."

Eli moved his voice through a range; like poetry, it had a delicate structure. Roberts would be listening to him and nothing would be happening, and then all of a sudden his head would click and he would have a miraculous vision and what was crooked straightened out. Eli drank some rum and pulled up some more sweet bermuda grass.

"Both Simes and James died the same way."

"That's a bad thing."

"They cut James's tongue too," Roberts said.

Eli studied Roberts for a long time. Then he stood and leaned against the Chevelle. Montego Bay was spread out below them to the north, and there were white hotels along the beach with green tile roofs, Gloucester Avenue curving along the beach where Roberts had sat and had his first Red Stripe. The palms bowed toward the water and there were oleanders in pink and red blossom lining the raised boardwalk.

"That so he can't talk when he get to Zion," Eli said finally. He spit on the grass and touched the rum bottle fondly and took another long drink, eyes closed. "Jah, they cut his tongue so he can't sing praise, jah, man. They cut his tongue so he can't sing. That's it, jah."

Eli had walked to the edge of the cliff, carrying the rum. There was a red dirt path winding downhill from the top and Eli paused on the edge, swaying slightly as if some reggae were going through his head. Roberts moved away from the car, all the glare from the metal and glass, and he could really feel the breeze, very strong, running right over the cliff. He was floating away from himself, thinking about Zion, the piece of skin cut away from James's tongue. What the hell did that mean anyway?

"Talk to me, Eli," Roberts said as the man slipped over the cliff and out of sight. Roberts could hear him moving through oleanders. Roberts scuffled downhill, getting pebbles in his shoes, and found Eli on his haunches again. They were on an outcrop shelf of rock and dirt, above the beach.

"You talk to me, man," Eli said.

Roberts sat beside the man. The volleyballers were shouting, having a good time. "Someone poisoned James. He was taken to the hospital and was recovering. Late one night somebody came into his room and slashed his throat."

"That simple you say."

"If you call that simple."

"Jah, man. What the police doing?"

"Their best."

"Jimmy still dead man."

"We can't fix that."

"No, sir, that's right," Eli said, drinking from the rum. "Everybody knows that. Don't you?"

"Yeah, I know that. But who did it?"

Eli sighed, drank rum. "Some rude boy killed him, that's for sure, man. Some damn old rude boy." Eli took the rum down about an inch, eyes squeezed tight. "Jah!" he shouted to the wind.

Roberts took the rum and pushed himself back to the edge of rock so he could sit down with his legs stretched out. He had screwed himself down, that feeling in his head, the tips of his fingers, like being drilled into hardwood with countersunk screws. It was too early in the day to be this tight, but he was going somewhere with Eli, hoping they'd arrive at a destination together pretty soon. Here they were out in the wind on the side of a cliff and Eli was mourning his friend, drinking dark *Anjeho.* "What is a rude boy?" Roberts asked. The gulls were hooting above them.

"Lotta rude boys down here, man," he answered. He made a sweeping gesture with one hand, an ellipsis of thought. It was an epiphany rooted somewhere else. "Jah, man, lotta these rude boys now."

"But who are they?"

"Outlaw man, you know."

"Drug dealers?"

"Rude boy who robs and shoots and loots."

"A gangster."

"You don't listen, man," Eli said. He was smiling now and Roberts could see clearly that he had two teeth gone from the front of his mouth. It had made his face slightly oval and shrunken.

"Try me again," Roberts said.

"Rude boys like the ratchet knife. They slash your throat and cut your tongue so you can't sing. Slashing and cutting and robbing is what they do."

The bottle was almost empty. Roberts was wondering if Eli would like to go down the beach and find a hotel bar and drink some Red Stripe, try to find a place to eat callaloo, some snapper, maybe lie around on the beach and talk. Eli had begun to hum to himself, waving the bottle. Roberts could see that the man was crying, big bright tears dropping from those weary eyes, very passionate, the guy articulating himself to the clouds and the gulls and the bright haze over the water that smelled of salt. Roberts let him sing, settling back in his rocky alcove. Below there were blondes on the beach, wearing tight bikinis, and a black man selling trinkets from a basket he carried on a strap around his neck. Eli had opened his eyes and was focused on Roberts.

"Fuck it, Eli," Roberts said. "I don't know what a ratchet knife is, either."

Eli laughed loudly, like a bray. "Machete man!," he cried. "The coconut knife, the sugarcane."

Now Roberts was sorry the rum was gone. Roberts was impressed with the odd mixture of grief and bewilderment, and the strange way Eli could still laugh, through all his pain. Every one of his emotions seemed admixed, grief, fear, confusion, and joy, these complicated surfaces, a psychology of cubism. Roberts was deep in the rum, watching Eli go on down the hill, kicking loose pebbles and rocks. He hurried after him and they hit the beach together where there were some fake grass huts, palm fronds piled over board frames, Jamaicans selling beer and suntan lotion and windsurf boards. Roberts found Eli squatting in the shade behind one of the huts, puffing on a thin black cigar. He handed one of the cigars to Roberts, gave him a light.

"I thought James would come home," Eli said wistfully. He had raised his voice to the sky now, sitting on an empty beer case in the shade. "Now my brother can't sing."

"James was a Rasta," Roberts said. He had lighted his cigar with some wood matches Eli had handed over.

"Jah, James was that. Not me, but he became Rasta down in Kingston." Roberts was in awe of the man's emotional complexity. There were tears on his face, he was smiling, talking to Roberts all at once. "Everybody need a voice, you know?"

"I think so," Roberts said.

"You got to sing and pray, jah, man?"

"I need your help, Eli. I really do."

"You want a Red Stripe?" Eli asked, laughing. Roberts took the hint and bought four beers from a vendor. He thought he might drink two, then take a swim and clear his head later. Eli drank half a beer in one gulp.

"You think a Jamaican killed James?" Roberts asked.

"Jah, I do," Eli said somberly. There was a fuzz on his chin. "With the ratchet knife. That's what a rude boy would do, you ask me. Cut his tongue."

"Rude boys are in London?"

"I never been there," Eli said.

"No, I guess not," Roberts replied.

"No, man, I ain't been to that place. I wouldn't know where to go if I did go there."

"Yeah, I know," Roberts said, drinking some beer. And Roberts did know the city of eleven million. He felt that way himself, coming into the cold place. He liked the lights and action, the theater and music, and he liked the smell of the place after a rain, but he was so alone. Eli had finished his first

Red Stripe and was opening another, Roberts still working on his first. It was fine beer, nearly ruby in color and very rich. "Sometime I'd like to know everything there is you can tell me about James." Roberts smiled as Eli relaxed against the plywood of the hut, his eyes bloodshot and his face covered by dust. Roberts smoked his cigar.

"How I gonna do that?" Eli said.

"Just start talking," Roberts suggested.

"How I gonna tell everything about a man? You know only God can do that."

"You're right," Roberts said, playing the game. "Just tell me about his life in Kingston. Tell me if he had friends. Tell me what he did for money. You say a rude boy killed him, maybe it all started in Kingston. Who knows, maybe James did something in Kingston that followed him all the way to London. If it is something like that, I'd like to know." Eli looked worn out, draining his second beer quickly, tossing away the cigar.

"Why some rude boy kill Simes Root?"

"Yeah, well, I don't know why."

"You find that out, then you know." Eli got up and edged out of the shade and stood looking at the volleyballers. The sun was overhead, the sky full of shimmering thin clouds. You couldn't feel much of the breeze down on the beach, under the cliffs. It was very hot, and somewhere a radio played loud *ska,* a hard beat that pulsed.

"What's a Rastaman?" Roberts asked. Eli had his back turned to Roberts, standing in full sun.

"Jah, man," Eli mused. "It means you go home to Zion. It means you pray yourself free, no more slavery, no more pain. You are part of a tribe and you can go home now." In an almost shy gesture, Eli turned to look at Roberts. "Oh, man, it means whatever you want it to mean. We went down to Kingston and James he wanted to be part of it. There are lots of boys doing that thing now."

"A Rasta isn't a rude boy?"

"No, man, no. They two different things, them."

"He had dreadlocks."

"Oh, jah, he wore the dreadlocks and he play the guitar and he smoke ganga. He laid about some, too."

"He had women then," Roberts said, smiling.

"Jah, he had some."

"And before he was a Rasta?"

"Oh, before that then," Eli said. "He was just like you and me then, man!" Eli showed his smile, jabbed Roberts on the knee. He took off for the dirt path up the cliff before Roberts could say anything else, running up the cliffs like a deer, singing as he climbed. Roberts tried to follow but he was staggered by the heat and the rum. He finally caught the man at the Chevelle, both of them leaning against the hood, choking and exhausted, laughing together. More cars were in the parking lot now and Roberts caught sight of the guests on the hotel veranda, some playing croquet on the side lawn, women in white dresses, men in blazers and gray trousers.

"I got to go see my brother," Eli said.

"Tell me more about James."

"Jah, man, I will. Don't worry now!"

Eli hopped in the driver's seat and tuned in another *ska* tune on the radio. Roberts noticed the dolls and conch shells pasted to the dash, like a shrine. They backed out of the lot and went down Sunset Drive, the way they'd come up, a narrow asphalt road hemmed in by logwoods and akees, this sharp cliff down to a ravine. There was something thick inside Roberts's head, in his vision, but he was happy, and he knew he trusted Eli now, even though the guy was driving too fast on the narrow road, making everything uncoil too quickly. The music was so loud it was distracting. Roberts thought they might have skimmed a guard rail once going uphill, but he wasn't sure because of the noise. Eli was peering over the steering wheel, rocking gently to the beat, just rolling with the music. It was a different experience for Roberts because Eli was crying out loud, big tears on his cheeks, and he was laughing too, high on rum and Red Stripe, driving way too fast in a brilliant tunnel of light and shade.

15

They were scaring the shit out of goats and chickens. They were scaring Roberts too, though he was softened up from the rum and two Red Stripes, but still, with the sunlight strafing him as they went uphill and through gorges thick with ferns, every time some goats scattered Roberts would crush down in the seat and close his eyes, expect to hurtle through the wind- shield in a blizzard of feathers, blood, and broken glass. They had gone through Montego on Gloucester Avenue like kami- kazes, parting the tourists, all the white-legged gawkers in bermudas with their necks piled with Japanese cameras. The Jamaican brothers on the boardwalk pointed and yelled after them, and waved at Eli, who pretended not to notice. Roberts watched the fruit and vegetable markets on the edge of town sear past like wildfires, and then they went along the north coast road where the beaches threaded out to isolated lagoons surrounded by white sand, waving palms, and then acres of red rock back of the road and then some more beach towered above by high rock cliffs where the logwoods and akees began. Eli insisted on stopping for more Red Stripe, and so Roberts bought six from a vendor at the side of the road, and threw the

beer in the backseat in a paper sack. He bought some sandwiches too, and a few mangos and oranges. For Roberts it was
like being imprisoned in a prism, crazy angles of light refract-
ing and reflecting in stupid succession, then the palm trees
roaring by and then some girls in bikinis waving and then Eli
laughing and turning up the radio. Cars passed them going the
other way, toward town, it was like a drunken battlefield.

Roberts was trying to clear his head. He wanted to talk to
Eli some more about James Root. He wanted to find out what
had started him on a road that led from Kingston town to a
dirty flat in London, try to get a feel for the guy who had died
twice. Roberts kept remembering the gray one-room bed-
sitter James had lived in, the dirty windows looking down on
Curlew Street. But right now Eli was in tune with the radio
ska, staring out through his mirrored shades, driving up
through scattered fields of cane, great ragged wilds of bloom-
ing poinsettias. Roberts thought they might disappear in a
vaporous cloud at the rim of a hill, and be gone forever.

But then Eli surprised Roberts by turning off the Port Antonio road and going up a rough dirt track that looked like a
goat path, all the jungle closing in, huge elephant ears and
some wild lime trees with ripe fruit. Eli didn't slow down, he
just bumped them harder over the rough tracks, it was like
riding a baby carriage over some lunar landscape, and pretty
soon Eli laughed harder and they bounced over a stone curb
and onto a narrow asphalt drive that wasn't divided by any
center line, the asphalt crumbled and diving downhill in
chunks where the rain had washed it away, the steep hills
dense with logwood.

Something engaged Roberts in the scene. The same blue
mist danced in the hills, and he wondered what on earth was
giving everything such a melancholy tint, an almost suffocat-
ing cast, even though the sky was bright with sun and the
clouds were illuminated and floating away in the distance.
This blue was an odd color, a hue that had seeped from the
ground and saturated the air, just the opposite from what he
expected, which was a tropical blaze day with a huge angry

wash of heat. It was just blue, this color climbing through the sounds of parrots and monkeys.

"What are you up to, Eli?" Roberts asked when they had come to a full stop. It was cool in the shadows and the sounds were muffled. Eli shut off the radio.

"See my brother, man," Eli said. "Like I told you." He hadn't looked at Roberts.

The things Roberts could see here were the shapes of the hills roiling away from him to the south. The other way there was a collection of shacks with corrugated tin roofs, some black men and boys kicking a football, a few of them staring now that they had noticed the ticking Chevrolet. And it was the faces that arrested Roberts the most, glances of emotional detachment, dark eyes. Roberts could hear their patois and it made him feel suddenly alone, even though Eli was sitting right next to him on his imitation sheepskin seatcover, his face relinquishing the alcohol, reflected in the windshield. *Those faces,* they were thin and haunting, he could see a lot of them now, maybe a dozen or more, through a clearing, in the dense blue smoke, and then some women too, bundled up in gray with bags of white hair wrapped in red cloth, but above all, the motionless stares poised between wonderment and anger. There was no other traffic, nothing to break the stillness but the sounds of the birds and the pitter-patter of the patois, as if all these people were suddenly disembodied. They were beings with a secret inner core. But mostly Roberts had thought himself way out in the country, in the sticks, and here were hundreds of people.

A dirt path led uphill and Eli took it, motioning for Roberts to follow. They went along slowly under a canopy of limbs. Eli had gathered up the Red Stripe and the sandwiches and the two of them were laboring up the dirt path at some level of interaction, maybe the trust Roberts hoped he'd develop. It was *something* to sit with a man in midmorning and drink rum and smoke cigars and sing and cry, it was something that could cement you together, even if it cracked later.

"Irie, mama," Eli shouted.

"Irie, Eli," answered a thin voice buried in shadow. "You come on up here, boy, now!"

"My friend Mitchell now," Eli shouted again, looking back at Roberts with his pinched eyes, smiling.

A frail woman looked down at them from the shelter of an overhang. She was standing beneath a sheer, water-stained cliff of black rock and Roberts could see a palm frond shack made of tin scrap and plywood, even some cardboard boxes. She was standing in a bare dirt yard where chickens scratched helplessly. Roberts couldn't identify the smell in the air, he knew that it was corrupt, a filth he wouldn't forget. When he got to the top of the path, and the old woman had walked over to where he and Eli were standing, Roberts was shocked at how incredibly wrinkled she was, like old newsprint, with a turbaned head and a black cloak over her shoulders. He was shocked too, because the woman was barefoot, it chagrined him, and he felt ashamed, he didn't know where to put his eyes. Eli kissed his mother on the cheek. "Mama, this is Mitchell Roberts," he said, proudly, Roberts thought.

The woman stepped back, embarrassed. Eli took Roberts by the arm and led him into the shack, which was really a lean-to that used the rock face as one of its sides. The whole room wasn't more than eight by ten wide, with some homemade shelves along one side wall, a cot, and one old-fashioned metal bed in another corner. Water had dripped down the rock face and was puddled in the dirt. While Roberts watched, shocked still, Eli kneeled beside the bed on which a man was lying under a thin blanket. Roberts thought the man looked like a cadaver, with bones that had been picked clean already, liquidless black eyes and the structure of his face so pronounced the skin had a paper-thin sheen. He could have been a newborn child, a sack of rocks, anything.

"Hey, brother," Eli whispered, taking the man by the hand. Eli opened his sack and produced a sandwich while the man on the bed smiled laconically. Eli peeled an orange and spaced the slices one at a time in a neat circle on the blanket, just on the man's heart. Roberts could have cried, he could hear the two men whispering in quick patois, a whole other language, it was like a familiar code, but it was too quick. The old woman had begun washing clothes in a wooden tub just outside the door to the shack, watched by a dog beset by flies and sores. Roberts waited for a long time, while the men talked and the flies buzzed around him, and then they went outside and Roberts watched Eli hand the woman a bundle of colorful Jamaican dollars and one of the remaining sandwiches. He handed Roberts a Red Stripe, and stood there in the damp chill, listening to the water curl down the rock cliff, having a sip of beer.

They were standing off to the side, drinking their beers. "What's wrong with your brother?" Roberts asked.

"Arthur is my brother," Eli announced.

"What's wrong with Arthur?"

"His lungs."

"Tuberculosis?"

"Jah, man, that's it."

"He should be in a hospital."

"You right there, my friend," Eli said.

"How long has he been sick?"

"Many years now." Eli was reporting all this in a slow, methodical tone.

"Has he seen a doctor?"

Eli looked down at the dirt. "What you know, man," he said. "We gonna take my brother down to big doctor in Kingston? We gonna put him in a clinic in Switzerland?" There was silence while Eli got himself together. "There nobody to see him, no money to pay for him to be seen anyway. You know?"

They finished their beers sitting on a log together. They shared some goat meat, and the strange tranquillity that shuttered the clearing. Roberts was trying to get used to the poverty, trying to get his senses back from the rum. In the back of his mind he knew there was a reason Eli had brought him up to this place. He could sense that it was something Eli had wanted to share with him, so that, tentatively, they could be equals for a few moments here in the forest. And now that

Roberts had settled down on the log with his beer he could see other hovels, six or seven of them, just like the one he was sitting in front of, each made of scrap tin and foraged cardboard, orange crates, and a trail of blue smoke sifting up from each where there must have been a charcoal fire. Through an opening in the forest Roberts could see a long valley that had been deforested, clumps of trees cut to the ground where skinny cows wandered like dazed survivors, all the wreckage in the midst of the beautiful forest. There was too much, it could drown you in your own contemplation of it. Then it hit Roberts. It was smoke that had tinted the air. Small fires in hundreds of hovels.

"What you gonna do, my friend?" Eli asked.

Roberts looked at Eli, who was pensive. Eli's mother was across the way in full shadow, pounding some rags against a wooden roller while her dog sniffed the sandwich. His notion of things had altered in the last few moments. Here in this incredibly poor clearing, way up in the mountains of Jamaica, he was finally glimpsing a portion of life that for him had always existed just below the surface of things, so that you had to microscope it to see it clearly. But it was there, like the blue smoke and the eight hovels scattered under the brow of the cliffs, those black faces in a sea of broken tree stumps. Once you could see it, it crawled all over you, it was as deft as the act of perception itself.

"Thank you for letting me come up here," Roberts said.

"No problem, man," Eli said.

"I think I'm beginning to get the idea about rude boys. Ratchet knives and machetes too."

"You stay around long enough, you understand Zion, jah. You see why them Rastas pray for freedom so much."

"So what I'm going to do is find out about James."

"So, you do that, man."

"What did he do in Kingston?"

"We went down there three years ago. James found a poor job in a record store on Orange Lane. When we went down he wasn't no Rasta man. He just sold records and he hang out on the streets, you know?"

"What about you? What did you do down there?"

"I walk the streets a lot, you know? I do this and I do that, and pretty soon I save about half what I need for my car. Arcadia, after James go to London, she give me the rest, she."

"You lived with James?"

"Jah, man, on and off. Sometimes he gone on the walk-about and he smoke for days. No sleep, just music and ganga. We had a place down on the railroad by Spanish Town Road. You know the thing, cement blocks they gonna use on the harbor, somebody steal them and put them up and then we move inside."

"And then James got involved with Rasta?"

"Oh, jah, involved," Eli said, smiling. It was a pleasant, wrinkled smile, very gentle and moving. "You got to understand. I bring you up here so you can do that. Everything around you make you hot and crazy. You got all this commotion and bother in Kingston, but there is nowhere to go. You got this rage against the government, but you ain't got no way to put off this rage. That's why so many boys going down with Rasta. You do that, or you loot and shoot, you get to be a rude boy, you know?"

Roberts was remembering the Bermondsey docks, how many black faces he'd seen there, it was the same thing, ragged gray skinny people peering out from an unknown locus, vexing, imploring, angry, hopeless. It scared Roberts inside, all these rude boys wriggling out from his microscope slide, like a spilled virus. And they were yearning down in the depths of their souls for freedom. And what did it mean, freedom? Escape to Zion? It was that, or this place covered with blue smoke, the residue of slavery, all the trees cut down for charcoal fire.

"Does the name Moseby Demeter mean anything to you?" Roberts asked Eli.

"He a rude boy?"

"I don't know. Maybe."

"Well, I don't know any Moseby Demeter from Kingston."

"James had ganga in London. You know how he came by it up there?"

"Jah, well, every Rasta got ganga. If you ask was James a rude boy, well then I say he wasn't no rude boy, me."

"The London police think maybe he was killed for something to do with ganga, or drugs. They're looking back to Jamaica. That's why I'm here. Did James have trouble with the Jamaican police?"

"No, I know he didn't. He was a fancy boy, but he wasn't no rude boy."

"You know somebody in Kingston who might know Moseby Demeter? You know somebody who might know what James was doing when he wasn't with you?"

"Now what you doing, man?" Eli asked.

Roberts had tried one of the goat meat sandwiches. The meat was stringy and flavorless. It made his mouth burn from the pikapeppa sauce. "Go down to Kingston," Roberts said. "Stir up the pot." He grinned at Eli.

"Ooooooooooh, man," Eli said, in a long perfect hiss that expressed incredulity and pleasure all at once.

"I want to dig for the real James Root. Find out what I can about Moseby Demeter, too. I want to shovel for a couple of days and go home. It might help my friend Hillary, and Arcadia as well."

"Kingston is a big town, man," Eli said. "I think maybe this whole island move there one day, you know?"

"Hey, maybe so. And maybe James was dealing ganga. That's what the police think. If so, I should be able to get a line on his friends."

Eli disappeared into the shack for another ten minutes, talking to his brother while Roberts waited outside. He wanted to say something to the old woman, who would wash her clothes, then smile his way, brush off the dog, and go back to work. Roberts didn't say anything, though. He didn't know what to say, so he watched Eli inside the damp hovel kneeling beside his brother's bed, feeding him orange slices and talking quietly. While Roberts watched, the clouds banked up over the forest head, big busted roses of clouds that had green edges and fluted purple dimples. Pretty soon it would rain and the rain would beat down through the trees and cover everything with a grainy tint. Roberts's skin felt clammy and damp, as if something was growing on its surface.

Finally Eli came out of the hovel and embraced his mother for a long time, kissed her, and she waved to Roberts shyly. They walked down the narrow dirt track and started the Chevelle and headed out of the forest toward the asphalt highway. Eli was driving without his sunglasses, and he didn't turn on the radio. The rain was sweeping up the valley like a murmur of silk.

"Jah, Kingston is a big town, man," Eli said reflectively. They made the Port Antonio road in fifteen minutes, riding on a shelf of red dirt above the beach. The water had changed color as the clouds moved in. It was slate gray and dark blue now, with shades of purple where the seaweed was bunched up. "So, you know, man," Eli said while they were going under a grove of banana trees, "I don't think you can get around a town like Kingston without some help."

"I'm used to big towns," Roberts said. They were running through cane fields now, all the hillsides splashed with poinsettias. In the lagoons were snorkelers, tanned women in bikinis lying on towels. It was another world down here, you wouldn't know the mountain world existed unless you went up into it, climbed through the blue smoke and saw the hovels. From down here the mountain people didn't exist. Roberts could see the bulk of a cruise ship way out beyond the swell line. The cruise ship was a world farther away still, so far away nothing but the casinos and swimming pools existed. "I'm sure I can find my way around eventually." They slowed to go through a tunnel. Roberts said, "I'm sorry about your brother Arthur."

"Jah, man, he is very sick," Eli said.

They hit town and went straight through it and up to Albion Road just as the rain crashed in the hills around them. Eli pulled off the road just below the wooden stairs up to Arcadia's shop. They were amid tamarinds where the road widened.

"You going to do this, man?" Eli asked, shutting off the motor. In the heat and rain you could hear it clicking.

"I told Hillary I would."

"You might get cut with a ratchet knife."

"It happened once in London. I'll be more careful."

"You didn't like it, no, man?"

"No, man, I didn't like it."

Eli faced Roberts across the seat. He was sweating in his polyester shirt, his face gleaming. "Then mebbe Eli better come with you, too." He gulped air, and put on his sunglasses, probably embarrassed. "You wouldn't know your way around too good."

"You think?" Roberts said.

"We go tomorrow morning then," Eli replied. "We take two hours across the mountains up by Mandeville. Down another hour or such and we be in Kingston. You can see some rude boys!"

Roberts was exhausted from the booze, but pleased, and shocked by the hovel experience. "I wouldn't ask you to do this, Eli," he said.

"I know, man," Eli said.

Roberts thought for a moment. "Did James have a woman in Kingston?" he asked. The rain had stopped already and sunshine was steaming against the black asphalt road. A puff of white butterflies floated across the road like a scarf.

"Oh, man, he had a few you know?"

They shook hands warmly, and Roberts got out of the Chevelle and walked up the wooden steps. From below, he could see Arcadia sitting on the veranda above him. She waved briefly, smiled, watching him from the shade, and he went on up through the hibiscus and oleander, giving himself time to think. He began to think about Hillary in London, wondering if it was rainy and gloomy there in the autumn, wondering if she'd gone back to work at Lincoln's Inn. There were tunes in his head, buried in the middle distances. Sometimes he was afraid of the music and sometimes he was too tired to be afraid. Right then all he wanted to do was sleep in a hammock, showered by butterflies.

16

Eli arrived at the hotel wearing a Monkees T-shirt and bell-bottom pants. Roberts was sitting on the balcony of the Port Royal Hotel on East Queen Street when he saw him driving along the crowded quay in his taxi. Eli doubled back around some parked cars, then drove through the square and parked in a bus zone near the traffic divider. Roberts had been watching him cruise around the square for about ten minutes while he looked for a parking place, until the man had finally given up and parked illegally. Roberts ordered some coffee and pastry, and got himself a newspaper, which was mostly cricket scores and bizarre political news. It was midmorning and he had been up for several hours already, washing himself in the irrigation ditch below Arcadia's house while the goat watched him in fascination. Then he had walked all the way downhill to meet Eli, get some coffee at the hotel and get ready to drive across the island to Kingston. The coffee came and he found raisins and currants in it, even a slice of chocolate on the side. After a cloudless morning, the sky had glazed over with clumps of cumulus that had blown in from the east. There was thick diesel smoke in the air, and there were higglers on the street hawking trinkets to the tourists. Taxis were honking wildly, and there were a lot of Americans gawking around in their suntan-oiled skins. The heat was like a pressure cooker, thick and tight.

The two men saw each other and waved, and Eli paused to talk to some of the vendors along the boardwalk. About twenty minutes later Roberts ordered more coffee, and some French bread and jam, still waiting for Eli to make his way through his friends. He had to laugh when he saw Eli wearing the Monkees T-shirt with its absolutely absurd stenciled drawings of the band playing guitars and jumping around wildly. Eli had slicked back his hair with brilliantine until it shone. He was wearing polyester trousers and tennis shoes, and he seemed happy and relaxed to be going down to Kingston. Roberts realized the Jamaican cab driver worked on a different sense of time, and that there was no hurry. Everything would be accomplished to its own rhythm. Eli sat down and sipped some coffee.

"Thank you so much, man," he said. "Ah, thank you, man."

"You mentioned that James worked at a record store in Kingston," Roberts said, trying to get something accomplished. "You can take me there, can't you?"

"Ah, man," Eli said, "that record store down on the quay of Kingston docks. When we get you to the Lime Grove Hotel, I gonna tell you how to get there." Eli smiled and broke off a hunk of French bread. "This is one nice record store. She is called Nasty Sound. How you like that?"

Roberts said he thought it was a good name. He was amused at the way people in Jamaica played with communication. A question would grow from a question, circling until the circles collided. He decided that Jamaica was a place that wore its spirituality directly on the surface of things. You could sense its history of piracy and revolt, exploitation and anguish. It seemed to speak through the blue smoke in the hills, as if the souls of dead slaves were rising through the air, as if the hundreds of years of cutting cane under a broiling sun were written on every face. Roberts began to get a sense for Zion, which was an expression of the desire to go home, to have peace, to be free. He thought about the slice under James Root's tongue, how somebody had cut it to stop the man's singing.

"Yeah," Roberts said, "I like the name Nasty Sound." He smiled and drank some coffee. "It has a charm."

"You find a rude boy there named Nathan who run the shop. James he work for Nathan. Nathan an awful rude boy, jah. You won't like Nathan. Why you want to talk to Nathan, anyway?"

"I'm sorry, but it's possible James was killed because of some connection to Kingston."

"James didn't sell no ganga. He was Rasta, and he might buy and sell, but not for no profit. Nathan, he gonna tell you that."

"And then I want to find out about Moseby Demeter."

"That boy I don't know."

"Maybe Nathan will know him."

"You be careful of that Nathan."

"Does Nathan have a connection to ganga?"

"Plenty," Eli said. A big diesel truck came up Gloucester Road, whirling the pigeons. The tourists scattered and the truck roared away down the street. "You going to find this Kingston town a different place. I don't think you will like it. It is very crowded and hot too. Not like here."

They finished their breakfast and Roberts put his clothes in the taxi. About an hour later as they were running down through the Cockpit Country, he and Eli *really* started talking to one another. Eli was driving and he had brought along a pair of mirrored sunglasses for Roberts, so that both of them were looking at the mountain-world through the same lens. Roberts would peel an orange and hand a slice to Eli, who would ask Roberts dozens of questions about America. They were driving along perilously narrow roads high in the mountains and they would meet trucks and cars that would almost nudge them over the cliffs. They met herds of goats being driven by children, lumber carts drawn by dogs. Roberts would be talking, and then he would see a Mercedes diesel loaded with lumber roaring up at them from the opposite direction, straddling the center line, and he would close his eyes and dig his heels in under the dash. The truck would whoosh past them and he would open his eyes to find Eli laughing wildly. The old Chevelle burned oil furiously, and it came inside the passenger compartment through a rip in the firewall. Finally, Roberts quit worrying and tried to enjoy the day for what it was, the wind and the sights and sounds, and the ragged blue patches of forest where the trees hadn't been cut. They talked about Eli's brother Arthur who was dying of tuberculosis, and they talked more about James Root too.

Outside the English colonial town of Mandeville, high up in the Cockpit Country, they had a pub lunch. Then they drove over the high ridge that separates the country in half, down through miles of forest and scrub farm country that didn't seem to have any boundaries, until they got to sugarcane country, lower down toward the coast. It had been cool in the hills, but by the coast it was hot and airless, and hotter still once they hit the outskirts of Kingston.

They went through suburbs of concrete shacks where dogs played in vacant lots and women were doing the wash in open trenches. The streets were unpaved, and on every corner there was an open-air bar where men were drinking and smoking huge spliffs of ganga. Roberts had asked Eli to share a room at the Lime Grove Hotel, but the man had shyly declined, telling Roberts that he would stay with a cousin who lived by the railroad tracks. Eli drove them through the commercial part of Kingston to the Lime Grove Hotel, which was down by the docks, and he helped Roberts get his bag into the lobby. Roberts watched Eli drive away down Spanish Town Road, stop at a light and turn and wave. Roberts didn't mind the hotel, which had a broken-down colonial feel to it, and he thought it would be nice to get a good night's sleep, have a rum and soda on the veranda, and watch the girls.

Roberts took a shower and changed his clothes and went

back down to the lobby and found a chair on the veranda.
Now he thought he was a world away from Montego Bay.
Rows of plaster and concrete buildings fronted the harbor,
directly across from the hotel. There were shops and open-air
stalls and vendors of all descriptions roaming the streets,
women hauling boxes of cut flowers, coffee, and roasted meat.
The street was filled with a mysterious music, with the smell of
flowers and garbage, and there were even chickens scratching
in the alleys. Roberts began to think of Kingston as a *ska* in
the head, but he was a long way from being able to intuit its
meaning. He admired the jumble of pastels and the thick
tumult of smells and sounds. After about an hour, and two or
three Red Stripes, Roberts saw Eli returning down Spanish
Town Road. He parked in an alley and came up to the bar.
Roberts ordered him a beer, and the two men sat in the shade
while Kingston bustled around them.

"So tell me what this Nathan guy does in Kingston. Do you
know where he gets his ganga?"

"He the man," Eli said. "He has some rude boys who do
business all over this town. You see, it is okay for a Rasta to
smoke ganga, but the rude boys do all the buying and selling.
Once you get a taste for ganga, you get a taste, you know?"

Roberts wondered openly how James had gotten his ganga
through English customs. Eli shook his head. "That's a different tune, and I don't know how to sing it."

"Do you suppose James was trying to do business, once he
got to England and couldn't earn any money?"

"I don't think so, man. Maybe he take a small amount in
his clothes and they don't go over him too good." The waiter
came around again and they ordered more Red Stripe.

Roberts began to wonder if it wasn't the other way around
from what he thought it was. He wondered if Moseby Demeter wasn't the source of James Root's ganga. That would be
plausible, but it wouldn't lead anywhere. Nothing did. Roberts noticed that Eli had tipped back his chair and was attend-
ing to some beautiful girls going by on the street. One of them
caught his eye and flashed a smile. "Oooooooooshee, girl," Eli

shouted at her. *"Irie* woman, *irie!"* The girl rolled her hips and smiled seductively. Roberts didn't know if it was a game, or if it was real. In Mexico, it was a game, based on the good-natured masquerade and the fondness for a tease. But here in Jamaica, the whole scene had a deeper playfulness that hid some kind of seriousness that might break out at any minute into an encounter. He liked the implications, the freedom of expression. The girl smiled up at Eli. "Foooool," she said. "Fooking fool, big fool!" Eli waved her on and the girl rolled away.

Roberts finished his beer, waiting for time to catch up to Eli and rope him back to the present. There was a pudding on the menu made with raisins, rum, and currants, and Roberts ordered two portions. "You ever think about leaving Jamaica?" he asked Eli.

"No, man," Eli said seriously. "I got to be here for my brother Arthur and my mother. They don't have nothing unless it be for me and what I make driving my taxi. You understand?"

Roberts nodded. He wondered if he had hurt the man's feelings. The pudding came and they ate it in silence and watched the street crowds.

"I think I got to tell you something, man," Eli said.

"Right, go ahead."

"James, he get his ganga from Nathan. And that Nathan, man, he is connected to some bad rude boys. Maybe even badder than this island got. I didn't want to say this before, because I didn't want you to get the wrong idea about James. He was a good boy, a Rasta."

"Well, I'll talk to Nathan. Maybe he knows who would want to kill James."

"Jah, man!" Eli shouted suddenly. "Man, that girl she going to break Eli's heart she keep shaking it like that." The girl had come back down the street. She was wearing pink stretch tights and a halter top. Her hair was wound tightly in braids and she had the longest eyelashes Roberts had ever seen. He thought she might be seventeen. Her whole appearance was silly and youthful, the halter top sequined with a penguin and pentagrams. But Roberts liked it. It made just the right statement there on East Queen Road along the harbor. Roberts didn't know what the statement was exactly, but it was right, sweet and insouciant and slightly reckless.

"When you get back on track," Roberts said, "we have to leave for the Nasty Sound." Eli watched the girl go all the way down the street until she disappeared behind a warehouse. The girl was aware of his look too, daring him to continue. Her rear end was very musical. "You were going to tell me something," Roberts said.

"Jah, we were talking about Nathan."

"So tell me about Nathan."

"You asked me how James got his ganga to England. Nathan he do that, man. James he bought some ganga from Nathan before he left, just to have a personal stash when he got there. Nathan he arranged to ship it over in a trunk with some records. He do that all the time, no problem. James paid him for the ganga and it was done. So, there was no trouble between James and Nathan. Nathan, he didn't kill James for nothing. There was no reason."

"I see," Roberts said. "But still, maybe Nathan knows whether James was having trouble with other people in Kingston."

"No way, man, I don't think so."

"But you don't know."

Eli frowned. "No, I don't know, man."

"Look, Eli," Roberts said. "I don't think he was selling dope in London either. But I have to find out anyway. I've seen the room he lived in. The London police said they found a few pounds, not enough to make any money from, just as you say, a personal stash. And besides, it wouldn't explain why Simes Root was murdered or why James's tongue was slashed. And it wouldn't explain how the ganga got to Demeter's room after the robbery. I'm just going to have a short chat with Nathan anyway because I promised Hillary that I'd do what I could to find out about James in Kingston. Then we'll come back and have dinner."

They went across the street and got in Eli's cab and then drove down the quay where the beach smelled of oil and diesel, up to Harbor Street where Eli started looking for a place to park.

The street was a jumble of bicycles, motorbikes, and push-carts. Eli finally found a spot in a driveway next to a ware-house, which was more a truncated alley that was covered in refuse. It didn't look safe to Roberts, it looked like the kind of place you could leave your car for an hour and come back and find your tires and radio gone, a couple of dirty kids smiling at you, telling you they didn't see a thing. Eli lit one of his cheap cheroots and pointed down the Kings Road to where Roberts saw a sign jutting over the street that said NASTY SOUND in hand-painted letters that tilted against one another. Four black men were loitering in the street, and some kids were kicking a football. Roberts tried to imagine how he would handle the scene, but he didn't know what the scene would be exactly, and so he didn't draw any conclusions. It looked very rough, and he thought back to the Zion pub when Arthur Lemon had come up behind him with a ratchet knife hidden down his leg. So, even if he didn't know what the scene was, he thought he knew the basic rules. Take care of yourself, cover your ass, tell a bunch of lies right up front. And some of the rules you made up as you went along. It wasn't that much different in the States. Same rules, different scene, you just applied the rules differently.

Roberts told Eli to wait for him. He got out of the cab and walked down the street, which had a sun-stunned serenity to it even if it was filled with garbage and fruit crates. You could smell brackish water and oil, and there were the sounds of gulls and ship horns. Roberts was getting cotton-mouth, and a film of sweat had developed underneath his clothes now that he was down from the balcony where there wasn't much breeze. He was self-conscious about his fear too, more ashamed than anything else, because the only thing he had to fear now were black faces staring at him as he came up the street, the guys gathered under the painted sign, the kids halting their game to watch his progress.

By the time he crossed the street he could hear *ska* music coming from the store. When he got inside, he realized how claustrophobic the place was going to make him feel. It was tiny and smelled of spliff and body odor and curry. And who was he, some white guy down on King Street in Kingston town wanting to buy reggae? The guy behind the counter was fairly big and wore overalls, no shirt underneath. To Roberts he looked like an NFL cornerback, long, muscled arms and a thick neck and some pretty good delts. But he was standing with his back to Roberts, and when he turned around, he didn't look like a cornerback anymore. He had a long scar that ran from his left eye down to the corner of his mouth and his eyes were glowing red, like maybe he had been born smoking ganga. Somebody had salvaged an old '50's hi-fi, and the music was blasting from it.

"I'm looking for Nathan," Roberts announced.

"Jah," the man said, "well you found him, I." Nathan put both hands on the counter, stood there like stone, as if Roberts hadn't made any impression. It made Roberts queasy, the one guy in Jamaica who didn't answer a question with a question, what a freak. He looked like a guy who operated in a different metaphysical time zone. "Well, man," Nathan said, impatiently. "You find him now." The man was being hard, tracing his tone with irony.

"You knew James Root," Roberts said. He made it a fact, he didn't want this conversation to run into questions and more questions. "I mean he worked here, so you know him, know James Root."

"Who you to come around my store asking me questions and all things like that now?"

"I'm a friend of his sister's."

"So now," Nathan said, haughtily. He smiled slightly, nothing special, and not warm. "You got a name, you?" Roberts told him the name, said he knew James too, a small-time lie. "Jah, well now," Nathan replied, noncommittal now.

"James is dead," Roberts said flatly. He wanted to see what kind of impression it would make on Nathan, just cold, surprise, what? "Murdered in London."

Nathan frowned. Roberts thought it looked like a genuine expression. Nathan went over to the hi-fi and took the needle off the record, scratching the music to a stop. Then it was supernaturally quiet, just some traffic noise from over on East Queen Road, thuds of foot against football. Nathan walked back to the counter. "Jah, well, you didn't say who you are now."

"I told you. I want to know who killed James."

"Jah, I don't know about that. Why you ask me for?"

"Somebody cut his throat. Sliced his tongue."

"Now that is something, jah."

"You sent James some ganga in a trunk. All the way to London."

"Who told you that?"

"Did you know a man named Moseby Demeter, say, two years ago here in Kingston? Big dirty rude boy with an ugly face? It's a guy who maybe deals ganga in London. Maybe you supplied him too?" Roberts relaxed, waiting for his questions to hit home.

"You be a fool, man, talking like that to me. What I know about some murder in London anyway? How you think you talk to me like that? Who told you all that stuff and nonsense, man?"

Roberts smiled. "Word gets around," he said.

"Jah, shit," Nathan said. His nostrils flared, his eyes screwed down, spinning out of control inside. "Mongoose!" he shouted. It made Roberts's skin crawl, all the spliff smell, how the kids had stopped kicking their football again and were staring inside the store window. "Mongoose!" he said again. "You damn fool man," Nathan said to Roberts.

A beaded screen parted in the back of the shop. Out of the corner of his eye, Roberts saw a tiny man enter the room with his hands at his side. He would come up to about Roberts's shoulder, close-cropped hair shining with brilliantine. A sense of déjà vu swept through Roberts, a dream that was more real than illusory, but something that spread conscious messages all over his psyche. The guy was shuffling toward Roberts, his name Mongoose, something that killed snakes, and when the guy got right behind him, Roberts whistled an elbow to the guy's eye socket, just below the right eye, so hard you could hear it snap against the cheekbone, *crack,* the hardest part of Roberts's body ticking against soft cheek, the crack meaning the bone had torn open, a tiny fissure that would run down to the mouth, past the nose, a crack that would make it hard to swallow for months, let alone see out of one eye. Mongoose went down like a sack, sitting on the floor, studying his hands. There was no blood, just a quick *pop,* and then the guy was sitting on the floor with his legs splayed, hands cupped over his face, immobile for the moment.

What was unusual about the scene was the machete. It had clattered to the floor, about eighteen inches long, like a sabre, the handle wrapped with electrical tape, a copper washer guard. Nathan hadn't made a move, and so Roberts went out the door and hurried down the street. The kids followed him partway, then they gave up and went back in a group, stared in through the open door at Mongoose. Lucky thing, Roberts thought, he'd played this game before, he knew the rules, shit, it was the same scene as in the Zion pub.

Roberts was halfway down the street toward the alley when he saw Eli staring at him, standing by the open door of the cab. Roberts hadn't known it, but his nervous system was acting up, heart racing, adrenaline sweat on his skin, but he was coming under control slowly. He decided he had learned something, that he was getting smarter in his old age. Once he might have ignored the rules, played it by heart. When he got up to Eli, he made a point of telling him to hurry, get the hell in the cab and get away. He thought they needed some distance between themselves and the nasty sounds behind them.

17

Roberts had a second-story room at the Lime Grove Hotel that gave him a view of evening in the harbor district. He had taken a nap, and dressed in some clean slacks, and then he'd propped open the French doors that looked over a false iron balcony to where the long eclipse of evening fell on the low buildings that fronted the quay. There were all kinds of colors out there, purple and golden light spreading over the water in Kingston harbor, which ended in a spit of land called Port Royal, with its white buildings and fort surrounded by arc lights. The sun was setting to the west and Roberts watched the railroad station house and the warehouses and shop stalls and back alleys plunge into a deep red glow, all the cul-de-sacs and narrow alleys that reminded him of New Orleans, prints he'd seen of bohemian Paris. The colors were spectacular, everything bulging against a patina, the ocean beyond the peninsula scarlet, almost surreal, and then the flat plain gleam of the horizon, which tapered to a string of yellow sheen and disappeared. He was sipping a Red Stripe, and fingering a small cigar made on the island, wondering how Eli felt about the gun, the one sitting in Roberts's lap, an oddball .25 Colt automatic that wasn't worth shit and jammed sometimes. He had brought it over inside his Gladstone, despite his customs worries, because he thought it might come in handy.

That afternoon Eli had sped away from the record shop without saying a word, just slipping behind the steering wheel while Roberts caught the front door and slid in beside the guy, the Chevelle running down the alley, down the street, as Roberts caught a glimpse of Nathan coming out the door, hands on hips, this look of anguished violence on his face. The man's expression was livid, like a photograph just emerging from emulsion, and Roberts didn't want to be around to see what it would turn out to be. They went down a block, around a sharp corner, and then had headed straight for the harbor district.

They were under some palms, waiting for a stoplight when Eli said, "Hey, man, what you do in there now?" They turned onto Orange Street, heading into New Kingston, lots of commuter traffic, people on the streets.

"You wouldn't believe it," Roberts said. They were stopped again at a red light and some kids came over the sidewalk and leaned on the cab, talking patois with Eli while Roberts listened to the hurricane of words. The kids laughed and taunted them both and then the light changed and they were off, leaving the kids pointing and laughing more loudly yet. There was something about New Kingston that Roberts liked instantly, the smells of curry and goat, the music in the streets, all the colorful garb and the language. He also liked the fact that it was *old*. Up here away from the docks were the colonial buildings and government bureaus painted green with gables and turrets and red piping colonnades, green tile roofs, and bermuda lawns and equestrian statues that gave the scene a frozen semblance, as if the English had just packed their bags yesterday and gone away. Trafalgar Park was like that, penny benches and loungers and old Rastas feeding the ducks.

"So tell me," Eli said, driving under the shade of an akee. "You see if Eli believe what you do."

"They were going to cut me."

"Ratchet knife, man, I told you?"

Roberts told Eli all about Nasty Sound, the guy Mongoose who'd come up from behind with a machete on his hip, the direct hit on the guy's eye socket. Roberts said there was a moment when he thought he might relax there on the sunny, garbage-strewn street, but then he'd heard Nathan call, "Mongoose!" and something came back from the Zion pub and out of the corner of his eye he'd seen this sad, skinny little bastard rude boy drop through the beaded curtain with a shiny edge of knife on his hip. That was when Roberts knew he was in for the bloody machete treatment.

"But I didn't learn anything from Nathan before the action started. Things happened too quick. He said he didn't know anything about James, his murder, but mostly he was angry."

"Jah, that's too bad," Eli said. They had pulled over to a cab stand on Trafalgar Park. The once manicured lawn was covered with paper cups, bottles of beer, dog shit, guys under tiny newspaper tents. There were new government buildings across the square made of concrete and black glass, but they had that already-used-up look of cheap construction and a damp climate. "You're lucky to get away from those rude boys now, you know?"

"But I do think Nathan knows something. I think he knows who was selling James his ganga, sending it over to London."

"Sure he does," Eli said. "I told you. The personal things come from Nathan."

"But where does he get it from?"

"Why you want to know? What good it for you?"

"Who killed James Root?" Roberts asked, question for question, following the rules.

"You think the man who sold to Nathan and James and Moseby going to talk to you?"

Roberts was really sweating, he just noticed it. They were in the shade, but it was unbearably hot. They weren't catching any of the breeze, and city buses were roaring around the concourse spitting streams of diesel smoke. *Ska* and reggae filtered down the side streets from bars and nightclubs, and a few storekeepers even put speakers in front of their shops and blared music out into the street. Roberts got out of the cab and bought two coconuts from a vendor who sliced each neatly in half with a machete. They sat in the cab and drank the coconut milk and Roberts followed suit when Eli began to dig chunks of meat out of the shell with a pocketknife. Roberts was sitting sideways in the car, with his feet outside on the sidewalk, trying to get some fresh air. There were mountains above the city, milk blue in the haze.

"What do you think, Eli? You think the guy who sells to Nathan will talk to me?"

"Jah, maybe not, if he cut out your tongue."

"That's a good thought," Roberts joked. Eli grunted.

"What you going to do, man?" Eli said.

"Let's go see Mongoose. You know where he lives?"

Eli tossed the coconut shells into the street. Roberts thought it was beautiful here, in a disheveled way, these bulky blue mountains covered by milky haze, Rastas asleep on the grass. "He's got a place down on Spanish Town Road by the railroad tracks." Eli was picking his teeth with the pocketknife, looking skeptical.

"You know exactly where?"

"I know where," Eli said, shaking his head. "I know the man from when I lived here. I know Nathan, all them rude boys."

"Then you stay in the car."

"That's fine with me," Eli said. They moved slowly away from the cab stand, going around the concourse of the park. Now that Roberts had a clear look, he could see that there were hundreds of people sprawled in the shade of the big trees. "But I tell you something," Eli said once they had skirted the park and were going through a residential district, "that Mongoose he's a bad man too, even though he's not so big."

"I know it, Eli," Roberts said.

"They call him Mongoose, 'cause he kill snakes, you know?"

"I'm not a snake," Roberts laughed.

They made it to Spanish Town in ten minutes. The poor suburb was spread around some barren flats, crushed coral and salt marsh waste. The sun was making a white-hot glimmer on the streets and there were stray dogs and children everywhere. All the buildings were either shacks, shanties, and lean-tos, or low, connected concrete slums one story tall where women were washing laundry and men were loitering in the available shade. Outside the bars, men drank paper cups of rum. Roberts couldn't decipher the smell, maybe barbecue and fermented sugar and diesel. Eli had parked in an empty lot next to a machine shop. He pointed down the road to some concrete bunkers painted pink and peeling in the sun, flat roofed and hot-looking.

"Anybody live with Mongoose?" Roberts asked.

"Just his old mother now. They all run off, his sisters and brothers. He come down here to lay up, you know?"

"Just wait for me here," Roberts said.

Eli flicked on his radio. "Don't be a fool now," Eli said. Roberts thought it had a note of affection, concern. Eli was tapping his palms on the steering wheel to some sweet *mento*.

Roberts edged out of the cab and headed across the street to grab some shade. Drapes and beads hung over unframed doorways. From what Roberts could see inside, there were dirt floors, sticks of furniture. A depressing heat and torpor hung over the whole place, babies cried. And then, going down the row, Roberts glimpsed a black face peering at him from inside one of the brick-and-concrete huts, an apparition, and it made him think of Arthur lying on his damp cot, the way his face had seemed disembodied, this guy dying of tuberculosis on the side of a mountain, someplace far away and unreachable. Roberts looked back at Eli, who was sitting in the cab, listening to the radio, watching.

Roberts got the right place and found the Mongoose lying on a pallet in the back of a room. The windows in back were barred and the barren dirt was musty and he was lying alone with his arm over the injured eye. He was breathing deeply, in gusts, in the dim light Roberts could see his skinny chest rising and falling. Roberts was shocked at the size of the room, so small. The machete was on the dirt beside the pallet so he kicked it away and kneeled down. Mongoose rolled over, tried to get up, but Roberts touched him down with a hand.

"Just don't do anything," Roberts said.

The man emitted a faint acknowledgment. He leaned up on his elbows to where Roberts could get a good look at his rubbery broken eye, already closed and chalky white around its rim. There wasn't any swelling in the cheek yet, but it was only a matter of time. For a moment, the guy looked for his ratchet knife.

"You go on, man," Mongoose said. "We settle all this later now."

"Not later, now."

"No go on now, man," Mongoose answered, louder. He had steadied himself against the concrete wall behind him. "You fool too much."

"I want to know two things," Roberts said.

"I tell you no things, jah."

Roberts took the man gently by the hand, an aikido hold he knew from the Army, the only bit of muscular trickery he had. As he put some pressure on the wrist, Mongoose tried to move but it hurt too badly and he settled back. Flies were buzzing thickly and it was so close and hot it could have been a nightmare if it wasn't happening already.

"Tell me who sells ganga to Moseby Demeter. Tell me if James Root was selling ganga in London."

"You crazy man, you."

Roberts stepped up the pressure, one quarter turn. "I'm going to break your fucking wrist," he said.

"No, sir," Mongoose said dully.

"I break this one first, then the other one."

"No, sir, you a fool, you."

Roberts pressed back the wrist and Mongoose pushed against the concrete. The beauty of the hold was its inevitability, the more you struggled against it, the more you hurt yourself. Mongoose lay back on the pallet, trying not to call out.

"You leave it be first," Mongoose said.

"Speak to me, snake killer."

"James Root a fool. He's not no rude boy."

"He doesn't sell. That's what you're saying?"

"Jah, I told you."

"And what about Moseby Demeter?"

"I know him, I."

"What about it?" Roberts turned it up.

"He try to be rude boy. Big man. Fool."

"He sells in London."

"What he can, you know?"

"Where's he get it?"

"Oh," Mongoose said, in pain.

"Where does Nathan get it?"

"Plenty of ganga in Jamaica," Mongoose said.

Mongoose tried to move. Roberts let the guy get both feet on the floor, then cranked back the wrist until the guy lay back down on the pallet very gently. There was a dreamy look in the one good eye. "Trinity Solange," Mongoose whispered.

"Trinity Solange," Roberts repeated.

"That's what I said, I."

"Tell me about Demeter."

"When he be in Kingston?" Mongoose asked. Roberts let the answer drift away. Mongoose said, "That man have trouble here, running around with his ratchet in his pants, trying to rob, you know? That's why he left here. He had too much trouble with the police, that what."

"He got ganga into London, though?"

"Not for a long time now," Mongoose said, very tired of the whole business. "At first, then he don't pay."

Mongoose had relaxed entirely, as if an electric current had passed through his body leaving him numb. There was a fixity in his look, but it wasn't anger, just a hole in his head that let out noise. "I don't know about that business, I. But Trinity Solange will get you, man."

"I'm sure," Roberts said.

"You are the same as dead now," Mongoose said.

Roberts dropped the wrist and backed out the doorway into brilliant sunshine. The streets were baked clean and he could barely see, it was that bright. Eli had edged the cab up the street, picking up Roberts halfway toward the railroad tracks, and they drove on down through the harbor district, then up East Queen Road where Eli let Roberts hop out in front of the Lime Grove Hotel. Up in his room Roberts took a shower and then a nap. In a couple of hours Eli came back to the hotel and Roberts took him up to the room, sitting across from the open French doors, sipping a Red Stripe and watching evening fall across the quays and warehouses.

Eli was looking at the .25 Colt. "Guns are bad trouble in Jamaica, man. You go to gun jail, you never get out, you."

"Guns are bad everywhere."

"You saw the signs at the airport? What you doing bringing a gun through customs?"

"Just crazed, I guess."

"Jah, man, that's for sure."

Sweat was cool against Roberts's skin. He could feel the air sucking against his clothes as the Undertaker's Breeze came up from the harbor. Some neon had blinked on in the bars and cinemas and the street was open to an orange hazy glow. Eli had his hands on his lap, looking worried and forlorn. He had on his checked trousers and Monkees T-shirt. "Who's Trinity Solange?" Roberts asked.

"Oh, man," Eli said.

"Come on, Eli," Roberts said calmly, smiling. "Let's go have some dinner. You tell me about Trinity Solange."

"That's a rude boy," Eli said.

Roberts was hungry, he envisioned some seafood, snapper in coconut milk, curried potatoes, a bottle of wine, maybe some music later. Eli didn't say anything for a long time as it got darker and darker in the room, in pieces, nothing happening and then the dark advancing, so gradually you couldn't measure it at all, the way it got dark in the tropics.

18

There had been a brief and violent rainstorm that woke Roberts, who had fallen asleep in a chair beside the open French doors. After that he paced the room for a while as the wind thrashed through the palms down on the harbor quay, the sky knitted by brief lightning scars, and then just as suddenly as it had begun, the rain stopped and Roberts could see dewy stars. Then it became a stunningly clear morning, sunrise over the pink houses and the fort over on Port Royal, across the water, all the tile roofs gleaming in the new sunshine and the sound of hundreds of parakeets screaming in the pet shop across the street from the hotel.

Right then, as morning rose, his conscience began to hurt, thinking back to the sound of the Mongoose, this hurtful sigh as Roberts leaned against his wrist, how some of the cartilage had probably given around the wrist as the sound wriggled up from the man and his eyes went dead with pain and fury, but with something much worse, humiliation, which was what Roberts thought about as the rain stopped and the sky cleared. Maybe, he thought, he was confusing two pictures in his head, one of Arthur lying on his pallet, the shrunken skull, skin stretched across the cheeks and jaws until you could see the guy's teeth even though his mouth was closed, this face like a spider monkey's, or worse, Holocaust survivor's, and this other picture of Mongoose turned with his face to the wall, there in the unmentionable heat and suffering all the shame of his pain, doing things a rude boy shouldn't do, which was talk because you hurt, and just then his wrist had popped.

Roberts showered and went downstairs dressed in his white cotton pants and flowered shirt, a Braves baseball cap on his head. A few men in white bustled around the palms in the lobby, mopping the floors, and sun was streaming in the open front doors and already there were guests on the veranda drinking coffee, buttering their toast. Roberts was feeling sympathetic for the Mongoose, but then he remembered the ratchet knife that had clattered to the floor of the music shop, the look of pure surprise and hatred on the man's face when he went down from the blow, back against the wall, how Nathan had glowered after Roberts as he walked quickly down the street followed by the stares of the kids who had stopped playing football. It was a look of hate, mixed with disbelief, that had come from these rude boys, Roberts remembered then, not feeling so badly for the Mongoose. These guys played by their own rules, it was part of the deal. You play, you sometimes get hurt.

From the veranda restaurant Roberts could see Eli standing across the street in the shade of the pet shop awning. It was going to be a fine morning, a little hot, with some puffy clouds over the water, the start of a hot day that looked like it might glaze over later, maybe by twelve o'clock, and then all the heat would be trapped in the city. But right now, sitting at a corner table overlooking East Queen Road, the table covered by white linen and a service of blue and orange china plates, his big cup of Blue Mountain coffee and orange slices with coconut sprinkled on top, Roberts was very content to watch the people in the street, the higglers, vendors, women in bright print dresses and huge gold earrings. There was a palm for shade, and just a riffle of breeze was blowing down the big mountain east of town, and there was a lilt of music in the air, *mento,* Roberts thought, because it had an acoustic resonance. Eli waved, came across the street, and sat down. He was wearing his Monkees T-shirt, some dirty tennis shoes, and for a time they sat there together eating fruit, enjoying the coffee, taking in the early morning. It felt fine to be up before it got too hot, watching all the sights and sounds of Kingston. Roberts was reading the papers, but all he got out of it were cricket test results, and the horse racing totals.

"Trinity Solange," Roberts said, looking over the newspaper at Eli, who was drinking coffee, studying the women.

"Let's not do that today?" Eli said. The parakeets had stopped their noise and Eli was staring at three beautiful women with fine asses, sauntering down East Queen. They were very young and tempting and it didn't take much imagination to regard them with awe. "Maybe we go up into the hills," Eli said, smiling, very nervous, "and I show you a chocolate tree." They weren't looking at one another now, Eli pretending to watch the girls, his head bobbing to the rhythm of their collective asses. "Now, you never seen chocolate trees, no, man?"

"We'll go see Trinity Solange," Roberts replied. "I have to go back to London pretty soon. You know that. You know we don't have time for chocolate trees."

"What good it do, go see that rude boy?"

"Look, Eli," Roberts said patiently. "I think a Jamaican killed James Root. I know rude boys sent ganga over to him in a steamer trunk. If there's a connection between his death and these rude boys, then Trinity Solange will know about it." Roberts put down the paper, poured himself some more coffee. Eli had left the girls to the street, they were turning the corner now, out of view.

"He's not going to tell you nothing, no?"

"Mongoose wasn't going to tell me anything either. I have to do these things for Hillary."

"You won't be twisting Trinity Solange like you twist Mongoose. This is a dangerous man, you know?" Eli was looking at Roberts now. "Besides, man," he said, "I don't want you to get hurt, you know?"

"Don't worry, Eli," Roberts said. "I don't plan on grabbing Trinity Solange. Nothing like that."

"You going to use that gun?"

"Only if necessary."

"Don't forget that gun jail now."

"It's the alternative that bothers me."

"So, let's go see the chocolate trees!" Eli exclaimed happily. He turned back to the street, conversation over. A girl about fifteen years old was sauntering by, dressed in a Day-Glo halter top and short-shorts, with big gold earrings and a short afro. You could see her ass in reflection in the pet store window, she was showing herself off. A ship's horn blew in the harbor and a spray of pelicans rose in the air just as Roberts admired the anthurium on the table, trying to keep his eyes off the fifteen-year-old, her marvelous round ass. In another country, he would be shot for what he was thinking. Somehow in Jamaica it didn't seem so evil.

"No chocolate trees, Eli," Roberts said. "Just tell me about Trinity Solange."

Eli sucked in some air, grinning fondly after the young girl. "This man is a Haitian," Eli said somberly. He frowned as if he had said something disreputable, shameful. "That tell you something about him, no?"

"You mean he's a rough guy?"

"Sure, you know that. But he's got him some money and some boys who do work for him now."

"What kind of business does he do?"

"He rob things and loots. Drugs too, you know?"

"How long has he been in Jamaica?"

"He come over when Baby Doc run off."

"After the overthrow, you mean?"

"This man is Ton-Ton Macoute," Eli said. "So you see he has money. He knows people here on this island. So when he come over he get to be a big boss. Maybe someday he go back to Haiti, but right now he make his money here. Not the same as Mongoose, you know?"

Roberts sat drinking his coffee. There was a silver pot of Blue Mountain on the table along with muffins and marmalade, oranges and ripe mango. "I'll be careful," Roberts said. "Just tell me about this guy. I've come a long way."

"Jah, man, I know," Eli said. He ate a slice of orange, trying to delay things. "Ah, this guy has a music house up in the hills by the University. How many people he got working for him I don't know." Eli pointed toward Long Mountain and the Botanical Gardens, a looming green hunk cradled over the city. Roberts could see the roads going up its side. "I can take you up there," Eli was saying, "but you better be careful now. This man is no fool. I don't know what he gonna do when you talk to him, when you say what you have to say. This can't be very good, no." He shook his head vigorously. "You know when I live in Kingston before with James we heard of this man. He come driving around in his pretty yellow Mercedes, you can't see in the window, and he strut around the town real big. You know he isn't like Nathan who is ignorant, yes. Trinity is Ton-Ton, he isn't ignorant. You can't trust a man like that. He is smart and he is plenty mean, ha."

"Do you know his main business?"

"Ah," Eli sighed. "Guns, man. Guns. Everybody want guns, everybody has got to get a gun. There is big money in guns, they bring them onto the island and sell them everywhere. He smuggles the guns in here, all over the islands. Trinidad, Cuba, Granada, Panama. The rude boys have their guns, guns everywhere. And let me tell you, Nathan going to talk to him about the Mongoose."

Eli brought the cab around while Roberts paid the bill and went upstairs. He wrapped his .25 Colt in a hotel towel and walked downstairs and waited until he could see Eli pulling down the street. He put the gun under the front seat of the cab and sat quietly while they went up through town and the park in a morning that was already hot. Kids were playing football on the park grounds and cops were strolling around in their blue dress uniforms, twirling batons. There was trash and garbage left in the park from last night, and Rastas were still asleep under many of the trees and benches.

Eli went up Old Hope Road about two miles, until all of Kingston was spread below them, white sun, green-and-red tile roofs, the railroad tracks leading down to the harbor and the quay, the harbor blue under the first of the haze. Beyond the harbor the sea was capped, and purple seaweed was bunched at the surf line, the horizon a black needle in the far distance. Way up in the forest above the city the air was cooler and morning fresh, and the foliage came right down to the road where the cliffs dropped away. You could hear water running downhill into what sounded like a falls, and then you could hear birds under the sound of the falling water. The grass was wet with dew and pretty soon they passed vendors at carts selling coconut and mango, other fruits Roberts had never seen. Farther up, by the University, there were guitarists on the roadsides, serenading, parading for dollars.

Eli pointed to a thick-foliaged tree by the road. "Now you see the chocolate tree, man." He tapped Roberts on the shoulder, laughing.

They were away from the sea now, around a line of ridges and hills from the water. Roberts had lost sight of Kingston and he couldn't get his directions quite right because they had gone around so many twists and turns. Then they suddenly crossed a wooden bridge above a tumbling creek. There were parrots in the logwood trees, and once again he could see the ocean, which had a purple cast, breakers striking a white beach, somewhere away from the city. They came to a field of lush cane and Roberts could see a circular building in some trees. The sun glinted against its glass windows.

"This is the place," Eli whispered. "Now I'm gonna tell you this Trinity is a quiet man. You come up to him and he ain't gonna say hello and talk to you nice. He gonna be thinking about cutting your throat. You hear me now good. You be one careful man, no?"

Roberts had a good feeling about Eli, the way they were

driving in the car under the dark canopy of forest, both of them sharing something special, a concern. "Thanks, Eli," Roberts said, not thinking of anything else to say. "You know I'll be careful. No problem?"

"Yah, mebbe so," Eli said. "You take the gun?"

"Not this time," Roberts said. He was watching Trinity's bar in the near distance, just over a rise between the cane fields. It had louvered windows open to the mountain breeze. Around a veranda some couples were eating under awnings. "There are a lot of people up here," Roberts said.

"Jah, he does a good business, you know."

"Nothing bad will happen. Too many people."

"Maybe so. You still be careful now. These rude boys are crazy, man." Eli had turned on his radio, searching the dial until he found some soft *mento.* Right then Roberts was focused on what he was going to do. It wasn't as though he thought he was a lion tamer, all he had to do was walk into a cage with a chair and whip. He didn't know what it was going to be like. He knew he wanted something definite to surface in this guy Trinity Solange, maybe get a glance at the guy's soul, even if it was a blank, he wanted the guy to lose a little blood. In his head he knew there had to be some connection between Jamaica and James Root, he could sense it there, just below the surface of all this calm, and he thought he could find a nuance of it if he could just stay calm and focused, use all his powers of concentration and not get sidetracked. Eli was listening to the tunes, clearly nervous, already in the grip of the *mento,* this lilting guitar music and soft congas that imitated the island breezes. There were some patois lyrics too, which Roberts couldn't understand.

They came to a stop just outside a wooden barrier where the cane fields stopped. Jacketed waiters came and went on the veranda and the fields were full of butterflies. Eli went down a shaded lane and pulled in back of the bar, switched off the engine. You could hear kitchen sounds, people talking, soft music. Eli pointed out the yellow Mercedes, an older model with darkly tinted windows.

"The man is here," Eli said glumly.

Roberts got out of the cab and walked around to the driver's side. "What does this Trinity Solange look like?"

"The devil," Eli said.

"Come on, Eli."

"Taller than you."

"Better looking too?"

"Jah, you," Eli said, half-laughing. "Blue eyes that look milky. He's tall and a thin guy, you know?"

Roberts placed a hand on Eli's shoulder. He liked the guy, he wanted him to know it. They looked at each other briefly and then Roberts walked around to the front of the bar and up three steps to the veranda where he was met by a bored waiter in a gray suit too small for him. Roberts was on the wooden porch looking through an open pair of doors. He could see inside the restaurant, which wasn't very large. He was sure he was looking at Trinity Solange, it had to be the guy, sitting languidly at a table in the back, pale blue linen pants and a rose-colored sports shirt, a light cashmere sweater tied around his waist, Pierre Cardin–style. He had a good-looking, narrow face set off by sharp blue icy eyes that had a rim of white, just like Eli had said. Back up on his head he had pushed some black Ray-Bans. It all had a strange effect, this efficient Haitian with slicked-back black hair and baby-blue eyes that looked like too-cold ice cubes. Funny, but Roberts noticed his shoes, Italian loafers with tassels. He walked over and stood right in front of the table, what else was there to do?

"I've been expecting you," Solange said.

Solange was a head taller than Roberts when he got up. He looked down at Roberts, speaking in a languid French accent, his words falling out casually.

"Why don't we have a drink?"

Solange smiled with his eyes, very strange. His face was pocked, it made him look tricky or diseased.

"As you desire," Solange said.

They sat down together and listened to a three-piece combo play island music for the tourists. A waiter came and Roberts ordered a Red Stripe. Solange told him to have rum and lime, "Much better to drink our rum," the guy said, smiling, trying to sound gracious. The waiter was a Jamaican teenager who looked ridiculous in his black suit. "Much better to drink rum on a hot morning like this. You might find it settles your nerves."

Roberts wondered where Solange got his information, probably from Nathan. Mr. Nasty Sound. "No problem," Roberts said. "No problem at all."

19

Roberts was aware of Solange regarding him, though his mind had wandered strangely, out to the broad bermuda-grass lawn that tipped down toward the cliffs, the tangle of bougainvillea and windswept royal palms that had been carefully cultivated to border the grounds, which curved in a semicircle and ended in a profusion of planted flowers, anthurium, poinciana, great heads of bird of prey. It was a perfect day up here in the hills above the University, the Botanical Gardens off in the distance like a mystical kingdom, as the white fleecy clouds bounced along in the Doctor's Breeze above the green ocean and faraway Kingston, lying nearly obscured beneath the forest—some tile roofs, the ships of the harbor, part of the Trafalgar Park a slash of misty blue. Here and there were puffs of diesel smoke from the quays. Roberts should have been tense, sitting there quietly as he sipped his rum with a dash of fresh lime, the restaurant quite loud with waiters and the windows bulging in the wind, all the clatter of tea pots and china. Solange had lighted a small cheroot and was blowing blue rings of smoke up from his nose and mouth, exhaling slowly in a practiced fashion, almost solemnly, watching the smoke rise and hover, dissemble, disappear. Whatever was on the man's mind was not apparent. He sat there with an untended expression, wholly motionless, it was odd.

"So we begin," Solange said in a hard, bitter voice. He tapped his cigar into a cut-glass ashtray and passed the ball to Roberts, who was absorbed in the day outside. "What is it you think you want here? You come up to my place, now tell me please what it is you think you want."

It was a good turn of phrase, what you *think* you want. It was the game of questions played a different way. "I like your place," Roberts said. "It shows class. You're doing pretty good here. Better than under Baby Doc?" Roberts smiled politely, question for question, smile for smile. He almost broke an involuntary grin, looking at Solange who was staring back at him in near disbelief, not enjoying the irony at all. Different from Haiti, all right, but Roberts wondered how much.

"You British have cheek," Solange said plainly. Roberts had to give it to the man, he was totally together, not like Nathan down in the record store who would have come unglued, called for the ratchet knives. "But I work hard for this place. Do you not agree that it is a good thing to work hard for something? You work hard for what you have, no?"

"I'm an American," Roberts replied, deadpan.

Solange glanced at the waiter who was leaning over the bar for an order. There was a shift in tone, probably Solange thinking how to make his mistake disappear. Roberts could sense his mind turning around, but he couldn't guess what the man would do, smile maybe, shoot him under the table?

"It's easy to confuse," Roberts added after a while, turning up the subtle heat.

The waiter served another rum and lime. The combo had finished a tune and announced a break. Outside Roberts noticed clouds building up over the mountains. It looked like it would rain later that afternoon, maybe in about an hour.

"I know you come from England," Solange announced, trying to gain some ground. "You fly into Sangster maybe?"

He had put down his cheroot. "So, you think it is funny a man has to work hard to get a nice place?"

Ball in Roberts's court. "You work hard, you get ahead. You work pretty hard in Port-au-Prince?"

"It is no laughing matter."

"Free enterprise, I'm for it. Enlightened self-interest, the invisible hand. I guess you've read a lot of Adam Smith."

"You think you can have fun with me?" Solange said. He was very calm. Up close the pockmarks were very clear, he had tried to cover them with makeup. Roberts was impressed with the eyes, the eyes of a torturer. "I could show you photographs," Solange said, "of people who had no fun with me. They are men who begged me to stop the fun. You know?"

"We're off track," Roberts said. "I didn't come to have fun with you."

"Then why you come?" Solange leaned across the table so Roberts could smell his cologne, bay rum, something sharp and definite. "Why you go down to Nathan's, make a mess down there? You think I gonna like such a thing?"

"I didn't go down to Nathan for a fight. Your boy Mongoose came up behind me with a ratchet knife. I knocked him down and left, that's all."

"Come on now, man," Solange said. "Why you come up here for? Why you think you can do something like this to one of my boys, down in the shop? And they say you asking about Moseby Demeter, that stupid boy owe me money?" Solange was fighting his Haitian creole. You could tell he was angry and sweating the emotion. It was dazzling Ton-Ton that showed in his eyes, which had screwed down tight to tiny glass orbs and glittered, something psychopathic you could sense that was just out of reach. "You tell me that," Solange hissed. The guy was giving off a cold aura, this shaft of something frozen that could go right through a wall. He took a deep breath, gaining some control. "You be a stupid boy, you think you can play with me." Solange could keep you off balance with his attitude. His words ran together and then he would relax and you could understand him, and then he'd be off again, this slippery lucid locution that had a hard French glaze. The only thing to do was to give up and admire the flow, let the event drive you toward whatever would happen. Roberts wouldn't have wanted to meet the guy above Port-au-Prince some dark night at a checkpoint where the Ton Tons got you out of your car, checked the glovebox, and marched you into the bush. This was an original, a guy who loved to see pain.

"I told you," Roberts explained. "Mongoose took a big chance and lost. It happens to everybody once in a while."

"Sooo," Solange said. "You catch the boy out, no?" Smiling, he sipped some iced tea and tried to light the cheroot, which had gone out. He took a long time with a gold lighter, then said, "What you go there for?" His face formed into a hard malicious grin, a grin that had heard screams and had enjoyed them.

"A man named James Root was murdered in London."

"So what, why you want to know?"

Roberts explained the situation, starting from the beginning. "His throat was slashed," Roberts said. "His tongue was sliced away after that. It sounds like an island job."

"Oh, jah," Solange said. "So why you come to me? Why you come down to Nathan?"

"James Root knew Nathan. Worked for the man when he lived in Kingston not long ago. I thought the past might have caught up with James."

Solange was thinking. Roberts tasted the rum, which was very good. The wind had come up and was banging against the windows and the restaurant was quieter, some of the people had gone outside.

"So maybe I tell you a story," Solange said. He pointed one long finger at Roberts. "You like to hear a story?"

"Why not?" Roberts said. "I like stories."

"Jah, why not?" Solange said smiling.

Another shot of rum and lime appeared on the table in front of Roberts. They were small shots of Bacardi dark with quarters of lime around the rim of a blue saucer. Roberts was feeling the rum in his stomach now, it burned, but it was giving him some courage. He thought about the gun back in the cab and wondered for a moment if he should have slipped it in his pants, if it would have mattered.

"I have to work very hard to get this business," Solange was saying. "All around you, you see this I have built with my own hands." Lies, Roberts thought, he took this away from somebody by force, came over from Haiti with his guns and drugs and money in a Swiss bank. "But you see I know lots of these men like James Root, this boy, you know. He's a simple kind of boy, not very smart, you know what I mean? But, like I say, if you willing to work, you can have anything you want, no? I think I can see in James somebody gonna work very hard for me. I think I can take him on in the record store, and then later he become a good boy for me. But then something happens to him, James, he smokes ganga all the time and he lay about too, mooning like he some cartoon boy. Then he's no good to me anymore." Solange leaned across the table again, blowing smoke from his cheroot. Roberts nodded, understanding at least part of this. Solange said, "So this stupid boy becomes a Rasta. This lazy stupid boy. So we can't use him anymore in my serious business. You know?"

"I don't know. Spell it out for me." Roberts thought he did know, but wanted to hear it.

"Man, you got to pay attention!" Solange said, singsong. "This James he hang around the street corners strumming his wooden guitar, mooning at all the girls. His head was dancing with ganga, he wasn't no good to nobody. He had songs in his eyes, this stupid Rasta boy." Solange tapped his cigar. "You know?" he said.

Roberts deadpanned, dropped another shot of rum into his stomach and felt it get hot immediately.

"He's a Rastaman," Solange said, leaning back. "This boy wasn't going to have trouble with nobody. He had the visions of Zion. He wanted to be free. That's all he wanted. Don't nobody want to kill somebody that stupid." Solange smiled, it was almost genuine. Solange was staring at Roberts with his ice-blue eyes, the smile that was so surreal, and those white teeth.

"So he didn't have trouble with you?"

"I told you."

"He have trouble with anybody here?"

"I'm telling you. No, you don't understand? Is that it, you don't understand?" Solange was perturbed again, his lips kept parting, then narrowing. "You go home. You stay away from my business from now on."

"Somebody in London cut his tongue."

Solange had begun to show some nerves. There was a vein of sweat under his nose, along the lip. The combo was practicing, not really playing a tune, just jamming. Roberts thought the music was something Cuban, pieces of a samba. When he glanced outside, Roberts saw the clouds growing darker in the mountains, bunching up in fists above the forest. He could barely see any of Kingston now, just parts of Port Royal, out in the harbor some ships. "Why you so interested in this stupid boy?" Solange asked. They were nearly alone, Solange had taken himself down a notch in tone. It looked to Roberts like things might get serious.

"I told you he was murdered. I work for his sister."

"You know about Duvalier?" Solange asked. It was asked to an empty room. Roberts didn't bother to answer. "You know about this doctor of the people? Since you do, you stop playing with me now. What you say?"

Roberts finished another rum. He sucked on the sweet lime. "James Root knew a man named Moseby Demeter. I want to know their connection. That's it."

"Ay, jah!" Solange said, obviously pleased. "This Demeter owes me money."

"Demeter is in jail in London."

"A good thing," Solange said.

"He's charged with killing a man. Hillary Root is defending Moseby Demeter. He says he was with Root on the night of the killing. That's all there is. That's why I'm here."

"Now, that's a funny thing."

"That's what I thought at the time."

"So why you care about Demeter?"

"Hillary Root is defending him."

"A woman . . ." Solange murmured, thinking the word to himself after he said it, eyebrows raised. "A woman lawyer."

"That's right," Roberts said, tiring of the scene. He thought it would be nice to get outside, get some fresh air before the rain. "She was appointed to the case."

"This boy going to jail," Solange said, matter-of-factly. Right then Roberts wanted to wipe the smile off Solange, grab a handful of rose-colored sports shirt. Solange crossed his arms and leaned back and spent some time studying Roberts, who was sucking another lime quarter. This talk was boring Roberts and he was about to get up when the first gush of rain hit the louvered windows and the jalousies in the door. It was a fine rain with a purple cast. Jumping over the trees, it seemed like a sheet, wind clicking in the royal palms. "This business is very personal, you say," Solange said behind the hush of the rain. The waiters were closing some of the louvers. Rain had swept inside, across the tile floor, you could smell it like decay.

"What did Demeter do for you?" Roberts asked, carelessly.

"You are too personal now," Solange replied.

"You know anybody in Kingston with a reason to kill James Root?"

"I told you, man," Solange said, raising his voice. "That boy was a Rasta. You think maybe it was me? I kill a Rasta over nothing? Rastas don't do business, I don't kill them. *But I kill that Demeter, I see him, I.*" Solange had retreated behind his blank expression, soulless eyes that were cold. He gazed at Roberts with a black and distracted stare, as if a plug had been pulled behind his head and everything was draining out.

"Fine, thanks," Roberts said. "Thanks for the rum."

"You get a lot of good information here, man," Solange said, "you think you should pay maybe?" Roberts wasn't paying good attention now, he was thinking back to Queen's Gardens, something he'd seen in the flat there. But nothing came of it, Solange kept talking quietly in the background, this whole process like a crossword puzzle without clues. For some reason he thought he believed Solange. "So now," Solange had been saying, "you don't answer my question. Who are you, you come in my place and get a lot of information and you don't pay? And you go in my music store and cause a fight too, no? Who do you think you are now?"

"I told you about that," Roberts said, getting ready to go.

"But you go back to Mongoose."

Roberts was surprised. He wondered how they had gotten to Mongoose so fast, only a few hours before. "The guy didn't tell me anything," he said.

"You went back to his place, yes?" Solange said.

Roberts hurried to the door, stood there looking through the jalousies at the socked-in sky and the hush of rain in the trees outside. It had gotten cooler and you could see the rain dusting the bermuda grass. He opened the door and stopped on the veranda, thinking, watching the overcast sky moving through the huge loop of forest rising away toward the mountains. He hoped it would rain down in Kingston, cool things off there too, get rid of the diesel smoke. He strained to see that far but couldn't, all he could see was the nickel-colored water sheening out toward the horizon and some sailboats swinging through the swells. Roberts considered going back inside, asking Solange what he meant about paying for information, but then he changed his mind. He tried looking through the jalousies, but he couldn't see the man anyway, even the combo had left the bandstand, they were nowhere. Only two couples were still eating, and the bartender was wiping down the bar while a bored waiter slumped at his chair counting change. Roberts hurried around the side of the bar and saw Eli waiting in the cab.

"Let's go, man," Eli said as Roberts got in the seat. They were crunching over the gravel parking lot. "That man Solange talk to you?" Eli asked breathlessly. Eli slowed the car in some shade. "You in there a long time, man."

"The guy talked to me. I'm expected to pay for the privilege. What do you think he means by that?"

"Jah, man, we know what he means. I told you!"

The cab was pinched between two royal palms, angled downhill. From where they were they could see a big white Chevrolet Impala, fins and furry dash and three big black men inside with sunglasses and woven cane hats and print shirts.

"Solange called James worthless. Too much of a Rastaman to have enemies. He said he'd kill Demeter if he could. That right?"

"Don't you worry about that," Eli said, looking at the white Impala that was parked at the bottom of a hill where the road curved. You could see the exhaust wisping away on the strong wind. Now that the rain had stopped the sky was like an onionskin over everything, very smooth. The cool was passing too, and Roberts found himself sweating inside the car. "Those are Ton-Tons down there, man, you know?" Eli was exchanging looks with Roberts, quick desperate glances that told a whole story. It was thirty years of fear from the island, stories of Papa Doc Duvalier, Baby Doc, and all the dungeons under the Citadel. "Sure now," Eli said breathlessly, "I seen these boys come out, and now there they sit in that car," nodding in the direction of the Impala. One branch of roadway went on down to Kingston, the way they'd come up, and another went uphill, curving, away into foliage on tight curves and thick switchbacks, all the way up the mountains away from the University.

"We can't outrun these guys to Kingston," Roberts announced. Eli told him that the uphill branch ran on to Port Antonio, sharp switches all the way until you got to the central plateaue, about twenty miles to where the road was flat and ran through cane and sweet potato country. Eli gestured uphill. "We better go that way," he said.

Eli slipped the cab onto the pavement and went uphill slowly, as if he were trying to become invisible, make his getaway without the Ton Tons. Down the road the white Impala moved imperceptibly from the shadows, crept up the asphalt, all the men inside tensed over the seats. The road went up through a deck of ferns where water seeped from rock beds, the pale puffy clouds straight overhead like a diaphanous hole, as if they were buried in soft green pillows. Roberts could see the Impala in the side mirror as they wound up some switchbacks, still going slowly, and he could see the reflection of the three black men on their windshields, variations of sunlight and shadow dappled, with ferns, a ballet he didn't wish to think about, or witness. Eli had been driving with both hands nailed to the wheel, like some kid's ride at the amusement park, concentration and concern on his face, this stillness all around that was enervating, a prehistoric forest that made Roberts feel cold. There were goosebumps on his arms and he could barely swallow.

They reached some upper flatlands, breaking from the forest into bright sunshine. Fields sloped away from the roadway and skinny cows ambled stupidly among the cut-down stumps of trees. Shacks were scattered on the hillsides, thin blue lines of smoke coming from their chimneys. It smelled of animals and garbage way up here, but once they got into full sun there was only the glazed metal smell of the car.

"They going to catch us pretty soon sure," Eli said, looking back at the Impala. "We got a long way to go to Port Antonio. Things gonna flatten out up here in cane country, pretty soon too."

Roberts fumbled under the seat for his gun, got out the small automatic and put in a clip. The Impala had gained ground, only thirty or forty yards behind now, following them around shallow curves, two of the black men in front, one in back, talking, pointing, sunlight patching over their glasses. They started up steeply again, oleanders closing in against the pavement, huge banks of bougainvillea, and just then a diesel Mercedes truck passed them going downhill, and then another, and then they were alone on another series of steep switchbacks, fifty-foot drops down to the roadway below, up and up.

"The next switchback you find," Roberts said, "stop dead around the end of a curve. Just stop, and I mean on the steepest part, something with pretty good cover from the oleanders." Roberts shoved in the clip. What he needed was a Magnum, something that could stop an elephant, maybe three Ton-Tons.

"What you going to do, man?" Eli asked, the crazy lilt in his voice going up through three or four tones. It was very hot inside the car now, with the exhaust blowing back through the firewall, all the sunshine against glass. There wasn't much breeze now. "Man, somebody catch you with a gun in Jamaica . . ."

"You think those guys behind us don't have guns? You think they want to drink some rum and play cards?"

"No, man, I don't think that."

"Then stop the car on the next steep switchback near the end of the curve. Just do it."

"What you going to do?"

"I'm going to get out of the car for a second. I'm going to open the front door, stay behind it. By that time the Impala will be right on us from behind. They'll be surprised and I figure I'll have about three or four free seconds. When I get back inside the car, keep your head down and get us the hell out of here fast."

Eli was shaking his head. Roberts had expected some kind of emotional debate, but Eli speeded up, opening some more distance on the Impala, and then they went uphill sharply on a switchback shut in by oleanders. There was a real tranquility in the hills, all the smoke like a pall hung in the logwoods, the way you could hear birds singing far away, parrots sliding around the trees, and the pure green stalks of cane in the fields ahead. Way down below, from where they'd come, you could hear the wind growling through the forest. You could see the crowns of the trees move, and Roberts thought he could have walked away from the Chevelle and gone to sleep in one of the sheltered lees of a field. Instead, he opened his door and crouched behind it, waiting.

Roberts slipped two shots under the grille. The Impala had come up behind them and stopped. The sound of the shots was high and hollow, like toy shots, *pop-pop,* fading away as the birds stopped chattering and then began again almost immediately. The two black men in the front seat of the Impala went down behind the dash. Roberts saw the back door of the car swing open, one big guy back there trying to get his legs out of the car, head peering over the edge of the backseat, this black face and a cane hat and two mirrored ovals in the shade, reflecting sunshine. Eli had crouched down in the front of the cab and was watching Roberts in fascination and dread.

The radiator on the Impala began to hiss. He again fired twice, two more quick punches under the grille as he hopped back inside the Chevelle and Eli gunned the car. Roberts heard a shot behind them, an explosion below the screeching of tires, and then they went around another switchback and everything was peaceful again. For about fifteen minutes they drove in mystified silence, coming out in highlands rimmed by mountains, cane fields slashed across in organized rows, and a store on a corner that sold soda pop, fresh fruit, and supplies. Two black cutters were out front, watching the cab. Eli pulled up in some shade and they got out, standing behind the Chevelle catching their breath. Pretty soon Roberts got two Colas from the store and they walked over to an irrigation ditch and stood beside the flowing water, drinking their pop, hardly talking at all.

It took a while, but Eli went to work. He dug around in the trunk of the Chevelle and found a license plate and began unscrewing the old one, putting on the new. Roberts drank his soda, standing under a faultless sky, listening to men chopping cane in the fields. Eli attached the plate and turned on the radio to some *ska*. You could smell raw sugar in the wind.

"What's with the license tag?" Roberts asked, getting back into the car.

"I got three or four plates, you know? Someday maybe you need them, jah."

"Let's go back home," Roberts said. "I checked out of the Lime Grove Hotel this morning. I don't want to go back to Kingston, do you?"

Eli smiled. "That was scary, man," he said. They listened to the *ska,* driving past miles and miles of cane, you couldn't see the end of it, only the rim of blue mountains and the sky. The music was the right sound for both of them.

"No problem, man," Roberts said, tossing the gun into an irrigation ditch, not looking back.

20

Roberts woke only once in the night. He had been sleeping in the hammock when it seemed to him he could hear birds, the goat straining at its tether, even monkeys, he wasn't sure what. He was covered by a muslin shawl, and as he lay there, not quite awake yet, he could see the remote stars drifting through winnowed streaks of thin cloud, and he could hear the ocean down by Montego breaking against the headlands. Almost immediately he drifted back to sleep and was fully awake some time later without having had any dreams, in a dawn that was luminescently blue.

Arcadia was in the kitchen fixing tea, humming softly to herself. The goat was watching him from down the hill, its ears pricked, munching on vegetable scraps, pieces of lime and lemon rind and oranges that had gone bad. There was no breeze in the night, but now, just as the sun rose, the wind was beginning to run down toward the ocean, sliding through the lemon groves like music, more blossoms floating down the hillsides. When the sun was fully up, the butterflies and hummingbirds would emerge.

He was limited by confusion, all around. Somehow, he

thought he could sense the source of it, just beyond his waking consciousness, something crooning to him gently, like a taste or smell, but he couldn't quite see it yet. As he lay there, in the clear blue dawn, he closed his eyes and tried to remove himself from the immediacy of his own experience, back to a point beyond the life of James Root and his father, really father-symbol, Simes Root, back to a place where the shock of their deaths had no reality, a realm in which he could think clearly and stand away from events so there was a focus to the foreground and everything close wasn't blurred by sensation. Quite suddenly, he stretched, enjoying the first warm sunshine of the morning and the softness of the lemon blossom smell, and he understood that he had been led astray by the obvious. A cloud of unknowing had descended upon him somewhere back in England, it was like being inside a fog. And in the sullenness of the last weeks, with all the murder, he knew that he had been trying to answer the wrong questions, he had been going down corridors with locked doors.

And so he came awake to his possibilities as a panel of sunshine advanced across the mountains, which seemed to symbolize his own progress. Relaxed now, he watched the wind flick through the palms down by the beach, and a flock of pelicans that had formed over the ocean, moving in a solid gray arrow along the line of seaweed. Now Roberts realized that he had been focused entirely on James Root, spending days wondering who had killed the man there in St. Olave's, trying to decide who had poisoned him in the first place. It was the wrong question! He began to see that the real questions focused on Simes, whose death had seemed so unreal and causeless. Causeless! Unreal! These words shimmered before his eyes, along with the lemon blossoms, and he thought back to London and he knew, suddenly, that the answer was there, that if he could understand the death of Simes Root, he would have his answer. The cloud will lift, he thought to himself. The question was not who . . . but why.

Just then Arcadia came outside carrying a tray with tea, sliced oranges, and mangos. Her voice was husky from sleep and she was wearing a flowered robe. Roberts thought her quite handsome there in the blue light, he could see Hillary in her manner. "Sleepy man," she said. "You've had a large adventure, now isn't that true?"

"I didn't learn much, I'm afraid," Roberts replied.

"This Trinity Solange, he killed no one?"

"No, I don't think so."

Arcadia poured tea and handed Roberts a cup.

"What about James?" Roberts asked.

"I took him up to a church in the hills yesterday. It's a small Anglican chapel my husband and I went to on Easter and Christmas. I'm afraid there's not much of a congregation now. Even I don't have the same beliefs as then. But it is a beautiful place above the ocean, on a cliff, and you can see Montego just over the tops of the trees. It's very cool there and Simes and I would go there for picnics when we were very young and stupid and in love. I'm glad James can be there, the caretaker was very kind."

"I'm sorry I wasn't there."

"No, please," Arcadia said. "I wanted to go alone, believe me. James was the son of another man. This had nothing to do with Simes, but I remember how it was there once. So, I needed to go alone and make my peace with the thing."

"Will you be all right?"

"Yes, I'll be fine. I've been here for many years now. I must be all right."

"It's very beautiful here," Roberts said. He took some orange slices and bits of mango. Arcadia was drinking her tea, smiling at Roberts who still felt sleepy, cocooned in the hammock. "Can I tell Hillary anything when I go back to London? I have to go back this afternoon, you know." Roberts was thinking how the world had changed, he'd be over the Atlantic in a few hours, moving through a frozen atmosphere that had no more reality than an abstraction. Modern life seemed an abstraction too, in which millions of deaths go unnoticed. In modern life you were always being torn away from something, moving toward something else. He thought of fifteenth-century music that had such a timeless faith, nothing would ever change. And then he thought of reggae whose chords expressed only flux and uncertainty. "Can I do anything for you in England?" he asked.

Downhill the goat was bleating for scraps. The sun was over the mountains and, surely enough, some hummingbirds came skittering through the lemon groves.

"Make Hillary come home," Arcadia said.

"I don't have that kind of power."

"I don't speak of power here. I speak of sense and happiness. The source of the rightness of things. With these things power has nothing to do."

"Hillary is very determined. I've tried to make her stop this trial she has to do. I've tried to tell her she's angry and depressed and needs a rest. She won't listen to me."

"She is stubborn, jah," Arcadia said, smiling.

"That she is."

"That's like me. Simes, he was not so stubborn. He had many qualities." Arcadia lowered her eyes. The dog had climbed onto the porch and was licking her ankles. "But Simes was not a stubborn man."

"Still, I don't have that kind of power. She wouldn't listen. It might even do more harm than good."

"You'll try for me?"

"You could write her a long letter." Roberts shrugged and smiled, took some orange.

"Oh, I've done that. Lots of long letters, you know?"

"What does she say about it?"

"She says that to leave England and return here would be an admission of failure. She is trying to prove something. She is trying to prove herself."

"And you say?"

"I say it is never a failure to come home. Home is our source of everything, don't you think?" Arcadia gave the dog a bit of muffin.

Roberts tried getting to his feet. He had slept in his clothes, curled up in the hammock, and now he felt stiff in his back, his legs. At the table with Arcadia, he sat down and buttered a muffin and spooned on some marmalade. It looked like Arcadia was about ready to cry.

"She's a strong young lady," Roberts said. "She's suffered two terrible shocks and she's been in a London hospital and she's had a terrible year at Lincoln's Inn. I can't tell you she's happy, you probably know she isn't. In all of this she's had her work and her father. Now her father is gone. Amanda and I have tried to get her to postpone this trial, but she won't hear of it. All through this madness she's been going to work, preparing her cases, appearing in court, and trying to deal with her grief. She's emotionally drained and she's been crying for a week, and God knows how long it's been since she's had a good night's sleep. Moseby Demeter is giving her a hell of a time complaining about her behavior. So, I don't know why she'd listen to me. She's that kind of strong, persevering person."

"You're right, I know," Arcadia said.

"On the other hand, how does she feel about Jamaica?"

Arcadia refilled the tea cups. You could hear motorbikes popping along the mountain roads, probably higglers and vendors going to work down on the beach, shop clerks and hotel waiters too. The sun was creeping board by board down the porch. You could smell the wood warming.

"Like everybody," Arcadia said, remorsefully, Roberts thought. "She loves her land, she hates it too. Lies can never be told about Jamaica, it is too fabulous for that. You know?" She smiled meekly, hoping Roberts would see.

Roberts was fully alive to Arcadia, to the hills that were full of sunshine. He ate some muffin, some marmalade, and washed it down with tea. "Do you feel up to talking about Simes now?" he asked.

"I think so."

"I know we've talked about him before. But something is snapping inside my head. I'm close to understanding this violence, but I can't quite see it. I've been thinking about this, and I know of no reason why somebody would murder Simes."

"There is no reason," Arcadia said.

"You're certain he had no enemies. You're certain that someone in Negril or Montego didn't hold a long-forgotten grudge?"

Arcadia nodded knowingly, thought for a moment. "Simes has been gone for a long time. Gone from me, from Jamaica. There is no reason."

"I'm sorry to say this . . ." Roberts began before Arcadia stopped him with a wiggle of her finger. "All right, I wanted to ask you about the tongue. It was cut or sliced."

Arcadia bit her lip. "It is that old Voodoo stuff. That is what it is. Sometimes in the backcountry, up in the hills, there are still people who practice this nonsense."

Roberts was puzzled. "How could it catch him in London?"

"It couldn't be. My son knew nobody who would practice Voodoo. Only those ignorant people in the mountains still do such things. James knew no one who practiced such a thing. His religion was different. He was raised a Christian, and he became a Rasta. That is a different thing from the old Voodoo."

"What about the tongue?"

"You never hear of this now. The government wishes to suppress such information. It hurts the tourist trade. They do not wish the tourists to think of Jamaicans that way, only as smiling people with open arms. But even now you hear of goats and chickens used as sacrifices in the old ceremonies. It goes on in Cockpit Country and back in the Blue Mountains. Those people have old beliefs and no hope. Superstitions like that harbor great woes. But my James did not go up to the mountains and he did not harbor such woe that he would call on superstitions like that. He had made his peace with Rasta. He wished only for Zion."

"I'm just groping for reasons. I'm trying to exhaust every possibility. I thought perhaps he'd become involved with someone crazy or superstitious enough to think killing his family, even Simes, would be ceremonial. I know I'm not dealing with a psychopath. I thought I might be dealing with ritual. Magic, incantation."

"No, no," Arcadia said, shaking her head. "The slice on the tongue is symbolic of the old Voodoo rituals. Those believers slice the tongue to take away the soul's music, its prayer, however blasphemous. It is considered a terrible deed in the Voodoo circles." Arcadia had finished her tea. The sun had advanced over her, she was drowned in its color. "Besides, those Voodoo people can't have the money to go to London, not no way, you know?"

Roberts sat back, thinking he was back to square one, where he was early in the morning, at dawn, when he'd begun to think. James Root had not been killed for money, for revenge, or for some long-unsettled score. He had not been involved with the police, and he hadn't been a dealer in drugs or guns. Even Trinity Solange had washed his hands of the man, he was that harmless to the rude boys. Whatever it was, Roberts was going to have to look deeper, he was going to have to look back to England because he was certain Jamaica had been exhausted as a cause.

He finished his breakfast and washed with water from a big porcelain jug in the back of the house. He put on his fresh London clothes, the flannel shirt and jeans, and rolled the flannel sleeves past his elbows. It was much too hot that way, but he didn't want to be at thirty thousand feet with cold, refined air chilling him all night over the Atlantic. And he didn't want to step off the jumbo at Gatwick wearing sandals and a flower-print shirt. He came around the back of the house and from the edge of the porch he saw Eli sitting on the top step. His overalls were clean and his hair freshly pomaded. Arcadia had gone down the hill and was feeding the goat more scraps, potatos and yams, some mango.

"You sleep, man?" Eli said from his step.

"Wonderfully," Roberts said, truly glad to see Eli.

"I here to take you to the airport."

"It's a little early."

"Arcadia here, she wants to go up to the church first. That's no problem, jah?"

Arcadia finished her business and they all piled into the Chevelle and drove straight up the hillside through a tunnel of ferns, huge stands of akee, until they reached a promontory from which you could see Montego Bay and the beach. There was a white Anglican church in a clearing of pepper trees, its white clapboards freshly painted, the grounds perfectly tended, gleaming in the clear sunshine. You could hear the wind click in the forest and you could see the graveyard, shelves of green, one red dirt grave freshly dug in a corner, beneath a wild lemon. They stood together beside the grave for a long time without speaking.

"Thank you for bringing James home," Arcadia said.

"I'm sorry for all this," he replied.

"Don't forget your promise now."

Eli had walked around the grave and was kneeling with a handful of its dirt. He held the dirt near his chest, eyes closed. "I'll do my best with Hillary," Roberts said.

A rim of tears formed in Arcadia's eyes. "What will you do back in London?" she asked, more to break her mood than anything.

"Hillary will do the trial. I'll help her with that. She's pretty weak right now, so just getting through the trial will be enough." Roberts was looking at the grave, its simple wooden cross, waiting for a concrete or marble replacement. It seemed a terribly short life, barely a wink in the eye of eternity. Roberts said, "I've been looking in the wrong place. I've been focused on James. I tried to see what he did to deserve being murdered. There wasn't anything. Then I focused on Simes, on how he was involved. There wasn't anything. Now I've got to focus on what I know, and take it wherever it leads me. I know your son was killed by a Jamaican. I believe Trinity Solange too, that he didn't have any connection with James. So, that's the one thing I know. And I know that Simes had no connection with any of this."

"And this matter on the road?" Arcadia asked.

"Strictly between Solange and me. He has a reputation to maintain and he was maintaining it. Nothing personal, and nothing to do with James. I knocked down Mongoose and Trinity Solange couldn't allow that to happen, not and maintain his control over his boys."

"Maybe you will never find out," Arcadia said quietly.

"No, Arcadia," Roberts said, taking her arm gently. "There is a reason for this. This killing isn't random. It has a rational explanation, even if the explanation is hard to see right now. The obvious came to mind and it threw me off in the wrong direction. Now I want to start thinking about the little pieces of the puzzle that I've ignored. I want to find out how it is that Moseby Demeter was with James on the night of the Zion robbery, if he was. I want to find out about the ganga in their rooms. I just have to jiggle these pieces and they'll fall into place. You have my word."

Eli had walked around the church to be alone, and had come back to the grave. "We going to miss that plane," he said.

They drove down into Montego and up Gloucester Street until they got to the airport. It was Sunday and the terminal was nearly deserted, just a few customs officials and police officers drowsing above cards at a table, some passengers for other islands. The jumbo would not be full. It was hot down on the waterfront and the wind had died and the low-ceilinged brick and concrete building was superheated, stirred only by overhead fans that bothered the flies. The ocean outside was glazed over with the heat. They were all standing at the departure gate.

"Thank you, Eli," Roberts said, genuinely.

"There is a bullet grazed my chrome fender," he announced proudly, smiling, showing Roberts his one gold tooth.

"We did good," Roberts said, embracing the man.

"God bless you, man," Eli said.

Roberts didn't want to leave. He wanted to sleep in a bloom of butterflies while the lemon flowers flew. "God bless you too, Eli," he said.

"You come back to Jamaica?" Eli asked, sadly, hopelessly, more entreaty than question. "And you find out who done this thing, jah?"

"I'll find out," Roberts called, embracing Arcadia, who had come around the departure gate.

"Take care of Hillary," she whispered in his ear.

Roberts walked onto the hot tarmac. Eli was across the gate smiling wistfully, thumbs under the straps of his overalls, a bit overcome by the strangeness of the airport. Roberts stood watching them for a long time, then turned and walked up the portable stairs.

LONDON

Shout the song of freedom now.
So that the words of our mouth,
And the meditation of our heart
Be acceptable in thy sight
Over I.

—MELODIANS

21

He ate breakfast alone in the kitchen. Coming to grips with his new reality had made him tired, jet-lagged. Everything seemed slowed-down, clutched at by the cold. In the night he had drifted into a terrible dream that featured the face of James Root dissolving slowly into the pock-riddled visage of Trinity Solange, in the background gunfire, and then on the couch he broke awake in a sweat, sleeping there in the Kensington Park house on a sunless morning. He had gone to bed in his clothes, and there was a two-day stubble on his chin and he could remember an airplane ride across the Atlantic, at the other end a gloomy predawn cab ride across a deserted London. Not in his wildest dreams could he imagine a city of eleven million so empty. During the ride across miles of gray housing projects and suburbs he had not seen a single human being, just rows of ghostly orange streetlamps, traffic circles, empty shops, huge monolithic public buildings. The cabbie was a frightened-looking Pakistani who said nothing, just giggling stupidly when they stopped at red lights, absurd in the emptiness. But when they had neared Kensington Park Road Roberts had felt strangely exhilarated momentarily, almost like coming home, and after he paid the cab driver he had bounded up the steps to the attached house and then he had found the note from Amanda. She'd had to go to her mother who was ill and she would be gone for perhaps a week, maybe more, depending on whether her mother's sickness was the flu or pneumonia. He was disappointed and annoyed, he wanted the woman to be there for him in the dim light, with some tea, a glass of whiskey and a kiss, something to make him feel a welcome, something to share with her, which was what he needed more than anything else right then.

The empty house unnerved him. Amanda had left a key under the mat and plenty of cold mutton and chicken salad in the freezer, a bottle of whiskey under the sink. She had made the note speak to him warmly, that was something, and it should have given him some consolation, but instead it made him morose. He didn't want to think about his cold cellar room, and so he brought some clothes and blankets upstairs and had watched the television all day long the first day home. With two hot baths and the bottle of Scotch, he drifted into a languorous unreality while he watched a football match, and by that time he knew he was getting drunk and didn't care. He telephoned Hillary and arranged to meet her the next morning. She seemed too tired and dispirited to talk. Their real difficulties were all ahead. He told her about James and his grave on the promontory above the cliffs of Montego Bay, and about Trinity Solange, and then they'd rung off. He didn't remember if he was slurring his words, but it didn't make any difference. In his exhaustion and despair, he was free of guilt for it, whatever it was.

He slept ten hours, maybe more. He ate some corn flakes and muffins and made some oolong tea, and then he put on a pair of slacks and a dress shirt, the only good clothes he had, and took the bus across West London to Lincoln's Inn to meet Hillary. It was a pewter-gray day with that universal Monday feeling of grim determination about it. All of the everyday faces he saw on the bus were long, the ticket sellers gruff, and he himself had a headache, a low hangover that made him slightly depressed and angry, and contributed to his Monday mood. He hurried through the Strand and found Hillary already at her desk working.

Sitting opposite her they shared an embarrassed smile that passed for a greeting. Roberts tried to discern her mood, but she was hard to read, and while he studied her face he noticed that it had taken on a plastic firmness, as if she were a woman who wanted nothing to pass from her eyes, no shared intention, no conviviality, nothing that would disturb the smooth flow of her mask. She did look tired, overworked, probably overwhelmed as well. Roberts spent fifteen minutes trying to tell her every detail of the happenings in Jamaica. She listened patiently, pausing to glance out of the north window, and once in a while she broke the lock of their attention by brushing her long black hair with one hand. More than ever Roberts thought that she looked young and vulnerable, despite her mask, and not like a woman who was going to have to handle a difficult murder trial. Her brown skin was milky, perhaps it was the cold autumn light in the room. She told Roberts that Simes Root had been buried in his churchyard at Wimbledon.

Roberts held his breath, counting beats, trying to think of something appropriate to say. He could taste the whiskey on his breath despite the corn flakes.

Hillary saved the silence. "Moseby Demeter is downstairs in a holding cell," she said. "He's pretty gloomy and down on me terribly, I'm afraid. He doesn't have much confidence in my ability, especially with all that's actually happened lately, with Simes and James and all."

"You told him about all of it?"

"I believe it's my ethical duty. Perhaps not, but I believe it."

Roberts looked up. He had been going over some police reports. "Look, I have some questions I'd like to ask Moseby Demeter. I didn't find out a lot about James in Kingston. I don't even know that there is much to find out about James in Kingston. But I did find out that Moseby was on the run from the police in Jamaica, and he owed Trinity Solange money too, and was probably running from that Ton-Ton as well.

That's why he came to London. I gather he was trying to be a rude boy in Kingston and wasn't having too good a time doing it. He owes Solange a lot of money and it wouldn't surprise me if Solange would kill him if he had half a chance. Ton-Tons don't make idle threats."

"You're supposed to be on Moseby's side," Hillary said.

"I *am* on his side. I thought you'd want to know his background in Jamaica."

"Oh, I do," Hillary said.

"But I have a lot of doubts about Demeter. I also went to Jamaica to learn about James. You know I want to help you find out who killed him and why. That's important right now."

It was so very cold in the office. Roberts wondered if the cold was a torture invented by English lords to test their subjects. Roberts said, "I think there is a strange connection between Demeter and James."

"It will have to wait," Hillary replied.

"But your brother . . ."

"We agreed, my brother will have to wait."

Roberts paused. "Have you spoken with Drummond lately? Has he told you how the cases are coming?"

"Just this morning," Hillary said. "I call him every day at the same time. I called him at his home on Sunday. I called him on Saturday. He expects my call. I'm afraid their search of the Bermondsey docks hasn't turned up anyone who knew any reason why my brother should have been poisoned. He was such a new arrival, I'm afraid nobody knew him."

"What about the hospital? Do they know how James was killed in his bed?"

"Nothing," Hillary said. The pale morning light was touching her face. It was an innocent face, but the eyes were blank. "I can't be distracted right now. Demeter is giving me all sorts of difficulties and the trial starts tomorrow morning. I want my brother's killer found, but just now, and for the next two days, I've got to concentrate on the trial."

"For God's sake, tomorrow morning?" Roberts said, surprised.

"The judge advanced the trial a week because of his schedule. We had no choice, really."

"What's Demeter doing to you?"

"He's complaining bitterly. I'm afraid he's sent a note to the judge, and he talks to the bailiffs and constables all the time."

"Complaining?" Roberts muttered. "You've worked your fingers to the bone for the man. I've seen this kind of shit pulled before. He's setting you up for a charge of incompetence."

"I know, Mitchell," Hillary said. "I've told him some of what we've done."

"Is your case prepared?"

"Absolutely," Hillary said. She turned and placed her forehead against the window glass, as if she were trying to cool a sudden fever. The room was diffused with blue light now, and Roberts thought about the mountains of Jamaica he'd seen, smoke rising through the forest in late afternoon. "All of the witness questions are prepared. I've got my case law submitted and I know what I'm going to argue. I could recite the police records and the autopsy reports to you from memory." Hillary looked back at Roberts. "I've even devised a few surprises," she said, smiling slightly. "And I've talked to Demeter at length."

"And what's wrong?" Roberts asked, truly amazed.

"He thinks I'm . . ." Hillary paused. She breathed deeply and turned back to Roberts. "He *thinks* I'm incompetent. He won't come out and say it to me, but he's said it to the judge, and he's said it to the bailiffs, and that's what he means nonetheless. He's been difficult all week while you were gone. I would try to prepare him for the trial, and all he would do was question my sanity. He kept asking if I was ready to do 'this thing,' as he called it. I can't work with him. He reads about these things in the newspapers and then he harps on each of them until I want to scream. It couldn't be worse between us. Perhaps I don't know how to handle people."

Rain splattered the window behind Hillary. There were pigeons huddled on the ledge.

"So let him have a new lawyer," Roberts said. Hillary looked at him, tight-lipped.

"No!" she said. "No, I'm sorry," she said quietly again. "I'm ready for this ordeal. I'm not being selfish, but if I thought I wasn't ready, or if I thought I was incompetent, I would withdraw. But I am ready and I can handle it. I've thought up some fine points for use in testimony and I don't want to be dragged away from the bar screaming and crying like a child."

"You don't think you're being foolish?" Roberts asked.

"You think it's my pride? Is that it?"

"I don't know."

"Well, I *am* worried about my pride. Why not? Of course I am. You don't think I worry about those wagging tongues following me down the corridors? Of course I'm worried about them." Hillary pressed her hands down the sides of her suit. "But I would not do this if I thought that in any way I couldn't give Moseby Demeter a sound defense. I just don't think anyone else can do as good a job right now, that's all. Even given what's happened to Simes and James."

"All right then," Roberts said. "Let me go down and have a talk with Demeter."

"I can't go with you," Hillary said. "I have too much work to do."

"Then I'll go alone. There are some things I have to talk to him about anyway. If you've got your case prepared you don't need me hanging around making grumpy noises while you try to work. Besides, it's cold as hell up here." Roberts had walked over to Hillary and was leaning against her desk. They were very close and he thought he could see in her Arcadia as a young woman. He had a sudden vision of pepper trees full of swallows, a premonition in reverse, all that leafy green alive with birds.

"Don't be harsh with him," Hillary said.

Roberts had to smile, it amazed him. Here was a woman

with an immense capacity to suspend her needs. He admired her for it, he didn't think he could ever do anything like it. In her place he would be filled with an enormous and debilitating anger that probably wouldn't allow him to move or think, certainly not to suspend his own needs, and here she was pleading with him not to be harsh with Moseby Demeter. Roberts thought about Eli, the first day he'd spent with the man, how they'd driven up to the hotel above Montego, drinking rum there in the bright sunshine, and how Eli had laughed and cried in the same breath.

There was a quality in that action that had amazed Roberts in the same way, something in Eli that had allowed him to carry his emotions on his skin, how their connections appeared level with one another, flowed each into each, like a cubist painting of a human face, many-sided and whole. He realized how terribly stricken Eli had been that day because of the death of his friend, and yet how solidly at peace he had been with his grief, how he'd carried his joy and his sorrow in the same emotional pocket. It reminded Roberts of a man he'd known on death row once, a guy who'd been sitting in his cell for years, waiting to die on the gallows. He'd gone gray from waiting, and Roberts could see that he wanted to die, he just wanted to walk down the corridor and get it over. It had been late fall when Roberts had gone up to the state prison to say good-bye to the man and when he got there he was sitting on his bunk listening to the World Series on a portable radio, worrying about the next hitter. The man's life had a whole substructure Roberts couldn't understand, but he admired it, and that's the way he felt about Eli and Hillary.

Roberts made Hillary sit down while he brewed some tea on her electric ring. He decided to tell her about Eli, their rum drinking on the edge of the cliffs, how much he admired the man, how much the man loved her brother James. He told her about Arcadia, the details he'd left out before, hoping that this would help Hillary. Hillary was drinking her tea, seeming more relaxed. Finally she walked Roberts down the hall and Roberts got an official pass to the basement lockup.

They were standing in the darkened hallway, waiting for the lift to come up. "Thank you for everything," Hillary whispered.

"I'm glad to do it. I mean it."

"Now don't be harsh with Demeter," she said, imitating a scold. "He's a rude boy and he's not terribly clean, but he's my client."

Roberts gave the woman a hug. He rode the lift down to the basement where he was met by two constables. The basement was a shock. Upstairs at the Old Bailey everything was high Victorian imperialist, dark wood, paste wax, and soldier portraits, while the basement had all the character of a modern insurance office, drop-ceiling of cork board, tile floor, modular cubicles on wheels, all powdered in a dusty white fluorescence that imparted a thin, almost transparent gleam. The constables made Roberts wait for twenty minutes while they retrieved Demeter from wherever they were keeping him on ice, but finally they steered him into one of the cubicles where Roberts found him shackled and sitting behind a metal desk wearing a gray jumpsuit. Under the light his skin had a pallor that surprised Roberts, and the man was smoking a cheap English filter cigarette. He smelled of sweat and his dreadlocks were matted.

"Jah, man," Demeter said when they shook hands, "so where is Miss Hillary now? She in the looney bin yet, man?"

"She has other cases on the docket," Roberts said, feeling anger prick his neck. "She's also busy preparing her legal strategy for tomorrow."

"That woman is crazy, man. She don't look good to me."

"She looks fine. I just saw her."

"Nah, man, I seen her all the time, you know? I hear about all this trouble she have, man. You know what I think?"

Demeter had the prison stare, red-eyed and desperate, abused by his circumstance. "No, tell me what you think?" Roberts said.

"I think the woman out of her bloody mind." Demeter fished another cigarette out of his crushed pack.

"Don't worry about it."

"You don't think I worry about it, man? I down here, I. Not you, man."

Roberts was really irritated now. "I didn't come down here to talk about Hillary. I've been in Jamaica this week."

Roberts detected mild surprise, an eye-cock against future possibility. "Oh, jah, man?" Demeter said, interested.

It wasn't warm as Roberts had hoped. The air was giving him goosebumps, cold-refined and almost palpable. Roberts could hear the air ducts whispering in the walls and he could hear the traffic outside, and the shuffle of feet and paper. It was like being captured by black-and-white film. A thought entered his head like a spike, an evocative memory of a film he'd seen once, *Invasion of the Body Snatchers;* it had scared the shit out of him when he'd seen these half-formed human beings lying asleep in seed pods, the malign look on their immature faces, pods white-cocooned with fiber, real life crying for help. Help, help. Roberts had gone home too frightened to go to sleep. The film was a sublimation of nothingness, very disturbing in an existential way. That was what it was like in this basement prison.

"Nathan and Mongoose say hello," Roberts said, hoping he could break the tension.

"You see those boys, huh?"

"How long were you in the dope business in Kingston?"

"Ahhh, now, man," Demeter said, flicking cigarette ash as if he were unconcerned.

"No shit," Roberts said. "How long?"

Demeter waved his cigarette, dismissing the question, another kind of smile on his face then, not a pleasant thing to see. Roberts thought that if he weren't shackled behind a metal desk, they might have gotten it on right there. It wouldn't have bothered Roberts, it might have been fun.

"Why you gone down to Jamaica now, man?" Demeter asked. Here it was again, Roberts thought, a question for a question, subtle shades of self-defense. Roberts was thinking how to break the chain of deceit.

"I took James Root home."

"And you see Nathan by accident, man?"

Roberts was getting a better view of Demeter now. The man was smarter, more subtle than he thought.

"I went down to Kingston. I thought I might find out if James was selling dope down there. Maybe find out why he was killed. You know, man?" Now that Roberts knew the guy was smart, he thought irony might unlock the stalemate.

"None of this involve me, man."

"You want to hear about Nathan and Mongoose?"

"Ahhhh," Demeter growled.

Probably yes, Roberts decided. "I asked Nathan about James but he said he didn't know anything. To be honest we were having a fairly friendly conversation about everything under the sun. The weather. Fucking Jamaican girls. The best ganga around, that kind of shit."

"You joking on me now, man."

"You know how it is, you eventually talk about everything, even friends in jail, guys you used to know, that kind of shit."

"Don't you play those words with me now," Demeter said. "What you want with me?"

"Oh, I talked to Trinity Solange." Roberts paused, waiting to see if there was an echo inside Demeter's head. The man glared up from the table, it was an ugly glare too. "Trinity Solange says you owe him a lot of money. I got the impression he would kill you if he could get his hands on you. Those Ton-Tons impress me as honest with their threats. *You know, man?*"

"So, man, life is hard, jah?"

"So, you tried selling dope in London?"

"Go on, man, you playing with me."

"This means nothing to you?"

"Nothing, jah."

"Tell me again about the man named Jimmy you said you were smoking with the night of the robbery."

"I told you."

"Tell me again."

"I see him in the streets, you know. He was a new boy on the streets too. That day it was cold and he say come up to my room, man, and smoke some of my ganga, and so I went up, I. We smoke some ganga and then we drink some rum. You know how it is."

"What time did you leave?"

"Late, man, late." Demeter had relaxed, showing Roberts a playful smile, setting things back on course. It was a mood Roberts could deal with. He would try to lay Demeter back far enough to surprise him again when the time came. The man looked about fifty years old now, but he was twenty-seven.

"What kind of ganga did James have?"

"Good Jamaican, man, it make you dream."

"This Jimmy is probably James Root. You know that?"

"Mebbe, man, mebbe so. Who know?"

"Yeah, well he's dead. Your alibi is dead."

"I know, man," Demeter said.

The trick was welling up in Roberts. He might be able to pull it if things got slippery enough. "Did you tell anybody where you were that night?"

"This mean something?" Demeter asked.

"If you told somebody you were with Jimmy, then it might be important at trial. Not the same as an alibi, but something." Roberts gave Demeter his full attention. "Like maybe your girlfriend?"

Demeter frowned hard, crushed out his cigarette, which wasn't quite gone. Roberts had a vision of the holding cell now, a narrow padded bunk, wash basin, crapper hole in the corner, about fifty degrees at night. There would be cockroaches under the basin and Demeter would have a cotton blanket.

Demeter raised his voice, angry. "What you talking about my girlfriend, man?"

"Your girlfriend, man," Roberts said. "The woman who stays in your room. You know?"

"There are lots of women, man."

"I went over to your place," Roberts said. "I know you're

a funky guy, but you don't wear lace panties and a bra, do you?" Roberts glanced at the clock outside in the hall. "I'm just fucking curious, you know?"

Demeter started another cigarette, something unconscious in his need system. "The woman is just a woman. She be around, not doing nothing."

"When did James lay the ganga on you?" *Here was the trick.*

Demeter surveyed Roberts like a coat of paint, his eyes narrowed. "I don't think you working for me, man," Demeter said. "Here I got a woman lawyer who is crazy and now you. The judge going to hear about this too." *You fail,* Roberts thought.

"Don't go tense on me," Roberts said. "When I was in your flat I saw this ganga that looked like the same stuff I saw in James Root's flat. Same grocery packing, same plastic sacks, same good ganga with flowers, smells like good shit. Good Blue Mountain shit, you know?"

"Hey, it's everywhere, man. Like fast food."

"So I'm right, huh?"

"Like I say, it's everywhere," Demeter said. "This Jimmy he wanted me to sell some of his ganga, that simple. He didn't know too many people, and he needed some money. So he say Moseby, man, you help me sell this ganga dope and you can have some for yourself too. That's the way it works around the docks, you know? You gotta friend. You help a friend. He your friend, he in need, you help him, he help you when you need help too. Simple."

Click, thought Roberts. *Simple.* It was a nice lie.

"So you met James and he laid the ganga on you?"

"Jah, man, what you think?"

Roberts got up and tapped on the door. The constable opened it and stood there waiting, bored. Demeter had crushed out his cigarette and was watching Roberts like a cat watches a perching robin. "See you tomorrow," Roberts said.

"That crazy woman lawyer, man," Demeter shouted, just so the constable could hear. "She not sane, now you. I heard all about her trouble, I gonna tell the judge too. She crazy!"

Roberts was outside, listening to Demeter rave. The constable took the pass and ushered him to the empty lift.

"They're all bloody crazy," the constable said.

22

Oh, an interesting lie. Roberts was awake at two o'clock in the morning, words running through his mind like fishing line on a silky stream. He was watching the chestnuts move in the wind, the words in his head. *An interesting lie.*

He had been asleep on the sofa upstairs in the Kensington Park house. For about two hours that night he had tried to be comfortable in the cellar, putting on some classical music from the BBC, pacing around like a monk, and then he had made some hot tea and whiled away another twenty minutes with a Robert Louis Stevenson tale, and then had put down his book and stared at the walls, feeling suddenly stifled and alone with himself. Pretty soon he went upstairs, abjectly and with some guilt, and had made an Irish whiskey and water and tried to watch television. He made a nest for himself on the sofa, piling together pillows and two afghan covers, and then buried himself in it while an old "Rockford Files" played on TV. He wasn't thinking about anything in particular, just the nagging loneliness, winding down from the long day in court. The parlor comforted him, paneled bookshelves full of Trollope and Dickens, the Irish hunting scene wallpaper, the black

216

baby grand piano in one corner and the bust of Beethoven. It was possible to think of this as a kind of temporary home, which was something he needed ever so desperately. He wanted to connect with somebody, or something, he didn't want to be dictated to by contingencies and moments, he didn't want to drift, he wanted a bond with his environment, a true surrounding in which he could wander like a familiar figure. The coal fire was casting slim shadows on the walls, a faint glow of red.

Very late he gave way to melancholy and drank another glass of Irish and watched the trees. Somewhere the moon had risen and a silver patina had formed over the park. That was when the wind rose too, and he could see the trees dancing in its envelope, and for a very long time he leaned back against the sofa and plied his imagination with whiskey that took him back to his childhood, a lyrical nostalgia that was mostly self-protection. But, after a while, he found nothing comforting about the past and he began to think about Demeter, how the guy had told such an interesting lie. He'd said that James Root had given him some ganga, the stuff in grocery bags and plastic sacks, nothing wrong with that, it was plausible, except that the time frames were wrong. It was a simple lie, Roberts could understand its telling. Guys like Demeter might lie for any reason, or none, it didn't have to be a major thing. But what made the lie interesting was its absolute uselessness. Roberts finally fell asleep thinking about it.

The next morning he showered and put on his slacks and sports coat and found his way across the West End to the Old Bailey again. The courts were as warrened as old bird houses, an intricate den of chambers and courtrooms and dark hallways impenetrable to the eye. He found Hillary waiting for him outside the main criminal court. She was neatly dressed in a beige suit and man's bow tie and she was leaning against a slab of oak, as if she might collapse at any second under the weight of her briefcase and her lawbooks, the huge folders in her arms. They exchanged smiles and he crossed the crowded hallway and relieved her of some of her load. She was wearing some makeup, but he could tell she was tired—there were black bags under her eyes, and her shoulders were sloping. She was as frail-looking as a china figurine. Lawyers were jostling around her, coming and going from the courtroom. He pulled her aside toward a stairwell where it was quiet.

Before he could say anything Hillary said, "There are two or three things you *must* do for me during the trial. I don't know how long the prosecution is going to take with its case, but please take notes for me all the time. I know they'll put on the autopsy expert first, and then the laboratory expert who examined the gun, and two or three constables who searched for the watch and gun. I suppose it could take all morning, or even longer."

"I'll be right with you," Roberts said, trying to be cheerful. Three men passed by them on the stairs, dressed in wigs and black robes. The Old Bailey had a polished Victorian glare to it, like a prison of amber. The noises were deafening, and you could hardly hear a word. "Do you want me to sit in the gallery?" Roberts asked.

"I've arranged for you to sit with me at the counsel table. For heaven's sake don't do anything or say anything during the trial. Just pass me notes and make sure I don't fall down from a faint. If the judge knew who you really are he'd throw you out on your ear."

"Americans aren't allowed?" Roberts joked.

"Not your kind of Americans. Without work papers."

Hillary vouchsafed a small smile. Roberts hoped she was going to survive, come out of her shell, just long enough to get through all of this. For a second he thought he saw a sheen in her eyes, through the red, something hopeful, as if she might be ready for a good fight.

"Are you going to call Demeter as a witness?" Roberts asked. He had briefed Hillary about the man's police trouble in Jamaica, he wanted her to be ready. Roberts didn't know anything about the prosecutor, but if he had done his homework he would know about Demeter's police record in Kingston. He might also know that Demeter had sold ganga in London. "I'm afraid his credibility wouldn't be very good."

"I'm not surprised," Hillary said. "I probably won't call him if everything goes as I've planned."

Roberts was surprised. "Good, I'm glad you've got a plan. Demeter is going to need one."

"We'll see then."

"How long will the trial last?"

"Two days, maybe less."

"Look, I'm still interested in Demeter's alibi. If I could find his girlfriend maybe she could help. Demeter told me there wasn't any girlfriend, but I've seen a woman's clothes in his room. If I found her and she would come to court and say that Demeter told her where he had been, would that help your case?"

"But the police were at his flat just after the robbery. Surely there wasn't time for him to talk to anyone before his arrest."

"But suppose."

"Yes, it might help," Hillary said.

"Then I may go off and try to find her today."

"But I want you around later for something important. There's something I need you for tomorrow just at the end of our case."

"All right," Roberts said. "I'll be quick."

"At the end of their case I know the prosecution will call Howard Boston. He's their star."

"The bartender."

"Right."

"What about my friend with the machete?"

"Lemon," Hillary said. "He's not as important."

"So, what do I do?"

"Boston is going to be an important and difficult witness. From the beginning his testimony has been the most damaging. For some reason he hates Demeter and wants to see him convicted. Treacle may be a different story, but as for Boston, he's going to fight me on every single point in his story. And Boston doesn't have any love lost for you, either. Boston will fall into the hands of the prosecutor like a baby in a cradle. This won't be easy."

"So, what do I do?"

A crush of lawyers gathered in front of the main criminal court, King's Bench. Hillary had pulled Roberts even farther away from the crowd.

"Now I've told you," Hillary said, "that you'll be sitting at the counsel table with me. Once I've gotten done with Treacle they'll call Lemon and Boston. I'm presuming they'll save Boston for the last because he's the main witness, the only one who really faced the robber. Boston was behind the bar at the Zion the whole time. Lemon came in from the kitchen and Treacle was sitting in the back all alone and drunk."

"But what do I do?" Roberts said impatiently.

Hillary stared Roberts down. "There will be a recess after the prosecutor finishes with Boston. I don't expect the direct examination of him to take very long because his story is short and to the point anyway. During the recess please come out into the hallway. You'll find three men standing there. Those men were hired by me and they'll be expecting to see you. You can't miss them, either. The three men are Jamaicans. Black Jamaicans. They'll be wearing dreadlocks, the whole Rasta business."

"You've got to be kidding."

"Not at all," Hillary said smiling. "It's all been arranged with the judge."

"I hope you have a strategy," Roberts said doubtfully.

"I suppose my strategy is reasonable doubt," Hillary said. Almost all the lawyers that had been standing in the hallway went into chambers in a single mob. Hillary told Roberts that when they all rushed out again it would be time for trial. She still had a satisfied look, but her shoulders were drooping now. "We've got Sir Edward Corcoran for a judge, and that's luck, I hear. He's reasonably fair and not likely to go to sleep on the bench and begin drooling on the indictments. I do think he's harsh in his sentencing, but as for procedures, he's as liberal as we could expect."

"You say you made arrangements for a recess after Boston testifies?"

"Oh, yes, the judge was quite helpful there." A gleam entered Hillary's eye, something watchful.

"These three men . . ." Roberts muttered.

"Never mind them now," Hillary said, interrupting. "The judge knows about them. Just usher them in. For the trial I've had the main witnesses, Treacle, Boston, and Lemon, all sequestered."

"Sequestered?"

"Yes, sequestered," Hillary said. One or two lawyers came out of the King's Bench chamber in a hurry. "They'll all be separated from one another and none of them will hear any of the trial. I've done that so they can't hear any testimony or consult about their own. If they haven't rehearsed their stories, then they won't have any chance to compare them and improve them. At least we'll get a relatively true version, or a moderately fresh lie. Either way, it's good for us and the judge granted my request and there wasn't much protest from the prosecutor."

Roberts noticed some color returning to Hillary. He kept thinking about the interesting lie Demeter had told, it was like an underground current, he couldn't see it, but its trace trickled to the surface if you watched carefully. By now Roberts was convinced that Demeter had gotten the ganga from the Root rooms, but he didn't know how he had done it, or why, or even when. He had been in jail for three months, so the dope could not have been in his room at the time of his arrest. Somebody had put it there recently. Roberts was thinking now, he sensed that Hillary had continued to talk to him. She was reminding him of the need to stay alert, to help with questions and cross-questions.

Roberts tugged at his tie, unused to the constriction. It was choking him. He saw that it was nearly ten o'clock now, the rush of lawyers going away from the King's Bench had begun.

"Who's the prosecutor?" he asked Hillary.

"An old bulldog named Fleming Jones. I think he was

South African British, come back to England after the Second World War. He's loud and patronizing and he's been around Lincoln's Inn since Robin Hood."

"Is he prepared?"

"Not all that well, I don't suppose. But he's got such a simple case it doesn't take much. Unfortunately he doesn't drink pink gin with lunch and he doesn't have a mistress over in Pall Mall."

"You sound like you know what you're doing," Roberts laughed. He was trying to keep Hillary alert with humor, he could tell she was getting nervous now.

"I don't really know," she sighed. "I've read so many of these legal handbooks. I've seen many trials like this from the gallery. But I'm frightened to death." She blinked twice at Roberts and seemed to empty of emotion. Roberts realized that her color was simple flush, that she was hyperventilating. "I'm sorry," she said as Roberts took her arm. They took a drink of water at a fountain in the hallway.

"Take deep breaths and become angry," Roberts said.

"You think that's it?"

"Especially the anger part," Roberts answered. "It's an old combat trick. Transfer your fear to the other side."

"At any rate, don't forget the Rastamen after Boston is examined."

"Hillary," Roberts asked abruptly, "what *are* you doing?"

"Just escort the Rastamen inside the chamber and bring them to where they're just behind the defense table. They'll know what to do from there, so just come back and sit down beside me. Don't be surprised at anything that happens. And, you won't see Demeter sitting in the dock either. He'll have been taken away."

"You won't tell me anything more?"

Hillary glanced nervously at the big oaken doors that led into King's Bench. Her breathing had slowed, but it still came in thick labored gusts, and her eyes were glazed. He quickly put his arm around her and squeezed and she put her head on his shoulder. She was all nerves, like a single strand of pulsing wire, her muscles tight as copper. Now more lawyers had come outside and were talking in a group. Roberts marshaled his thoughts, trying to get everything into one place without any critical filter between him and the source of his sensations. He kept thinking that if he could see the murders as a piece, if he could make them subject to his intuition, the way one might feel one's way toward a jagged piece of picture puzzle, the one you couldn't find until you stopped looking so hard and allowed the forms to guide you, then he could *sense* the reasons. As it was, he was staring at the puzzle pieces, unable to sense their forms. *He was being too clever.* The answers were barred to him by his intelligence. If only he could hypnotize himself, free his mind to the possibilities.

Hillary was halfway to the chamber when he came to his senses. He caught up with her and together they walked down the polished marble aisle. The room was supernaturally Victorian, high-ceilinged and decked with portraits of judges, flags, every section mullioned and divided by intricate gates and barriers. Roberts had never seen so many nooks and crannies and he was shocked at how high the judge's bench sat above the parties. But it was the prisoner's dock that caught his attention, a circular cage of wood that seemed utterly isolated, the center of attention. On one side of the chamber high mullioned windows sifted a diffuse gray light that seemed to hover in the place like a ghost. Hillary had gone around one of the barriers and was laying out her tools, the lawbooks, police reports, charts and diagrams, a list of direct questions and carbon copies of her notes, a Xerox of the autopsy, lists of inventories. Near the bailiff's bar Roberts could see the exhibits, the gun, some folded quid, Treacle's stolen watch. He was standing there adjusting to the grim light when the bailiff called order and the judge entered.

After ten minutes Roberts got to sit down. Two constables brought Demeter in through a side door and deposited him in the dock. He looked less fierce now to Roberts, just a small Rasta sitting quietly in a gray suit with a white shirt, no tie, his black dreadlocks spilling over his shoulders. Hillary smiled at

Demeter, who didn't return the smile. Roberts took a deep breath to settle himself and the chamber began to fill with other people, the prosecutor, reporter, two or three deputies. Roberts didn't think he'd be bored, but after an hour of testimony from some police constables he used the first break to tell Hillary he was going. He walked outside and found a Persian rotisserie on a corner away from the law courts and ate a quick sandwich and drank some apple juice. The day was flat and gray with a light drizzle that came from clouds you couldn't distinguish. It would drizzle and then it would quit and Roberts could see his breath.

Because he was restless Roberts decided to walk all the way to Demeter's flat. He didn't mind getting his sports coat wet, it wasn't all that cold, it was just chilly and it felt fine to walk through the streets all alone. He had gone toward Tower Bridge, and he could see the Bermondsey docks in the distance. He stood on the Embankment looking across the Thames. There were gulls above the river and some tour boats going by. The light seemed artificial. He walked across the bridge and found Gainsford Street, and then Curlew. Roberts was trying to live on his instincts, without expectation, listening to his body and the secret voice inside his head, the one that whispers late at night just as you drop off to sleep. He didn't want to go back to the Old Bailey and hear two or three more hours of testimony about the autopsy, watches, and guns. He knew the law well enough to know it wouldn't help to be there, he'd just waste time. He would go back when it would do some good.

Walking across Tower Bridge he didn't know what he'd find in the flat. When he got to Gainsford he found the same grim street and the same grim row of ramshackle buildings. He could smell bacon and egg, the musty odor of the docks, the sour smell of wharf garbage and salt water. Going up the stairs, Roberts had a déjà vu, an instinctual foreboding. But he broke into the flat anyway and found the same two grimy rooms. Then he was surprised by a smear of dried blood in the middle of the floor, about six inches around, some of it dragged away from the center of the circle. It had the abstract intensity of a de Kooning, something that mirrored deep angst. The blood had meaning for Roberts, it teased him, made him cold.

He left Demeter's flat and walked across the Bermondsey docks until he got so wet from the drizzle that he hailed a cab.

23

Looking infinitely puzzled and confused, James Treacle was answering questions from the prosecutor. Roberts tried to hear but the man was barely audible in the huge chamber, and once or twice Roberts made notes and passed them to Hillary who would glance at them, nod, then return to her utterly transfixed state, upright at her chair, fully focused on Treacle and his words. Roberts couldn't believe the woman could concentrate that long and that hard because he was already weary from his part in it. Roberts doubted she would notice an earthquake if one shook the chamber, tumbled the marble bust of Blackstone from its high perch, if the ceiling caved in around them. It took about forty minutes for the prosecutor to finish up, partly because everybody had a hard time deciphering Treacle's patois, this dusting of the truth that was being recorded word for word by a court reporter working overtime with French and Jamaican idiom. Roberts felt sorry for Treacle too, the guy had worn his secondhand tweed pants, a shirt yellowed from too much laundering, and tennis shoes with pink laces. He was in constant motion, fingering his green-and-black Rasta tam, putting it down on the rail in front of him, picking it up, doing it over again.

Roberts had lost track of time, as if the whole scene was being acted out under water, just a dull gray day that was flaking away like dusty paper, like history. If you listened you could hear traffic on the street outside, some sirens, bus bells, but nothing real, nothing palpable. "I believe it's your witness," Roberts heard the prosecutor say. The man named Eric Fleming Jones bowed slightly toward Hillary, beet-red claret face, black robe, dust-ridden white wig, a man out of a Hitchcock film.

"Pretty superficial stuff," Roberts whispered to Hillary. Demeter was sitting in the prisoner's dock, narrow-eyed and small, almost nonexistent.

"Treacle is frightened of the whole experience. He wasn't a good witness." Hillary collected some notes, an outline of her examination. She was wearing a black robe too. She left wet marks on the counsel table where her hands had been.

"Mr. Treacle," she said, marching toward the witness stand. The room echoed faintly. Wind bleated against the windows and Roberts could see leaves drifting down. England was shedding, going blank gray for winter. "May I ask you what your employment is, sir?"

"Jah, well I got no work now," Treacle said, muffled. The judge had leaned back, probably bored. "They is no work for me in London, now you know?"

"What do you do all day at home?"

"I do nothing, jah."

"You have a wife, is that correct?"

"Sure now," Treacle said, brightening.

"Is she employed?"

"She chars," Treacle said, fingering his tam.

"I refer you to the day of the robbery," Hillary said. She was standing in front of Treacle, Roberts couldn't see the man now. "Tell me what you did that day."

"Sit in my room."

"You listen to music?"

"Jah, sure," Treacle said.

"What kind of music?"

The prosecutor bounced out of his seat like a greyhound. He was pudgy, out of shape, true Colonial South Africa. "Is this all necessary, your Honor? We'll be here all week with questions like these."

"I don't know if this is necessary," the judge said. "But tell me if you have a legal objection to the question."

"Well," Jones said, "I don't quite see the point."

The judge smiled slightly. "You mean you don't see the relevancy of this line of questioning?"

"Quite so," Jones said.

"Overruled," the judge said. "Please proceed."

Hillary exchanged a glance with Roberts. He was very proud of her first minor victory. "What kind of music were you listening to, Mr. Treacle?"

"Just Capitol Radio."

"All day?"

"Just about, jah," Treacle said.

"You smoked some ganga, didn't you?" Hillary spoke very gently, slightly embarrassed for the man.

Treacle had looked appealingly at the judge just as Fleming Jones sprang to his feet again. "I must say!" the prosecutor shouted, apparently quite put out and angry.

Hillary circled Treacle while the judge thought about the objection. Roberts was beginning to enjoy the scene. The quiet bothered him, and he was tired, but Hillary was showing guts. "Overruled," the judge said finally.

Treacle frowned. "You know about the ganga, jah?" he said.

"I can't hear you," Hillary said.

"Jah," Treacle said.

"That's yes," Hillary said to the reporter. "So you smoked ganga all afternoon," she continued. Jones frowned but sat back in his chair, listening. Roberts thought he might get up again, a flinch passed his face, but then he relaxed.

"Jah, pretty much so," Treacle said unhappily.

"That's a yes," Hillary said.

"I must say," Jones shouted again. "Not only is this woman putting thoughts inside my witness's head, but there is no relevance to any of it."

The judge leaned forward over the bench, peering down through a cocky pair of square bifocals that were absolutely precocious. "I have no difficulty seeing the relevance of this line, sir. If you don't, I can explain it to you for the benefit of the record."

Jones dropped to his chair like a rock.

Hillary said, "You *do* drink rum, don't you, Mr. Treacle? I mean as a Jamaican that's no problem, is it?" Roberts certainly admired the approach now, gentle, cautious, but right on target, too.

"Jah, no problem, miss," Treacle said. The man had settled in the witness chair, you could barely see his head above the gate barrier.

"It is common in Jamaica to smoke ganga and drink rum together, isn't it?"

"Jah, miss."

"At what time in the afternoon did you smoke your first spliff, Mr. Treacle?"

"Spliff?" the judge said. "That is definitely a new term for this court."

"Spliff," Hillary said calmly. "A marijuana cigarette that's actually quite huge."

"Yes, quite," the judge said. "Please enter the word on the record if you will."

"Again," Hillary said, "what time of day did you smoke your first spliff, Mr. Treacle?"

Treacle sighed deeply. He glanced around the huge chamber as if he expected some help, someone or something to transport him away from his confinement. The light in the room had gained a moony, surreal transparency. Treacle said nothing for a long time and Roberts noticed it was getting cold in the room.

"Was it in the afternoon?" Hillary asked.

"Jah, maybe."

"More like in the morning, yes?"

"Jah, I'd say so, miss."

"How long does it take you to smoke a spliff?"

Treacle chuckled gently. "Sometimes a whole hour, miss. Sometimes you lose track of the time, jah?"

"You smoked ganga all afternoon too, didn't you?"

Treacle was fingering his tam again, probably wishing he could hide behind it. "Jah, I'd say that was right now."

"Five or six spliffs in all?"

"Jah," Treacle said, defeated.

"What happens when you smoke ganga, Mr. Treacle?"

Fleming Jones was on his feet again. "I must say, this whole line calls for a completely subjective opinion that is without medical foundation. And it isn't quite fair." The prosecutor had his hands behind his back and was pacing back and forth mechanically.

"Now, I'll explain this to you, sir," the judge said. "The defense is attacking the credibility and reliability of a witness that you called to the stand. She is attempting to show that this man's judgment and his identification of the defendant might be wrong because of drugs and liquor. Does that explain the matter sufficiently to you, counsel?"

Jones made a noise like a dog bark. He sat down and crossed his legs and pushed back his chair. Roberts had laid down his pencil. He probably didn't need to make any more notes. When he looked up, Hillary had made her way back to the counsel table, and was putting down her notes. She caught Roberts's eye and passed on around the table.

"What time did you go to the Zion pub?" Hillary asked.

Treacle shrugged. "I don't know, miss."

"Was it dark outside?"

"Jah, it was dark."

"Had your wife come home from work?"

"Jah, she just come home now."

"You often go to the Zion when she comes home from work, isn't that right?"

"Jah, most of the time."

"So, you were smoking ganga for four or five hours at home alone and then your wife came home and you went out to the Zion pub?"

"Jah, miss, probably so."

"That would be five or six spliffs then?" Hillary was speaking very quietly. You got the impression she was sorry for Treacle too, not wanting to embarrass him, just needing to get a job done, something she had to do.

Treacle thought for a moment. "Jah, miss," he said.

"You had some rum that day too?"

"Jah, miss."

"Did you have a bottle that day?"

"Only part of one, miss," Treacle said, laughing.

"Part of a liter?"

"Jah, miss."

"Did you finish the liter before you went down to the Zion pub that afternoon?"

"Jah, miss."

"Let me ask you," Hillary said. She moved over to the witness stand, pausing just in front of Treacle again. "What happens when you smoke a spliff?"

"Objection," Jones shouted. "I don't see any foundation for that question."

"Please be more specific, Miss Root," the judge said.

"Very well," Hillary said. "How did your music sound when you smoked ganga?"

Treacle glanced at the judge for help. The judge told the man to answer. "The music she float," Treacle said.

"And you float too?" Hillary asked.

"Jah, that's for sure," Treacle laughed.

"Do you hallucinate?"

"I don't know, miss," Treacle said.

"Do you see things? Have visions?"

"Oh, jah, man," Treacle said, "that's for damn sure!" Jones had stood, but then sat back down because the answer was out. "You see the good things on ganga," Treacle added.

"That's why the man smoke the stuff. He wants to see the good things."

"About your rum that day," Hillary began. "What kind was it?"

"Just that old rum," Treacle said.

"Was it Myers's dark?"

"Jah, I think so, now you say it, miss."

"That's one hundred and sixty proof, isn't it?"

Treacle looked puzzled again. He shrugged.

"The witness wouldn't know," Jones said.

"Answer if you do," the judge said to Treacle.

"Mebbe I don't know," Treacle said.

Hillary walked back to the counsel table and took out her briefcase. She opened it and produced a bottle of Myers's. "I'd ask the court to take judicial notice," she said.

"Proceed," the judge said.

Hillary walked to the dock and placed the rum bottle on the rail just in front of Treacle. "This is Myers's dark, yes?"

"Jah, miss."

"Tell the court how much rum was in the bottle when you started drinking that morning."

Treacle touched the bottle on its shoulder.

"That much?" Hillary asked.

"Jah, that's right now."

"Read the label for me, Mr. Treacle," she said.

"I can't do that," Treacle said.

"Well, all right," the judge said. "I can read it for myself if necessary."

Hillary said, "And your rum bottle was empty when you left for the Zion bar that evening?"

"Jah, that's right," Treacle said.

"How many drinks did you take in the four or five hours you were drinking in your room?"

"I don't know, miss."

"Then take a guess," Hillary said.

"The witness has answered the question," Jones said from his seat.

"Sustained," the judge said.

"All right then," Hillary went on, "were you drinking rum from a water glass that day?"

"Is this necessary?" Jones said, still seated, taking a very superior and bored air.

The judge smiled. "Is that an objection, sir?"

"Jah, from a water glass," Treacle said, before there was anything further from Jones.

"Five or six glasses?"

"Jah, maybe so then," Treacle said.

"And how does rum make you feel?"

"Good, miss," Treacle said.

"Yes, I imagine so. But what does it make you feel?"

"I told you, miss."

"No, you told me how it makes you feel. Now, I want to know *what* it makes you feel. Do you understand, James?" Roberts was touched by her use of the man's first name. "You have seen visions on rum, haven't you?"

"Oh, jah, miss," Treacle said just as Jones got to his feet again, this time too late.

"Objection!" Jones protested.

"Do sit down, Mr. Jones," the judge said.

Hillary strolled back to the counsel table and picked up a sheet of notepad. Roberts could see that it was blank. Hillary studied the notepad, and then walked back to the witness dock with the paper held behind her back. "You know, Mr. Treacle, I've spoken with your wife about that same night. She said you were drunk when you left for the Zion pub."

"Objection!" said Jones, clearly angry.

"Sustained," the judge said. "This question assumes facts that are not yet in evidence, Miss Root. If you wish Mrs. Treacle to testify, you must produce her, have her sworn, and allow her to take the stand for cross-questioning." A moment passed and the judge smiled at Hillary directly. "Or you may have to rephrase your question."

Hillary pondered for a moment. "Your wife is a fine person, isn't she, Mr. Treacle?"

"Oh, jah, miss."

"If your wife told you that your behavior indicated that you were drunk the night you left for the Zion bar and a man was shot in the bar, could she be relied on to tell the truth?"

"I don't understand you, miss," Treacle said, truly dumbfounded.

"Your wife is honest, isn't she?"

"Oh, jah, miss."

"If she had ever said you were drunk, it would be true, wouldn't it?"

"Jah, miss."

"Were you drunk that night, James?" You could see Jones trying to think of an objection.

"I must say," Jones said distractedly.

"I'm afraid she's got you there," the judge said.

Treacle looked down, ashamed. It was very quiet for a long time. "Jah, well, you know how things are, miss," Treacle said finally. "I was drinking rum, jah."

"Is that a yes?"

"Jah, probably."

Hillary grabbed the liter of Myers's and walked back to the counsel table and plunked it on the wood so that it made a loud, reverberant sound. Roberts thought that the gesture was made for Jones, maybe for the judge. It was a nice touch. The woman's eyes were closed tightly, as if she were trying to control her breathing, stay on her feet, like a runner straining for the tape on guts and instinct. She turned around, using the counsel table for support.

"Did you have any money when you went to the Zion pub?" Hillary asked, nearly shouting across the distance.

"Only some shillings, miss," said Treacle, clearly relieved that the subject had changed.

"How many shillings?"

"Just a pocket of shillings."

"Four or five shillings then?"

"Jah, that would be right, miss."

"And your wife," Hillary said, this time quietly so that you had to strain to hear the words, "gives you rum money every night when she comes home, doesn't she?" Hillary smiled pleasantly at Treacle, *It's all right.* Treacle looked terribly dejected, morose.

"She has the work," Treacle said.

"And how many glasses of rum does the money get you when you go to the Zion?"

"That many," Treacle said.

"Come on, James, please."

Treacle nodded. "I can get four or five, then the man Howard he gives me some sometimes too."

"And did you drink that many glasses before the robbery that night in the Zion?"

"Yes, miss," Treacle said weakly. At this point, Roberts had the impression you could ask Treacle any question at all, and he would have answered compliantly, just to get the experience over and done with.

"So you had no money left when the robber came in?"

"I was drinking my last rum, miss."

"Was it dark inside the Zion pub when you got there?" Hillary asked.

"Jah, miss."

"In fact, it's always quite dark inside the pub, isn't it, Mr. Treacle?"

Treacle seemed utterly lost, not in thought, but in another realm of being entirely. Somewhat gently, Roberts thought, the judge reminded him to answer, and then Treacle began to speak, gesturing with his hands, telling the judge, perhaps nobody in particular, telling, perhaps himself, that it was always dark in the Zion pub, even on nights when there was music playing, when there should be joy, *irie!* It wasn't like Jamaica, where everything took place outside, under the palms along the beach, where a man could take some air and listen to God's music, the trees and the water. *It was too dark,* Treacle said while Hillary waited for him to finish. Even Jones was too stunned to speak. Hillary looked as if she wanted to interrupt the man, give him some comfort, end his defense of his life, but she only walked back to the counsel table and leaned against it, waiting.

When Treacle finished she said, "Where did you sit when you went into the Zion that night?"

"Where I always do," Treacle said.

"In the back, opposite the bar?"

"Jah, miss."

"Who else was in the Zion when you got there?"

"Only Mr. Boston and me, miss."

"That would be the bartender?"

"Jah, miss."

"And where was the dead man. Mr. Calliope?"

"He was back in the kitchen with Mr. Lemon."

"How long did you sit there before the robber came in?"

"Must have been a long time."

"An hour?"

"Jah, miss."

"More?"

"Mebbe, miss."

"And when the robber came in, who was in the room?"

"Old Calliope he come in, I think."

"Just you and Calliope and the bartender?"

"I think, miss."

"And you had almost finished your four or five rums?"

"Jah, miss."

"And when the robber came in, what did you do?"

"I just sit, what you think, miss?"

"Of course," Hillary said. "And the robber had his back to you most of the time, didn't he?"

"Mostly, miss," Treacle said.

"Please tell the court what you heard when the robber came in the Zion."

"He said he wanted the money, jah."

"But what did he say?" Hillary walked up to the witness stand again. "Tell us what his exact words were."

"I want the money," Treacle said uncertainly.

Hillary had some official papers in her hands. "What would

you say if I told you that Mr. Boston testified to the police that the robber said: 'I kill you, fool, if you don't open that cash money drawer right now!' " Hillary laid down the police report in front of Treacle, investing it with magic. Roberts was thinking that Hillary had, after all, learned something from her student days at the Academy of Dramatic Arts.

Treacle looked at the police report in front of him with dull fascination. "Well he could have said that, jah."

"You don't really know, do you?"

"I object," Jones said, halfheartedly.

"I don't know why," the judge said. "At any rate, I'll overrule the objection. Please proceed, Miss Root."

"Now tell me what happened next," Hillary said.

"He took the money and he shot Calliope."

"Of course he did," Hillary said gently. "But tell me *exactly* what you remember."

"Seem like poor old Calliope he come out from the kitchen with Mr. Lemon behind him. Calliope he step around the bar, he, then he stop."

"And the robber took your watch?"

"Jah, he come over and he did that too."

"Did he say anything to you?"

"Probably, miss."

"You don't remember do you, Mr. Treacle?"

"I think I do."

"But you were drunk."

"Jah, that's so . . ."

"And it was Mr. Boston who told you what happened during the robbery, wasn't it?"

"He talk to me about it, jah."

"And when you identified Moseby Demeter as the robber, you did it because Mr. Boston told you it was true. Am I right?"

"No, I think it was Moseby all right."

"You think, but you're not sure."

"Pretty sure."

"But it was dark and you were drunk and the man had his

back turned most of the time and there were tables and chairs
between you and the man and you'd been smoking ganga for
five hours and drinking rum for that long as well and you can't
remember accurately what the robber said and he was wearing
a mask."

Treacle said nothing, it wasn't even a question he was expected to answer. It was so still in the chamber that Roberts
could hear traffic again, sounds he associated with evening
London, buses snarled back on Oxford street in the thin yellow glow of the streetlights as the fog swirled in from the river.
"No more questions," Hillary said.

"Very well then," the judge said. "Mr. Jones, unless you
have any questions on redirect examination, I'll call the court
into adjournment for the day. It is late, and we've done a lot
of work." Fleming Jones waved a hand passively.

Roberts watched the constables escort Demeter out of the
chamber. The man shuffled away, pausing to glance at Roberts. Hillary was halfway down the marble aisle and Roberts
hurried after her, out into the foyer of the Old Bailey. There
was nobody in sight, only Fleming Jones sweeping by them
without speaking, followed by a breeze of cigar smoke and old
leather. Hillary was leaning against one of the columns, holding herself up against all the fatigue.

"You were wonderful," Roberts said.

"I'm shaking so badly."

"Never mind, you destroyed Treacle."

"Yes, perhaps," Hillary said. "But I hated it. Treacle is just
another Jamaican immigrant with nothing to live for. I should
be helping him, and here I am in the Old Bailey making him
into a drunk and a liar."

"Not a liar," Roberts said. "Treacle was wrong. It was your
job to set the record straight. You did a wonderful job and you
did nothing dishonorable. Don't buy into that."

"I know you're right. But I still feel for Treacle."

"You really did your homework, didn't you?"

Hillary smiled shyly, all worn out. "I did talk to his wife,
you know?"

"You did all this when I was in Jamaica, didn't you?"

"Well, I couldn't just do nothing."

"Where did you learn those tactics of yours, walking up to a witness with a blank sheet of paper while he thinks you've got some kind of statement? The idea of the bottle of rum? The police report?"

"Reading novels," Hillary said softly.

They walked over to Lincoln's Inn together, and then up to Hillary's ice-cold office. Roberts started some tea on her electric ring while Hillary began to open a package that had been delivered. Outside in the quadrangle, Roberts could see that it was deserted, all the cobbles covered by wet, fallen leaves. While he made tea, he thought about Amanda for the first time that day, since the trial began. He wondered if she were thinking about him too and a loop of doubt stripped through his heart, went out to her, and came back unanswered. He felt that his love was growing vague, like falling leaves, soon the tree would be barren, though it had been beautiful during the event. Ah, he shrugged, dipping in two oolong tea bags.

Hillary was in the corner when he turned around, slumped to her knees. She was holding the opened package in front of her, a shoebox that had been wrapped with brown string— inside the box a dead cat with its throat slashed. There wasn't much blood. It was just an alley cat with matted fur and cold, glazed eyes.

24

It was Drummond who asked him to freeze the cat. Roberts thought it was creepy. "Do it," Drummond said after they'd been talking for fifteen minutes that night, Roberts using the downstairs telephone while Hillary slept. "Do it, the bloody thing may come in handy. We're working on your slasher over here." Roberts tried to listen. "Do it now," Drummond had repeated.

Now that they were in recess, and it was finally quiet in the chambers, Roberts had time to think about what he'd done, been forced to do really, just sit by himself and ponder with his thoughts twisting down to the heart of the matter, deep inside himself. It had been a long morning in trial, Fleming Jones leading Howard Boston through all the details of the whole robbery at the Zion pub, how Calliope had been brutally shot dead. Roberts thought the prosecutor had done a pretty good job and now that the judge had called a recess and Hillary was having a breather in her office there came a prolonged period of utter silence. Boston had glared at Hillary the whole time on the stand, his eyes focused like holes of fire in his head. Roberts had sat at the counsel table all that time, trying to concentrate and take notes of the testimony when he could, passing them to Hillary, little ripostes that might come in handy, but what he noticed most was the hate in Boston's eyes as he continued to stare at Hillary, even when the man was asked a direct question. Fleming would ask, Boston would nod in acknowledgment, and then answer in his low bass voice that sounded like an accusation somehow. Roberts thought the tactic might be getting to Hillary; several times she had glanced at him, then she would read his notes, touch his hand, almost afraid to look back at Boston who would be booming his bass over the whole courtroom like a whip crack. Fleming Jones was using the trick too, letting the voice settle over the chamber, then asking another question, putting himself between Boston and the silence, just enough time to hear some cars way down on the Strand. And then Jones would ask another question, there would be some traffic noise, and then Boston would answer the question.

When it was over, after about two hours, Roberts thought about the cat. This ragged muff of a thing frozen in Amanda's fridge. It made him sick to think about it, but he had done the thing Drummond had asked, and now he was remembering it during recess, while Hillary went upstairs to get some rest. She was wearing her black robes and she had put her hair up behind her head in a bun. She looked very competent and professional, even if a little pale, but pretty good considering how much she had been through in the past two or three weeks. Once or twice she paused to take long drinks of water, but then she would go back to paying attention, saving her consciousness for events that were happening right in front of her. It was a trait that Roberts admired, he himself never could have done it. In fact, what was happening to him now was more typical, these images of the dead cat coming through his head like laser beams, breaking whatever defenses he had, and he was seeing the pictures clearly. It was happening again.

The evening before Roberts had spent about fifteen minutes just holding Hillary. He had squatted to his knees so that he could see her face, and gently he had taken the box away from

her. She had held it in front of her with the top of the shoebox
in her lap. The dead cat had been wrapped in a *Daily Mail,*
and Hillary had unwrapped the newsprint, thrown away the
string, and the dead cat had come tumbling out, uncoiling
from its paper coffin. The cat was there in the box when
Roberts went over, lying on its back with just a few drops of
blood on the shoebox, a gash in its throat, some saffron-
colored fur matted around the wound and a pink tongue
leaking from its mouth, and of course, those cold, glazed eyes.
Hillary wasn't looking at the cat, not even at Roberts, she
wasn't looking at anything really, she was just staring out at
the black trees. Roberts told her to put down the box and then
he tried to take it away from her, but she was holding on to
it with an iron grip. He didn't want to force her, and so for a
long time he didn't say anything while Hillary sat transfixed,
not even moaning, something that keyed Roberts to her psy-
chological state. But after a while she turned her head and
focused on him with an utterly abandoned gaze, like someone
who had survived an unspeakable horror. She bit her lip and
handed the box to Roberts.

Roberts made her drink a cup of tea. She still hadn't spoken
and he was worried. Awful thoughts were piercing his skull
now, things he didn't want to mention to the woman. Could
she continue the trial? As far as he could tell, she had done
very well with Treacle and she had managed to destroy him as
a witness. She had demonstrated that the man was high and
drunk, that he'd been sitting in the back of the darkened Zion
and hadn't really seen a thing, and that his whole story had
been told to him by Howard Boston. It was a seed of doubt
that was sure to grow. But could she go on?

They stood together while Roberts helped her with her coat,
the cold room surrounding them. "Who's doing this to me?"
Hillary said finally. She put her head on his shoulder, her voice
a solitary whisper. Roberts could feel her body against his,
how frail it was, this ripple of fear in her shoulder. "Who is
doing this?" she asked again. Roberts put his arm around her
then, helping her to the lift. They went outside and found a cab

and right away dashed across the West End in the failing autumn light. Roberts didn't tell her what he suspected, they just rode through the evening traffic without speaking, Roberts watching the city sweep past on reflected glass, down Oxford Street behind rows of red buses, past Hyde Park where the lamps were finely visible through a haze of trees, gulls winging up over the Serpentine. It was a sad evening, you could feel the weariness of the city too. Roberts wanted to breathe life into Hillary, into the city, but he didn't know how. Telling her his suspicions would only drive her deeper into her self-consciousness. He didn't want that. He wanted her angry, not inert. He wanted her ready and able to fight, as she'd been during the first phase of the trial. At the Kensington Park house he took her upstairs and made her drink a huge whiskey.

About ten o'clock that night she came back from wherever she'd been in her mind. She was lying on the sofa with her blouse loose, her shoes off, pillows behind her head. Roberts made her some minestrone soup from a can and she ate three spoonfuls, and then put down the spoon. Roberts pulled up a chair and watched her doze again with the huge sky out the window like black velvet and a few stars hazy like powder. He had made a coal fire and it was warm in the room. When she sat back up it was with jack-in-the-box abruptness. There was a sliver of light in her eyes and her hair had come unpinned and was going wispy on her neck. "I don't care what they do," she said coldly. "I'm going on with this trial."

Roberts was surprised by her calm. There was nothing desperate in her voice, no trace of fear. She said it with the matter-of-factness of someone reading out a train schedule.

"You are remarkable," Roberts said. He leaned over and kissed her cheek. It was an antiseptic kiss that embarrassed him, but he meant it and the woman smiled. "You are a bloody miracle," he added, sitting back up.

That was when Roberts went downstairs and froze the cat. It took him ten minutes to find some wax paper, but he finally did and wrapped the cat up in it and tied it with string. It was like working with rancid bacon. There were some peas and a bottle of Russian vodka in the freezer compartment. Roberts cleared out the peas and vodka, then put the cat inside and just stood there looking at the fridge with its ridiculous package inside a compartment the size of a breadbox. His feelings were growing elusive, as if the moment had no spirit of intention to it at all. It was just Roberts the camera staring at a white-walled fridge with its one bright eye staring back through the roast mutton and brick of Stilton. He finally closed the door and went back upstairs to be with Hillary. There seemed something crawling on his skin, though, insects or worms, and he was nearly sick right then. When he thought about it, he decided it was the wet cold fur that smelled so terribly. . . .

Just then something thunderous gloved Roberts and sucked him back into the space of his inner thought, then rebounded and left him in open court. He could sense Hillary standing behind him, touching his shoulder, and he placed a hand over hers and left it on his right shoulder, feeling the cold dry surface of her skin, much colder than the air in the room. It was a gavel that had come down and the judge was standing high above them at his bench and Roberts realized too late that he had failed to stand. A constable was bringing Demeter into the courtroom through a side door and Roberts saw Boston marching down the marble aisle toward the witness dock.

"How are you feeling?" Roberts whispered to Hillary when she sat down beside him. Her breath seemed dry and papery. Thin as ice. She nodded.

"You may proceed, Miss Root," the judge said. Roberts was noticing the room, its equipage of justice, the cold detachment you could slice. Barred shadows covered the room from its mullioned windows, giving every object a harsh, overproduced look, as if it were a movie set and the actors were trapped with their lines. "I trust you won't take the whole of the afternoon," the judge continued amiably.

Boston sat down. Moseby was looking down on the scene, just a head and shoulders above the dock.

"Very well, your Honor," Hillary said, walking around the counsel table. She was standing in the middle of the shadows now, halfway between the counsel table and the witness stand, appearing very small in her robes. Roberts kept thinking about the frozen cat, the vividness of the images amazing him. He was, he thought, finally achieving an openness to experience, the kind of photographic stance he had sought, something that might lead him to the answer to all this death. Something Hillary had said: "Who is doing this to me?" *They. Me.* While Roberts pondered this, Hillary was examining Boston, he could hear her questions, subtly distorted sounds coming at him. He knew he should have been making notes, exercising his attention in the straight-linear way of everydayness, but he was drifting in circular patterns, like a hawk descending on its prey, while this huge courtroom battle played itself out in front of him. And then he realized the obvious. *The victim here was Hillary.* This whole thing hadn't been about James Root, or about Simes. It hadn't had its locus in Jamaica.

When Roberts looked up again, Hillary was circling, walking around and around, asking Boston questions. He tried to pay attention for a while, but something was piercing his skin, a knowledge that was small and sharp.

"And how long had you known Moseby Demeter?" Hillary asked.

"Since he come over from home, you know?" Boston said.

"How long would that be?"

"Three years, maybe more, jah."

"Did you ever visit his flat?"

"Course not, you know that. Moseby he trash."

"Were you his friend?"

"No, miss, you know that, such as you. That boy was a rude one. Him."

"So, you weren't his friend. And you didn't visit his flat. Is it fair to say the only times you saw him, he was in the Zion pub?"

"Sure, that's right now."

Hillary walked back to the counsel table. Roberts swallowed hard, trying to hold back his excitement. He wanted to fly away now, go down to St. Olave's hospital and start some payback coming to Hillary. God, she deserved it.

Hillary stood off from the table. "Do you know if Moseby Demeter wore jewelry?" she asked.

Boston looked up at the judge on a rubbery neck. You could tell the question had stopped him. Fleming Jones rose from his seat. "Once again, your Honor," Jones said, "I fail to see the relevance of this question." Jones cast a wise glance at Hillary.

"Do you have a purpose, Miss Root?" the judge said.

"Yes, I do," Hillary replied.

The judge nodded. "You may answer the question, Mr. Boston," he said.

"Maybe he did," Boston said.

"How about rings? Did he wear a ring?"

Boston hooded his eyes now. Roberts was amused, you couldn't see Demeter's arms, his hands.

"Maybe he did, why should I care?" Boston said.

"Did he wear a watch?"

"Maybe he did," Boston said angrily.

"Do you want me to intercede?" the judge asked Hillary.

"No, it's all right. Thank you." She had moved closer to Boston now, they were nose to nose nearly, Boston doubled up angrily in his chair. "Right now, Mr. Boston," Hillary said, "what's your answer?"

Boston placed both hands on the rail and peered over it at Hillary. They were inches apart now, a steady intent of hate on Boston's face, a film of sweat too. "That man he killed my Calliope, you know? What do I care if he wear no watch, or if he do. I? I know he killed him, I."

They went at it for five minutes, just like that, Boston answering with questions, smudges of anger passing his face each time, Hillary at him steadily. It was the Jamaican game of question for question, but Hillary had played it before, it didn't faze her at all. Roberts admired the woman's stamina,

a trait she must have inherited from Arcadia. Here was this
tiny woman looking cold and pale, hammering away at a huge
Jamaican bartender.

"May we have a recess, your Honor?" Hillary said at last.
Late-morning sun was streaking the courtroom now. The trees
were rippled in the wind, leaves dusting down, an airplane
overhead droning.

"This court is in recess," the judge said. "The constable will
sequester the witness and take away the prisoner." He had
stood, halfway down from his bench. "Shall we say about ten
minutes?"

Hillary sat down next to Roberts. "You did great," Roberts
told her. "You've got Boston looking like a liar already. He
doesn't know if Moseby wore a watch or not. He also looks
like he has a grudge. And he probably didn't have any better
look at the killer than anybody else there."

"I think that's true," Hillary said, scratching out some
notes on her legal pad. She sounded tired now, as though she
might have another hour or two of battle before she collapsed
entirely.

"The watch thing was entertaining," Roberts remarked.

"Boston stumbled, didn't he?"

Roberts smiled and touched her shoulder. Her neck was as
knotted as a fist. "What are you up to?"

She put her head down on the counsel table, entirely exhausted. Roberts noticed her breathing was more regular and
deep. "It's time to get our friends from outside," she said.

Roberts went down the aisle between the empty gallery
rows. Just outside the chamber he found three Jamaicans,
each about six feet tall, rangy, with black dreadlocks down to
their shoulders. They flashed nervous, jittery smiles and all
were dressed in white shirts and gray woolen pants. Roberts
introduced himself and they shook hands.

"This some way to earn ten quid," one of the men said.

"Jah, you say," said another.

It shocked Roberts when they put on the masks. They wore
devil faces made of red rubber held in place with a band.

Roberts stood and stared for a long time, wondering what anyone would think who saw them, wondering what the judge would think too, but realizing what Hillary was doing now. It was a tremendously clever thing and he had to hand it to her, taking these kinds of risks in her first trial. Standing back from the Jamaicans, he almost laughed out loud because they looked ridiculous. But he led them inside the chamber and down the aisle, and directed them to stand just behind the counsel table as Hillary had told him to. Hillary looked back in recognition, then turned around to her notes.

In another few minutes the bailiff called the court to order and the judge came back to the bench. Boston was led inside from another room and he took his place again in the dock. You could see him stop, look at the Jamaicans. When Hillary walked over to Boston she was looking down at her notes. This was going to be a test for Boston, one he would have to pass all alone.

"I direct your attention to the three men standing behind my counsel table," Hillary said in a loud strong voice. "Do you see them clearly, Mr. Boston?" Demeter was not in the dock.

"Sure I do," Boston said. He glanced at the judge, who didn't return it. "This is a funny trick now."

"These men are wearing masks just like the one the robber wore that night, isn't that true?"

"I guess," Boston said glumly. He had hunched forward in the witness box, giving himself some weight.

"Tell me which one is Moseby Demeter," Hillary said flatly.

Fleming Jones was slumped in his chair, staring away at the gray light in the back of the room. This whole scene had been concocted by Hillary, by herself, there was no prosecutor who could possibly object. Hillary repeated the question, this time even louder than before. Her voice made an echo that came back once.

"You must answer," the judge said. "If you know."

"Jah, this is a pretty trick," Boston said.

The Jamaicans stood motionless. They were grotesque in their masks.

"Do you know which one is Demeter?" Hillary asked again.

"Course I don't, you know that," Boston said.

"But you know what the robber said to you?"

"He said, 'Give me that cash, fool,' that's what he said, jah."

"All right," Hillary said, turning to the Jamaicans.

"Give me that cash, fool," one of them said. The others repeated the phrase.

Boston closed his eyes and seemed to relax. "Which will it be, Mr. Boston?" Hillary said, her back still turned.

Boston gestured to the Jamaican on the right. "That one there," he said. Hillary walked around the gate and placed her hand on the shoulder of the man who'd been chosen. All of them removed their masks. Boston shrugged and slumped down a bit, bathed in the gray light. Roberts sensed that the moment had gotten away from Boston, that this film had broken and was wiggling wildly on the floor while bulbs flared and popped. The Jamaicans were standing with their masks in their hands.

Hillary said, "Did you tell James Treacle what to say in this case? Did you?"

"No, I never done that. You a fool if you think that." Boston gestured, as if to wipe away the question.

"Nothing more," Hillary said to the judge. Fleming Jones dismissed the witness and sat waiting for the judge to say something.

Hillary was sitting next to Roberts now, her hands wedged under the table, as if they might soar away if left alone. Roberts wanted to put his arm around her again. The Jamaicans went away down the aisle, Roberts could hear the oaken chamber door whisk shut behind them.

The judge hunched forward, looking at Fleming Jones. "Ordinarily," he said, "I'd take this matter under advisement. It is quite a grave thing we have here. But all I've heard today has given me dangerous doubt about the guilt of this accused.

In the first instance, I've got only a watch and some folded quid as evidence that a robbery took place. These were found in the accused's flat, of course, but nothing connects him with the Zion pub beyond that. The watch, while more directly tying him to the robbery, still isn't conclusive as you know. And while it is suspicious that the weapon was found in a trash bin just outside his flat, this too proves nothing conclusive. Taken together, the demonstrative evidence just isn't enough to find a conviction herein." The judge leaned back, thinking.

"It has always been true that the eyewitnesses in this case were the most important factor here. Mr. Treacle, while quite honest in his own way, proves to have been quite drunk at the time." The judge cleared his throat, "And perhaps more than that, who knows? At any rate, it is arguable that he was told what to say by Mr. Boston. He's as much as admitted it. And as to Mr. Boston, I've seen that he couldn't identify the man in the mask and he couldn't tell the difference even when confronted by spoken words. I must say that the test concocted by Miss Root is both quite ingenious and quite effective. Hopefully, it has done its obvious work of justice." Here the judge shifted his gaze to Demeter, who had been returned to the dock. "As for you, Mr. Demeter," the judge continued, "frankly I have my doubts about you. Perhaps you did this thing. But it is not my duty to judge on the possibility that you did this. I must judge on the fact. Therefore, it is my duty to discharge you."

Hillary smiled and hugged Roberts. There were huge tears in her eyes that refused to fall. Already the judge had left the chamber and the constables were releasing Demeter, who glided up the marble aisle. Roberts guided Hillary up the aisle too, then outside where they found Demeter propped against a window frame smoking a cigarette. The man was wearing gray woolen pants, a white shirt, no rings, no watches.

"You're a lucky guy," Roberts said to Demeter.

"Maybe so," Demeter said.

"Good luck, Mr. Demeter," Hillary said.

"The luck come to you," Demeter said. "You know you

were crazy all through this thing, jah. Say, if you hadn't come with these tricks, old Moseby he would have had another trial. That's for sure." He smiled strangely, then shuffled away down the long corridor. Roberts watched him disappear down a stairwell.

"God, I'm so tired," Hillary said.

"I'm taking you to the Kensington Park house."

"I just want some sleep."

Roberts looked out the window, down into the courtyard where Drummond would be. He saw a police car, the little Cortina that Drummond drove, and some immigration officials in blue uniforms. They would arrest Demeter, take him away in one of the vans. After that, Roberts didn't know what would happen.

25

Providence put Roberts back in the Wimpy Bar across from St. Olave's hospital. He was sitting at a window seat looking across at the hospital facade, backlit like a movie set, only more ominous, like the grainiest black-and-white frame. The weather had tried to be sunny in the morning, but had settled back into a streaky gray that would move bilious clouds along on a stiff wind, and Roberts could tell that it would be gloomy before too long. He was having some toast and marmalade, some black Formosan tea, trying to adjust himself to predictions he was making about the future, where he would be in the next twenty or thirty minutes, as if there were a crystal ball inside his head and he could consult it for free; it would uncloud, and there would be his future, his fate announced on a fluff of glass.

The first providence was Moseby Demeter himself, the guy slouched over the windowsill the day before at the King's Bench, looking down at the street, wearing that laundered white shirt with bits of tobacco on the breast. Roberts remembered how callous he had looked, with a smirk on his face, a grim wry smile, telling Hillary how he'd have gotten a new trial because she was so crazy, yes. The man had jabbed an index finger at Hillary. Roberts thought about popping him good, putting a red bruise under his ear, watching him sit down hard and roll. At that bitter and irreducible moment all the foreboding in Roberts had vanished beneath the racket of his harsh words. *A new trial,* the words were like a train wreck to Roberts, and suddenly, watching Demeter tap his cigarette against the marble sill, Roberts had a new respect for the violence in Demeter's past, the violence in his future too, the man's disrespect for anything and everything decent. Roberts knew he was seeing an absolute psycho, this guy who had strutted out of the courtroom like a cock, and was already on the lookout for another victim. Roberts almost uttered an audible oath, but it wouldn't have meant anything. Besides, he knew Inspector Drummond was waiting for Demeter out in the yard, along with some immigration officials. That would have to do for then.

Providence made Roberts call Drummond too. Sitting down in the Kensington Park house, thinking about the dead cat, Roberts had called the inspector. Roberts had to hold on for about five minutes before he answered the phone. Something took hold of Roberts when Drummond said, "Look here, old man, we have absolutely conclusive proof that the same instrument that was used on James Root was also used on Simes. Same instrument, same murderer, don't you think?" Behind Drummond Roberts heard Scotland Yard ticking away, soft vibrancies that filtered and cooed, tape recorders, stenotypes, air vents that robbed and resupplied. By the time Drummond launched into his explanation, Roberts had sped ahead. Samples of blood and tissue from James were found on the wound of Simes. The murderer had used the same weapon. It had been cleaned in soapy water, but it hadn't been thorough. Science had outdistanced the act, you couldn't fool the microscopes and chemicals. Yeah, true innit? Modern life was catching itself on the rebound, the language had even changed, transvestites were cross-dressers, tanks were assets, there was DNA testing that showed you your own character from a bit of sperm, this twisted molecule that lit up like a light show. Before the perp was done, he was stamped out of some machine downtown, the cops were on the way. Everybody lived in a petri dish.

But, the main providence was the frozen cat. Roberts had been thinking about it for a long time now. He had almost dropped it before the trial, the cat angle, because too much was going on for him to think. But that second dead cat had whispered to him from across the waste of its death, two cats, two men, it was the sanity of syncopation coming to his ear and finally he understood it all. Hillary was the victim, no one else, not Simes, not James. If Hillary had come undone, if she had become emotionally overwrought, then Demeter would have gotten a second trial, another chance, and who knows, maybe some of the witnesses would have died. If you thought about it, maybe Howard Boston would be the next with his throat slashed. After he called Drummond, Roberts had opened the freezer and had looked at the dead cat, these cold, glazed eyes peering into nothingness, and something had whispered to his deep unconscious, this feeling right out of Poe. At that moment, Roberts knew that Hillary was the victim, that Demeter was the real perp, that somewhere in London there was a killer doing the bidding of Moseby. And Roberts knew he had to find out who it was before Demeter disappeared forever. It was Drummond who suggested meeting at the Wimpy Bar across from St. Olave's. The inspector had some real hard news, maybe Roberts would like to hear it in person? He said he would.

And so Roberts sat in his window seat waiting for Drummond to show, thinking back to the weeks before when he'd sat at this same table with Amanda, that Saturday morning when they'd come down to see James Root, the guy who had died twice. Then he'd gone over to the hospital, seen the dead man, and had come away shocked. Roberts remembered the soggy toast and the foul oolong with skim milk, the egg and bacon smell on the waitress too. Now he had a chill and was trying to find some sun in the window, but there wasn't any. Maybe the chill was permanent.

Roberts sipped his tepid tea. *Horrible.* There were reflections on the surface of the glass, a window full of cunning fluorescent light that was so sharp it seemed to gnaw right through the bone. The Wimpy Bar seemed to sum up modern life, in a different way from police science, but good nonetheless, all sharp angles and discomfort, mediocrity and speed and the anguish of faceless conformity. Drip, drip, drip, your life is gone, sir, time to retire, sorry about that. Pity, isn't it? Oh, well. Outside the window Roberts saw Drummond dodging across the Jamaica Road, topcoat zephyred as he ran by a news kiosk, then up the sidewalk like a wingback, this tight, small figure in natty tweed. Drummond came inside the Wimpy Bar followed by a gust of dank wind, smiled, and sat down across the table.

"Been here long?" he asked.

"Twenty minutes, not long," Roberts said. "I came early anyway. Something jumpy is inside me wanting out."

Drummond made an unidentifiable noise. His nose was red and runny. The cockney waitress came and took the man's order, a Scotch egg, cup of white coffee. When it came, Roberts could barely stand the sight of it. For a while they talked about the weather. The man had a sharp, pointed face, cheeks sunken, his hair parted hard right and plastered down with oil. They seemed to have a faint psychic connection somehow, as if there were other voices beamed at them, something subtle and catalytic. They were leaving their fingerprints on each other, maybe someday they could dust themselves and become friends, you never knew. But it was a start for Roberts, his first self-made friend in London, a sign that he was having a life after all, something different from existence in the cellar on Kensington Park Road. There had to be an ontology at work here. Otherwise, why would Drummond have let Roberts come along on whatever this was that was happening?

"We picked up Demeter," Drummond announced. "This chap was mad as a hornet, he was. But your information was right on target. He entered the country illegally and his flat was full of cannabis. Good old Jamaican ganga. The chaps at immigration are having a go at him right now, and by tomorrow morning he'll probably be in Kingston." Drummond had loosened his tie and was digging a fork into the Scotch egg. "Don't suppose you'd care to explain how you got into Demeter's *locked* flat?" The word "locked" Drummond had spoken while looking outside at the lorries on Brunel Road. "Or how you knew about the animal blood on the floor, and the cannabis in plastic bags?" Drummond smiled wanly.

Roberts drank off his Formosan. The act was automatic. He hated the stuff. "I broke in," he said.

Drummond waited while some lorries plowed down into the Thames tunnel. "Yeah, well, at least you're honest about it, I'll give you that."

"Why not? Two men are dead. I want the person who killed them caught and punished."

"You think you know who did all this mess?"

"It was Demeter himself," Roberts said.

Drummond raised a practiced eyebrow. He made another gash in the Scotch egg, revealing a rotten green planet of yolk. "Demeter was shut away in Wormwood, old man," he said with a mouthful of crust. "You aren't telling me he turned into a bat and flew over the bloody wall?"

"Something like that."

"That's a good trick, that."

"Suppose you tell me what you're thinking, why you asked me to meet you here. What's going on? Maybe between the two of us we can decide what to do."

Drummond swallowed some coffee, washing down his egg. "By the way, how is young Hillary doing?"

"I took her home to Kensington Park. I put her to bed and she looked as if she would sleep for a week. She's completely exhausted. She buried her brother and her father and now she's at the end of her rope. It would stupefy a normal person. I'm surprised she's doing as well as she is."

"Someone looking after her?"

"A close friend."

Drummond nodded thoughtfully.

"Demeter is behind all this," Roberts continued.

"All right," Drummond said, "I'm listening."

"You agree that these killings weren't random."

"Yes, I've told you that."

"Then there was a motive."

"That's the logical conclusion, old man."

"Well, I've spent a lot of time trying to think why anyone would kill James Root, why someone would poison him too. You remember he was poisoned the night before he died in the hospital?"

"Of course," Drummond said. "We've canvassed the entire Jamaica Road area. Gone round to every flat and council house and pub in the whole bloody neighborhood. Couldn't find a soul who knew a thing about the poisoning."

"Well, I went down to Jamaica Road looking for clues myself. And I went to Jamaica, just to find out about James from his mother and one of his friends. I wanted to see if anyone there had a motive to murder him."

"And you found?"

"Nothing. There wasn't a soul in Jamaica who would have a single motive to kill James Root. No grudges, no women trouble, no police record. He was a simple Rasta. He liked music and the guitar and he worked in a record shop. That's all."

"I presume you inquired about Demeter as well?"

"Yeah, he's a petty criminal. He wasn't even reputable enough to be a rude boy down there. He got his one big break in the rackets from a guy named Trinity Solange. He bought some dope and didn't pay the man back. I have the feeling Solange would kill Demeter if he could find him. Other than that, I didn't find anything out about Demeter you probably didn't already know."

"Right you are there. A few arrests, some time in gun jail. Nothing much."

"But there are a few things you don't know."

"Such as," Drummond said.

"Before the trial began someone killed Hillary's pet cat, a little calico. I'd taken her home one evening and she saw it hanging from the wash line. I cut the poor thing down and buried it in the back garden. Then two days ago, someone delivered a dead cat to her office in a shoebox. That's the cat I told you about."

"And you conclude?"

"A personal terror campaign."

"Yes, I quite see the point. Personal terrorism."

"But why?"

"Why indeed?" asked Drummond.

"Yes, well there are other facts. Demeter has been complaining all through this about Hillary. He's told her to her face that she was incompetent. I discovered he's passed notes to the judge complaining about her performance. He's done the same with his jailers. He seems intent on making everybody know that he believes she is unbalanced. And he seems pretty well informed about all her troubles. During their trial conferences he pushed her so that she could barely work with him. Even after the trial, standing out in front of the courtroom, he told her he would have tried to get another trial if he hadn't been acquitted. It should have been a celebration, he should have been thanking her, and he was telling her she was lucky."

Drummond pushed away the remnants of his Scotch egg. "You wouldn't join me in some apple crumble?" he asked. Roberts said no. He wondered how anyone could eat such a meal.

"I think Demeter concocted this whole thing to increase his chance for another trial. Maybe he gets convicted, maybe he doesn't. It's a close call and he knows it. So, he plans to terrorize his lawyer, make her crazy. He has witnesses to her emotional stress. I've seen the look on the man's face and he's a pure psycho, I'd bet on it. He's facing life in prison. What kind of risk would he take to avoid that? How far would he go? I think he orchestrated this whole affair."

Drummond leaned back in his chair. The waitress came back with the apple crumble, a day-old mess covered by yellow sauce. "This presupposes he did the Zion robbery and that he's got help from someone on the outside."

"Yeah, I think that's the deal."

"Can you prove it?"

"No, I can't prove it. If I could have proved it, I would have talked to Hillary. I don't know any more about the robbery than she does. Than you do. She did a hell of a job in court. She's going to be a good lawyer. Demeter got lucky."

"Do you have any ideas?" Drummond was frowning, looking outside. The big clock on St. Olave's had struck four o'clock. "I mean we're dealing with a fellow who's been acquitted of a charge that he should have been found guilty of doing."

"That's right."

"Pity," Drummond murmured.

"Yeah, pity." Drummond had bent over his crumble, working at it distractedly. Now Roberts was moving down the aisle of his fancy, which was composed of conscious anger. "The bloody bastard didn't have to kill anybody." The waitress had come back and was startled by the words. Drummond smiled at her and she wandered back to the kitchen.

"But really, old man, look here," Drummond said finally. "We know Demeter was in Wormwood all this time. He was definitely behind bars when James Root was murdered, and Simes too. We can't give him credit for those jobs until we find out who was helping him. If it's true. So, the question is, who?"

"But I'm right about Demeter. I know it. I feel it."

"The inner light of intuition," Drummond said.

"Look, Drummond." Roberts said. "When I broke into Demeter's flat I told myself I was looking for something to help him with his alibi. It was mostly bullshit, but there was a grain of truth in it. Still, I broke into the flat and I spent some time looking around."

"Go easy," Drummond said.

Roberts sensed an arc of pain behind his ear. He fingered
the machete wound that was like tight bulbs of sewn matter.
"First of all," he said, "I found the packages of cannabis all
wrapped up in plastic and paper. They were just exactly like
the packages you found in James Root's room. Same plastic
bags, same grocery sacks. It was the right amount for one
person to have carried away. Nice and neat. Now, who do you
suppose took it from Root's room over to Demeter's flat?"

"Not Moseby Demeter," Drummond said.

"Yeah, it couldn't have been Moseby Demeter. The coppers
were right on Demeter's trail after he robbed the Zion. He was
arrested that night, and your people searched his flat. There
wasn't any cannabis then or you'd have found it. Weeks later
I find it in the closet. That means somebody took it from
Root's place after the robbery, while Demeter was in jail.
Somebody, but not Demeter."

"Yes, I see what you mean. I don't suppose you'd have an
idea of who that might be?"

"It's a woman," Roberts said sharply. "I've seen her stuff
up in Demeter's flat. She's the one who killed Hillary's calico
cat and she's the one who butchered the stray and sent it up
to Hillary at her office. And she's the one who poisoned James
Root and then killed him later at the hospital when he didn't
die the first time. And she's the one who slashed Simes too.
She's also the one who took the cannabis from Root's room
and stashed it in Demeter's closet. *And the woman wears orthopedic shoes, like a nurse."*

Drummond touched his chin. "A woman who works at St.
Olave's," he said.

"Like that. Demeter has her under a spell. Demeter has
special power. The woman is crazy. Your guess is as good as
mine. But that's how it falls out." Roberts sat back then, tired
as hell, trying to think. Some peach-hued clouds were drifting
over Bermondsey and you could hear the misadventured
traffic out on Jamaica Road. The machete wound was bother-
ing him again, and he kept thinking about Hillary, who had
freed her father's murderer. And now Demeter would get on

a plane for Kingston in the morning, walk out in the sun a free man.

"All right, lad," Drummond said. "I should tell you I've been working on this as well. From a different angle, but it's the same problem. From the beginning, it seemed to us that the person who killed James had to have a way to get inside the hospital in the middle of the night. Thorny problem, if you think about it. Then I began to think that the murderer was *already* inside the hospital. We've been working through the hospital records for a week now and there are seventeen or eighteen people who work at the hospital and are immigrants. And only two of them are from Jamaica. The rest are South African, Nigerian. Asian. Lots of Indians. One of the Jamaicans is an old woman who's been in England for twenty years, a grandmother of five who works in the kitchen. We've checked her out and her family as well. The other woman is named Lucille Voltaire. They have no record of her at immigration."

"She's an illegal."

"It would seem."

"What about her?" Roberts asked.

Drummond nodded out at St. Olave's where some ravens had settled on the grounds. "She works in the evenings on the housekeeping staff. She comes in at four in the afternoon and leaves at midnight. She has the run of every floor and keys to most of the major rooms. She's about twenty-four years old and looks to have been in England for at least a year. We don't really know."

"She could have come over with Demeter."

"She could."

"She could have stolen a scalpel from surgery."

"She could," Drummond said. "But it's bloody impossible to tell for sure. There are thousands of instruments in the hospital and impossible to inventory the lot."

"She might be the woman in Demeter's flat."

"She might at that."

"Then if we can talk to her, make her confess, we can stop Demeter and charge him with murder."

"That's the idea, lad."

Roberts put a thumb on the window. It left a wet print. "We going after her now?" he asked.

"That's why I got you here," Drummond said.

Roberts smiled. "Thanks for that."

"I thought you deserved it. For Hillary." Drummond was searching his pockets for change. "Look, immigration has our friend Demeter right now. They want him out of the country by tomorrow and if there isn't any reason to hold him on another charge, they're going to deport him. We have to find this Lucille and talk to her right now. Otherwise, Demeter goes off to Kingston. Oh, we might be able to get him back, but it would be messy. And if Lucille won't panic, then it might be weeks before we have enough to charge her in court."

"Yeah, sure. I don't suppose immigration could forget about him for two weeks. Lose the key."

"Not much chance. Immigration had their eye on him from the time he was arrested. I'm afraid there's nothing you or I could have done to prevent it."

"I don't want Demeter to get away with this."

"Then let's go see Lucille Voltaire."

"I've still got a frozen cat for you," Roberts said.

"I think we can use it," Drummond said. "Miracles of modern forensics and all that."

They walked out to Paradise Street to where they could see the Brunel tunnel. Roberts had been right. After such a nice day, it was going to be a gloomy evening.

26

They wandered the vast black corridors of the hospital for twenty minutes, maybe thirty, going down polished halls that had the rainy look of runways. Roberts could hear the mumble of sounds all around, some vacant conversation, kitchen noise, metal against glass. Drummond told him there were men stationed at certain posts, and he caught glimpses of them, down sideways, in aisles, lurking near exits. Roberts kept thinking about Demeter, how the man looked when the immigration officials had put him in their Ford van, this guy who was tethered to his past, perhaps going home. He wanted desperately to find Lucille Voltaire, force her confession, make her scream the truth until it drowned Demeter too.

Down in the basement they stopped under a bulb of pale light. Drummond had unbuttoned his overcoat and was pinching his rooster throat. "You let me do the talking, right, mate?" he asked.

Roberts didn't answer as a constable approached them in the near dark. The two men talked and there were hushed conferences elsewhere. It was like standing inside a tube, light leaking in at either end. Two flares advertised HOUSEKEEPING over a double door. The tinkle of kitchenware and the groan of pipes.

"Right then," Drummond said.

"Right," Roberts answered stupidly.

Drummond paced off ten steps and paused in front of the double doors, peering in one of the porthole windows. Roberts came up behind.

"That's her then," Drummond said flatly while Roberts stood on tiptoe, looking inside the explosively lighted room. The light went back and back, through racks of towels and sheets, boxes of supplies. A woman was standing there peacefully in a white hospital smock, hairnet on her smooth skull. She had a tapered face with pocked skin and hard, coalish eyes. Her hands were manipulating some towels, strong hands. Drummond pushed open the doors and they went inside the room together as the woman continued to heap towels on a rolling tray. She looked up and stared at them coldly. The air had a humid thickness, fresh wash and soap, the smell faintly mercuric. At twenty feet the woman was coiled into a pose.

"Hello then," Drummond said.

The woman dropped her eyes nervously. "That's right then," she said meaninglessly.

"Like to ask a few questions," Drummond said quickly, before the woman had finished her non sequitur. "If you wouldn't mind, that is."

Curling away to one side, Roberts gave himself a few feet in which to be a witness. He could see two or three other hospital workers back in the washroom.

"What is it then?" the woman said. She had pushed a clutch of fresh towels to her breast.

"You'd be Lucy Voltaire?"

"Lucille, I," she said. She was looking at Roberts too, dull thoughts on her face.

"Lucille then," Drummond continued. "You know a chap answers to the name of James Root?"

"Not him, no. Never heard of him."

"How about Moseby Demeter?"

"What do you want?" she asked. She was dropping the towels one by one onto the rolling tray in front of her, plumping the pile, an automatic-pilot response. "I done nothing, I," she said after a silence. "And who are you?"

Roberts recognized the cadence of question for question. Balls of questions piled up like towels. Drummond snapped open an identification wallet, his badge there, and he told the woman his name. "Right then, suppose we chat about James Root? That be all right?"

"I don't know that man, I done told you, I." The woman had her back against the towel rack, stiff, eyes focused.

"I think you do," Drummond said.

"Now I done nothing, I."

"Then you have no reason to worry."

"No, not I."

Drummond buttoned his coat, a gesture of insignificance to plod against time. He took three steps ahead. "So you wouldn't know who killed James Root then?"

They were stranded that way. Roberts didn't know how they were going to progress against the strain, how events might come apart against their separateness, how the discrete phenomena might form. But it was funny in a way, how it happened, this loud burst of amorphous sound followed by a cloud of white blur, towels exploding down from the racks behind the woman Lucille Voltaire, and then the rack falling in a metallic crash just as Roberts felt his feet sliding back as he bounced against the swinging door, which gave slightly, then held against him. When he leveled himself against the door he could see the woman for an instant as she closed on Drummond, who was toweled like a fog-bound freighter, and then the dart of the woman's arm and the rude flash of a ratchet knife striking a fuzzy arc. It was happening on the level of spirit, sound, action, flow, and then echoes split his ears as he stumbled again trying to get up in a whirl of activity, feeling the doors give way behind him again so that he couldn't stand properly, and so he sat down hard on his rump, being stumbled on by Drummond who cursed nastily once and was quiet.

A second or two passed and the woman struck at Drummond, who was on his knees, partially draped over Roberts. Drummond cursed again as the knife hit his arm, just below the shoulder, and Roberts managed to kick out and cuff the woman harmlessly below the knee. He slid back but the door moved and he was too far away to kick again as he scrambled, seeing the knife flash. All that was left of the woman were the sounds of her footsteps disappearing behind washing machines and racks of linen.

"Bloody hell," Drummond muttered.

The man was pale, leaning back against the wall above Roberts. There was shouting down the hall, Roberts could tell a constable was running down the tile floor toward them. One of Drummond's coat arms was torn away from its seam and the man was staring down in disbelief at his own wounds, the ragged tweed attached to the shoulder by a few strands of thread, some blood pooled on the floor. A constable was leaning in against the weight of the door.

"My best Scotch wool too," Drummond said.

"I'm sorry," Roberts said as the constable shouted something inaudible. "I should have warned you about the ratchet knife trick."

"Should have warned myself," Drummond said, separating his coat sleeve with two fingers. "Quick as a cat, that one," he said.

"Quicker, you ask me," the constable said, one head inside the swinging door.

"She can't get far," Drummond said, still examining himself, breathing heavily as he sat on the floor.

Roberts made Drummond stand still while he and the constable looked at the man's wounds. There were two deep X's on the upper right arm and biceps, a smaller slash where part of his suit coat had been torn away at the sternum. The constables were spreading out through the acres of fresh and dirty laundry, combing through the racks and washing machines and piles of soiled bedclothes. Two more constables came inside and stood by the door.

"This was a bit of bloody foolish overconfidence," Drummond said, now standing, watching his men fan through the housekeeping areas. Roberts helped with the overcoat, got Drummond to his feet. One of the constables came back and shrugged.

"You try the loo?" Drummond said. The constable shrugged again. "The loo then," Drummond said, following the constable to the ladies room.

Roberts entered third. In the fiery antiseptic glare he could see rows of stalls, wash basins, some chairs made of plastic and waste bins, mirrored walls, and ashtrays. It didn't take long to see the open skylight above the last stall where the woman could have climbed up on a toilet and gotten outside. Four constables stood helplessly by while Roberts climbed up and looked out the skylight and saw Brunel Road. There was a flight of concrete stairs leading to street level, some trash piled up and an iron rail outlining the sidewalk above. It had gotten dark on that side of the hospital and there was a wedge of moon over the quays.

"Nothing," Roberts said, climbing down.

"She's got off, bloody hell," Drummond said. He turned to the four constables. "Get off now and check all around the hospital. One of you check with the administration and see if she has a vehicle." When the constables hustled out Roberts was alone with Drummond. He took a wet towel and began to swab Drummond's gashes. Drummond angrily tore away his coat sleeve. "This is a lesson in police procedure, what?" he asked.

"You going to be all right?" Roberts asked.

"Sure thing," Drummond said wryly.

"Then let's go after her."

"She can't get far. My men will find her."

"Eventually," Roberts said, finishing the sentence. "Look, if we don't find this woman and make her confess tonight, then Demeter goes back to Jamaica a free man."

"They'll find her, don't you worry."

"She'll go back to the Demeter flat."

"You think?"

They went outside the housekeeping room so that Drummond could sit down on one of the hard benches in the hall. A constable was telephoning from a nurse's station, and more men appeared at the end of the tube of light. In time a nun came back with one of the constables and made a bandage for Drummond's arm. Drummond grumbled about his stupidity while the nurse worked away. "What makes you think our Lucille Voltaire will go to Demeter's flat?" he asked.

"She's got no money," Roberts answered. "She's wearing a white smock from the hospital and a hairnet. She hasn't got a coat and it's going to be cold tonight. I assume she doesn't know yet that Demeter is with the immigration people. She'd want some clothes and some money if she has any. I saw her clothes in the flat so I know she's been living there, or at least using it for a while."

"Ouch," Drummond said, glaring at the nun. A constable ran down the hall and whispered in his ear. Drummond pulled away from the nun suddenly. "We've got out an alarm for the woman," he said. "But my men haven't found her on the hospital grounds. She doesn't own a car."

"Let's go to the flat," Roberts said.

"As soon as this creature lets me," Drummond said, looking up at the nun.

She finished up in five minutes. Roberts fidgeted on the bench, desperately impatient, angry at himself for being so slow when he saw the ratchet knife. Hadn't he learned anything from Howard Boston, from Nathan? He kept seeing the flick as the knife came out, a scowl on the woman's face. And there Roberts was on his backside, looking up as Drummond covered his face with one arm, the one arm now gashed into two X's. Drummond hurried away from the nun and Roberts followed him down the hall and outside the basement of the hospital to the car park where Drummond had an official Cortina.

They drove past Southwark Park and around St. Olave's until they got on Jamaica Road going west again back toward the wharves. There was a heavy evening traffic of lorries and buses, and people jammed the street in front of pubs and shops. Mist was rising from the Thames like a pillar of dust, as if horses were running far away. The clouds were still back-lit by the sun and you could see the tip of Tower Bridge. Roberts was riding in the front seat next to Drummond who said nothing, steering them down Shad Thames, going along the wharf until he parked in a warehouse drive about a city block from Demeter's flat. The buildings gave the appearance of leaning toward the center of the street. It made Roberts feel claustrophobic, as if the sky were closing in.

"We need to be circumspect," Drummond said, turning off the key.

"That sounds good," Roberts said.

"Some men will be posted downstairs just in case. The train stations are being watched and immigration is being alerted too, just in case she makes it to the underground, the boat train, anything else. There is no reason to take risks now. She'll be caught, don't doubt it."

"But Demeter leaves the country tomorrow."

"Yes, that's quite true."

They got out of the Cortina. Roberts's breath slipped away in the clammy cold of the quay. "What do we do if she won't talk tonight?" he asked.

"We have some other evidence of her guilt. I've sent a chap over for your frozen cat. We have the tissue samples from the knife or scalpel. She's had access to Root's room at St. Olave's. If we find the scalpel she's done for. If we don't, then we'll need perseverance and a spot of luck."

"We don't have time for perseverance. Demeter is going to disappear into Kingston tomorrow. There are a million or more people in Kingston."

"Seven hundred thousand," Drummond said.

"All right, that's a lot anyway."

"There are police and courts there too."

"I don't know," Roberts muttered.

Roberts could hear tugs out on the Thames. He was dispirited, feeling the muted logic of justice grinding down against them, trying to share Drummond's hopeful tone, knowing he meant it, knowing it was designed to give them some solidarity. "Let's get our payback," Roberts said to Drummond, who had started walking away now, down the dark street.

The whole block was deserted, not a soul in sight, hardly any light at all. There were pubs and shops on Jamaica Road, but back here were council flats and warehouses, abandoned buildings, some betting parlors closed for the evening. An icy chill was funneling in from the river and as Roberts watched Drummond ahead of him, coat torn off at the shoulder, he thought how uncomfortably cold the man must be. He felt as if they were being watched, as if pairs of eyes were wandering along with them down the street, but when he looked, he couldn't even see the Pakistani woman in the off-license. It was a pure premonition, this feeling that haunted, gave your skin a film, this existential dread that was caustic. When they got into the passage the bulb was out above the stairs. Roberts wondered if that was intentional, and he could feel his heart race as they went up the stairs in near-total darkness.

Drummond nodded, motioning Roberts to the side of the door as Drummond leaned on the jamb, listening, pushing his foot against the door until it slid open about six inches. The man peered inside, frozen for a second, as if in prayer, and then he touched Roberts on the arm, gently, something that was designed to give them both confidence. There was a sour odor that Roberts remembered now, pickapeppa sauce and jerk meat, mildew, sweet ganga smoked for months, seeping from the walls. Drummond pushed on the door and it was wide open now and Roberts could see the broken sofa, a recliner, and in back of the main room an iron stove, the small fridge. The grimy window looked out on some warehouses in dull, motionless order under a gray glow from the city. Both men listened like cats at a mousehole.

"Drummond again," the man shouted into the flat. There was no reply. "Lucille Voltaire, come on out."

Nothing. Roberts had expected a ratlike scurry as the

woman moved, probably tried to flee again, maybe out the window where the constables out in the street would run her down. Drummond had stepped into the open door.

"Wait a second," Roberts said, touching Drummond on the shoulder.

"We've got to go in," Drummond said. "I don't think she's here, but I wish I'd brought a bloody lamp."

"I smell something," Roberts said.

"A terrible rot is what you smell."

"No, wait," Roberts said again, this time taking hold of Drummond's overcoat, physically pulling him back from the door. "Burned candle wax, you can smell it."

"Yes, now that you mention it."

"Somebody's just put out a candle."

"Let's go, lad," Drummond said.

For a long time they stood stock-still in the main room, waiting expectantly. They were like maneuvered planets dense with gravity, it was that scary, a dream you refused to have that kept coming and coming. The wound on his neck was hurting Roberts, probably where the sweat was salting it. He remained back as Drummond moved over to the closet and began to rummage around in it. Then he shuffled into the back room where he knew there was a mattress on the floor, some drawers, an old shower stall with a plastic curtain hiding it. The total dark was cut by ribbons of gray light from outside, light from Jamaica Road over the rooftops. The drapes were torn and Roberts began to think they'd missed Lucille Voltaire, that she'd come and gone, that she was already somewhere else in Bermondsey, hiding in a council flat, staying with friends, that she'd disappear into the underground of immigrant life and they'd lose her forever, they'd lose Demeter as well, the logic of justice would close out James Root and Simes, the book would hammer shut. Maybe the woman would turn up in Leeds or Manchester, maybe not. Roberts knew he was cold and that the wound on his neck hurt.

Roberts could hear Drummond slam the closet door. "Nothing in here," the man called out.

Later Roberts remembered the moment it happened, how the light was coming in under the drapes, how he'd seen some shadows on the walls and had thought how odd they were shaped, and how much his machete wound was hurting him after all this time. The moment was like a frame of film, this locked departure from all time, a particle of the eye. But just then, as the shower curtain exploded out toward him, Roberts was not thinking at all, he'd given up hope of finding Lucille Voltaire, and then the curtain folded in on him in a rush and he was falling back through darkened space. The plastic clung to him and he tried to shout and then a sharp pain wired through his chest. A great weight seemed to tug him down. Bucking backward he tried to get the woman off his chest, straining to push his legs under him so he could achieve some leverage before he was cut to ribbons, feeling another sear of pain under his chin. He didn't know how long he was that way, on his back under the shroud of plastic that stank of mildew and soap, as if time had collapsed and there was only a huge star of pain and blackness at the center of everything. It was amazing, trying to free his own arms, all of it was taking place in another zone.

Just then he heard something else that shattered his senses as his ears went numb. The weight on his chest stopped moving and another silence took its place. The woman had straddled him, her head on his shoulder. It was obscene. Roberts pushed her away. Drummond was looking at him, upside down.

"Here now," he said. "Let's see how you are."

"What happened?" Roberts said.

Drummond dragged the woman away from Roberts, pulling her body full-length across the floor, unwrapping her from the plastic curtain. Roberts felt cold, sweaty too.

"I shot her," Drummond said finally. Drummond was testing the woman's pulse. She was lying stretched out in her white hospital smock, orthopedic shoes, still wearing the hairnet.

"I didn't know you had a gun," Roberts said.

"I do, and I did. Didn't want to use it, though. Bloody crying shame."

"I'm glad you did," Roberts whispered.

"She was going to cut your throat."

Roberts's coat was slashed at the lapel, some blood soaking his undershirt. He could tell there was a nick on his chin too and now Drummond squatted next to him and was taking a long look. Drummond had a scalpel in his right hand.

"Is she dead?" Roberts asked. He had pushed himself up against a wall and was sitting where he could see the Jamaican woman, the curl of blood behind her head. Her features were very clear, fine smooth skin, flared nose, wide lips.

"I'm afraid she is," Drummond said quietly. "Bloody hell and all that."

A huge rage took over now, Roberts began to shake, whether from fear or relief or anger he couldn't tell, it didn't matter really. The pain didn't matter, or the torn sports coat, or the nick on his chin. Lucille Voltaire had been shot through the crown of her head. He could see the wound clearly now, a horrible bluish gap on the top of her skull. Drummond must have fired from directly above while the woman kneeled over Roberts. There were bits of bone and blood splattered on the base of the shower stall. Roberts felt a great relief and sadness. "She's dead," he said to nobody in particular.

"Yes, well," Drummond said meaninglessly. He was examining the hospital scalpel. "She was using this on you. I don't think we'll have a problem proving that it was the same one used on James and Simes. She's definitely the one working for Demeter on the outside. We've got our murderer at least."

"I guess so," Roberts admitted. "But we'll never know what made her do it. And Demeter will be in Kingston tomorrow morning having a beer in the sunshine."

Drummond laid down the scalpel and opened Roberts's coat. "You're all right, lad," he said. "She couldn't get much of a hack at you through all that plastic and wool. You're a lucky man all right. This woman had to be some terrible fanatic to kill for Demeter, and then to try to kill us both when we came for her. We'll never know for sure."

"Yeah, I'm lucky," Roberts said, more to himself than to Drummond. He was trying to think what he'd tell Hillary. *Oh, I'm so sorry. Your brother and your father were murdered and the killer is dead. Yeah, and the mastermind is free. Sorry, I did my best. I did my best.*

Drummond said, "Lucille must have come over with Demeter. She must have poisoned James to get the ganga and then when he didn't die it was a good piece of luck for them that he was brought to St. Olave's where she had a job. Maybe it started out as a way to get his ganga, but it turned into a plan to give Demeter a second chance at a trial. She killed Simes and she killed the cats. What a woman, God."

"Well, it's almost over now," Roberts said. Drummond had given him a handkerchief and he held it to his chin to stop the blood. A neat flap of skin had been sliced away. It would scar, and he would remember it every time he looked in the mirror. "So Demeter goes free. He goes back to Jamaica."

"We have no evidence to hold him," Drummond said. "Probably never will have."

"Yeah, that's right," Roberts said. He was thinking that he needed Amanda now, more than ever before. If it had been war he could have stalked Demeter, killed him with his bare hands, cut his body into pieces, worn severed ears on a chain around his neck. He could smear himself with blood and drink until he was drunk. He could parse his soul for God. But it wasn't war and he couldn't.

"Let's get you out of here, lad," Drummond said, helping Roberts to his feet.

Roberts let himself be walked outside to the Cortina where he waited a long sad time alone.

27

He made Amanda wait in a working-class pub on the Gold-hawk Road, past a roundabout where evening traffic streamed like silver fish. She was puzzled, not wanting to be alone, even for a moment, and she gave Roberts one of those perplexed frowns, but he made her wait anyway, though she insisted on sitting just inside the front door at one of the round tables so that she could relax on one of the long divan-style seats and look out the front window at the street. That was fine with Roberts; he wanted to be able to see her as he walked away, thinking he would have some luck, she might bring it to him solely because she looked so vulnerable and pretty. The last thing he saw before he walked away, heading for the post office, was the lovely gesture she'd made taking off her beret, the way she'd brush back a strand of hair, the gentleness of her hands, the smile that made a question.

The day before he had gone home and waited with a whis-key, sitting in the darkened parlor downstairs with the sun setting behind the chestnuts in the park, the room filling with shapes. Just then a cab pulled to a stop at the curb and Amanda got out and he saw her with her overnight bag, and

275

his spirits had lifted suddenly and all at once, as if he'd been injected with a powerful drug. The cabbie was lifting two suitcases out of the backseat, and he rushed outside to embrace her, getting jabbed with her umbrella as she turned and uttered a breathy shriek of surprise. He felt as if someone close to him had returned from a terrible foreign war. Hillary had gone back to her flat, and Roberts had been forced to tell her everything about Demeter and Lucille Voltaire by telephone.

Now, after a difficult night during which Roberts had hardly slept at all, he and Amanda had walked down Notting Hill all the way to Shepherd's Bush, through the evening rush hour, arm in arm and silent, on through the autumn sunshine, both of them dreading their meeting with Hillary. When they got to the dreary Watney-owned pub on a corner of Goldhawk, Roberts made Amanda wait near the door while he went across to the post office and sent a telegram, which took him perhaps fifteen minutes. When he returned to the pub he found that Amanda had ordered two brandies. She had finished one cigarette and had put her coat around her shoulders because it was cold inside the drafty and ill-lighted pub. Her face showed how anxious she was, how uncertain. Still, Roberts thought, coming in the front door, seeing her there waiting for him, she was very lovely. Her freckles were so nice, and her oval brown eyes too. He could have looked at her for hours. Instead, he sat down and drank one of the brandies right off. Sunshine was sifting through the windows and you could see the frayed carpet, the miserable fake medieval chandeliers, the spotted glasses hung above the bar like butchered rabbits. Amanda covered his hand with hers.

"What on earth were you doing in the post office?" she asked.

Roberts smiled and leaned across the table and kissed her cheek shyly. She returned his smile and touched the gray-blue gash in his chin, where a dimple might have been. "Nothing really," he said, trying to avoid the question. "Come on," he said quickly, before another question could follow. "We've got to go see Hillary right now. She wanted to see us."

"Is it urgent?" Amanda picked up her beret. "Is she in trouble? Is she all right?"

"I don't know. It sounded urgent, but she didn't sound as if she was in trouble. She wanted to be alone last night, and then when she telephoned today she seemed in a rush to see us. It couldn't wait apparently."

Amanda drank some brandy and shoved the snifter across for Roberts, who finished it. He had on a sweatshirt and a sports coat, and the brandy had warmed him, but he was still cold. It was always cold in the Watney pubs. There was nothing cheerful or English about them. The floor seemed damp and the air had a rinse of permanent cigar smoke. Roberts paid for the drinks and they went outside and down Coverdale Road, past flower stalls, a green grocer's, a licensed betting parlor where a dozen men stood in blue light in front of a chalk tote board. Clouds scudded over the buildings, fretting the sidewalks with shadow. Amanda stopped at the end of Coverdale and pushed Roberts back against a stone wall.

"Does Hillary know everything about Demeter?" she asked. "I mean, does she know he's off to Jamaica right now, that he'll probably go free. Does she know there isn't any proof he was involved in the murders?"

Roberts closed his eyes, just briefly, delving into something other than the immediate. "She probably does," he said finally. "I told her what happened, she can draw her own conclusions."

"Actually, you can't be sure that the man did the Zion pub robbery, can you?"

"I know he did."

"But you can't know, can you?"

"I don't know it like I know the sky is blue. But I know it the way I know there are penguins at the South Pole, even though I haven't been there."

"Yes, I understand, Mitchell, but maybe Demeter wasn't actually involved."

"Look," Roberts said, seeing his breath just as the sun

passed behind the rows of flats on Coverdale, "I told you about the watch that was stolen from James Treacle?"

"Yes, of course."

"Treacle told me his watch didn't run. When the trial was over I went up to the bench and wound it. The watch found in Demeter's flat didn't run."

"I see," Amanda said, tugging Roberts out into Coverdale again, up to the flat. She rang the bell and they went inside and up a flight of stairs to the landing. Hillary was at the top, looking down at them as they climbed, standing in the door when they reached the head of the stairs.

Her hair was braided into cornrows, Jamaica-style, and she was wearing a flowing flower-print blouse over white cotton pants and sneakers. Mostly, Roberts noticed the huge red circular earrings and bright red lipstick, not to mention the two packed suitcases on her bed. The room was bare, without plants or pictures on the walls, and it had been recently cleaned, everything looked scoured. Amanda embraced Hillary.

"So," Hillary said, sitting down on the bed next to her packed suitcases, thumping her sneakers together little-girl-style, "I'm going home. I'm leaving England." She sat there looking down quietly.

"Tell us about it," Amanda said. Roberts walked over to the window and looked down at the ash heap in the back garden, just where he'd buried the calico.

"I'm going home," Hillary said again firmly.

"How wonderful," Amanda said. "Isn't that wonderful, Mitchell?"

"It's wonderful," Roberts said.

"I'm leaving just now for the airport. That's why I was in such a hurry to see you right now. There isn't any way I can tell you how much I appreciate your help and support. Mostly I want to thank you for being my friends." Roberts came back from the window and sat down on the bed. He touched Hillary.

"Your mother will be happy," Roberts said.

"She doesn't even know yet. I'm just going to go home and surprise her. No brass bands, no fanfares." Hillary held out her hand to Amanda, who took it. They were making a circle in the room. A brow of sunshine had come in, just the last of it. "I hope you don't think I'm running away from anything. I'm a lawyer and I have a profession, and right now I have a need to be in my own country. I don't feel English and I don't feel Jamaican." She smiled gently, almost bashfully. "I think I'll feel better about myself if I go home. I hope you understand. I hope you don't think I'm a failure."

"You're a damn fine lawyer," Roberts said. "What you did here qualifies you as a hero."

"Mitchell told me what you did," Amanda added.

"Yes, but a guilty man is free," Hillary said.

"You don't know that," Roberts lied.

"Well, anyway," Hillary said, brisking away the comment with her hand, "my radio taxi is due here just now." She swallowed hard and stood up. "I want to go down alone and I want to go to the airport alone. I do hope you understand." She bit her lip, holding off her tears. "I do so want to see you both again. Sometime."

Amanda held her again, and Roberts kissed her cheek. He was delighted with her transformation. She had crystallized, metamorphosed into something seriously beautiful. Roberts knew she was going to be all right, that her life would make sense. That was all you could hope for, after all. Amanda had gone outside and was waiting on the landing. Roberts was about to leave when Hillary pulled him back inside.

"I know about the watch," she whispered. "I know Demeter was behind everything. Don't worry." She kissed him hard on the cheek and he could feel her salty tears. "Let's just live with it," she said.

Roberts hugged the woman so hard he could hear her heart beating. He wondered if he *would* see her again. She would go home and be a lawyer in her country. It was where she belonged, and he knew she would succeed.

He walked outside with Amanda and they crossed Shepherd's Bush to the south and walked all the way to Holland Park under barren sycamores. The houses of the rich were being ignited by the setting sun, and a wind had risen. Arm and arm they went up High Church Street, through a churchyard where there were mossy tombstones, then across a cricket pitch and a rose garden. For some reason, Roberts didn't want to go home right then. He didn't want to be inside, even though the wind was cold and the sky was gray.

They sat down on a bench overlooking a slope of hill. Down the long decline they could see empty playing fields, shuttered shops.

"She'll be fine," Amanda said. She had moved close to Roberts and he could sense her nearness emotionally. "She's very strong. I only wish I knew what has happened."

"Demeter killed the man Calliope. He did the Zion robbery. Hillary found a way to get him acquitted, and it was a damn good job." Roberts put his arm around Amanda. "From what I've seen of her in court, she has a long fine career in front of her. Jamaica will be damn proud to get her."

"But what on earth is going on?"

"Demeter has been in prison for six months," Roberts said. "He's been sitting in jail probably knowing that he was going to be convicted, thinking of ways to get another chance. He came up with the idea of ruining his lawyer, making her crazy, and then later getting another trial. He'd known Lucille Voltaire for a long time, probably lived with her too. They came over from Jamaica illegally at the same time."

"The woman who slashed you."

"She was on the outside. She started her campaign by killing James Root. That had a double purpose anyway."

"Double purpose?"

"Both of them knew that James Root had some ganga. Lucille Voltaire wanted it, probably just to sell. She found a way to slip him some poison, probably in a cup of tea. When he became ill, she took away the ganga and left him to die. But he didn't die, and was taken to hospital where it looked as if he would recover. But, of course, she worked the night shift at the hospital. She stole a scalpel and sneaked into his room and finished him off by slashing his throat. She couldn't have James Root survive to identify her as the one who'd poisoned him. So, she killed him that night."

"Dear God," Amanda said.

"And then it came to Demeter that this was the start of his campaign to destabilize his lawyer, make her truly crazy. Lucille Voltaire killed Hillary's cat."

"She killed Simes."

"Yes, probably meant only to slash him. But he was old and he died."

"And about the tongue?"

"Lucille was probably from the hills of Jamaica where some Voodoo still survives. It was one of the things that made me think that a Jamaican had killed James. Drummond came to the same conclusion working independently. And he began a search of the hospital records for a Jamaican who worked at St. Olave's. When we talked at the Wimpy Bar, we converged."

"And Lucille sent Hillary the second cat?"

"Just more pressure. Maybe they thought they could kill Boston later, if they succeeded in getting Demeter a second trial. Who knows? They were both crazy enough to do it. Drummond has told me that it was animal blood on the Demeter flat floor that I saw when I went in there the second time. So we know that Lucille Voltaire killed the cat and sent it to Hillary. The scalpel she used on me was the same one used on James and Simes."

"Can't they arrest Demeter, put him on trial?"

"Double jeopardy," Roberts said. "He can't be tried for the Zion pub robbery and murder again. And we'd never be able to prove he inspired Lucille to do the other murders. She's dead, there isn't any evidence."

"But he did."

"Yes, he did. I can feel it in my bones. No doubt."

Amanda took his hand and held it for a long time. "What

on earth were you doing for fifteen minutes at the post office?'' she asked.

"Demeter is being deported to Jamaica. He's already on his way. He's going home a free man.''

"And?'' Amanda said. "This is terrible, but maybe Hillary doesn't know.''

"She knows,'' Roberts said. "Back at the post office I sent a telegram.''

"What on earth?'' Amanda said.

"There's a guy in Kingston named Trinity Solange. He's a Ton-Ton Macoute from Haiti, a very bad guy. Demeter screwed him on a deal and he said he'd kill Demeter if he could. That's one of the reasons Demeter left Jamaica in the first place. I've telegrammed Solange Demeter's time of arrival, his flight number, everything.''

"Oh, dear,'' Amanda said.

"I couldn't live with things this way,'' Roberts said. "I just couldn't live with it. Solange will kill Demeter. I couldn't stand it any other way.''

"Let's go home,'' Amanda said. "I'll cook us some chicken. I don't want you in the cellar tonight. I want you upstairs with me tonight.''

Roberts felt empty for a moment, just as he heard the sound of a jet overhead. An old man walked by, sweeping autumn leaves. It was getting to be winter now, and Roberts's thoughts turned to Eli Churchill, the way the man had smiled at him, buried in the sound of swallows. He could smell the lemon trees of Jamaica. He imagined Hillary in flight, heading toward her horizon.